SLIPS
CATCH

Published in the UK in 2023 by DR Enterprises

Copyright © Douglas Roberts 2023

Douglas Roberts has asserted their right under the Copyright, Designs and Patents Act, 1988, to be identified as the author of this work.

All rights reserved. No part of this book may be reproduced, stored in a retrieved system or transmitted, in any form or by any means, electronic, mechanical, scanning, photocopying, recording or otherwise, without the prior permission of the author and publisher.

This book is a work of fiction, and except in the case of historical or geographical fact, any resemblance to names, place and characters, living or dead, is purely coincidental.

Paperback ISBN 978-1-7399182-2-4
eBook ISBN 978-1-7399182-3-1

Cover design and typeset by SpiffingCovers

SLIPS CATCH

DOUGLAS ROBERTS

About the Author

Educated in and around the London Counties, Robert Utting alias Douglas Roberts never received a good report from his English teacher, but if there had there been a class for innovation then he may well have emerged with an accolade. Unfortunately no such course existed in the 1970s and all an individual could do then was what was called 'daydream'. But some of those memories stuck and emerged a few decades later. Born during the classic year of 1955 in South London, as the only son of Lieutenant Colonel Bernard Utting he listened avidly to his father's exploits. As a youngster one rarely pays much attention to the older generation, but such were the quality of his adventures from world war two, the rugby cricket and hockey pitches, the snooker clubs and even the dance floor, that one felt as though one was actually there with him.

Robert and his wife have been living in Surrey for the past forty years and he is now passing the mantle of family innovation onto his three sons. Being able to pass on humorous anecdotes and other memorable stories in written form is a blessing that humans have over other creatures of this world, so he will continue to provide what is hopefully some entertainment.

There is still much more yet to come.

About the Series

Detective Inspector Patricia Eyethorne OBE is now employed by Special Branch. Justin Crawford, formerly of the diplomatic protection squad, is happily engaged to her, and unless crime suddenly ceases overnight, then their marriage plans are going to be put on hold again. Having successfully foiled a political assassination plot against Maurice 'bloody' Hamilton MP, secretary of state for Northern Ireland, their reputation for discretely rooting-out corruption in the highest circles of British government has sky-rocketed. It really didn't help that while they were saving Hamilton's life, he had tried to rape Patricia and have Justin thrown into jail, but undeterred, they successfully emerged as silent heroes.

Their lives quickly revolved around numerous requests from various government departments at a breathless pace and now they were having to defer their wedding plans yet again. What they really wanted was a quiet weekend to actually sit-down with a calendar to pick a date. It was not to be as a terrorist-led conspiracy to control financial aspects of the metal market emerges, and this one requires extreme tact that Patricia and Justin are now renowned for. Despite their diligence, it still comes as a complete surprise that Hamilton is once again involved.

Foreword

Everyone will find themselves under a spotlight at some time during their lives; even if it is only for two minutes. Organisations find it almost impossible not to be visible all of the time, and governments, while claiming to be overt, go to extraordinary lengths to hide certain facets from us. For our own safety of course.

Before the invention of the printing press in the fifteenth century, information was generally passed from one to another either by parchment or word of mouth and one can easily imagine this taking some significant time over distances. Certainly, the telegraph then the radio speeded this process up, but thanks to the inventor of the microchip, information can now circle the globe in milliseconds; reaching tens of millions simultaneously. This is very useful to make an announcement but most unhelpful if one has something to hide.

It seems as though even a hiccup in Buckingham Palace is news in a remote Pacific island, and recently the likes of MI5 and MI6 have come under far more scrutiny than is healthy for their remit. Hence the need for subterfuge.

The Parliamentary and Diplomatic Protection Squad (PaDP) does what it says on the tin very well. They are bodyguards in the main but are constantly in the limelight and consequentially hampered; criticism goes with its territory. In any event, it often needs to gather nefarious information, and to do that means being able to step out of the gaze of the media. Among others mentioned in this book is the Diplomatic information Service (DiS) and is one such possible organisation that maintains itself under the radar, ostensibly under the auspices of Special Branch.

One pervasive organisation is the Organization for Security and Co-operation in Europe (OSCE) which manages to encompass aspects of all of our lives. I'd lay odds of one hundred to one that you never knew of its existence, and while this truly frightening behemoth is overt with an official website, it would not be able to function without being fed information. That information by itself is useless without interpretation or utilisation and is generally subject to political interference, which just so happens to be the subject of this book. If the reader takes the time to look up this organisation, I defy them not to drop their jaw.

Our capable heroes, Patricia and Justin, don't really have time to look forward to the day when they can say that they lead average lives. In the meantime, they carry out their duties with relish as there's a certain Maurice 'Bloody' Hamilton to deal with.

Organization for Security and Co-operation in Europe | OSCE

Chapter 1

Today's Lesson

This wasn't training. This was suicide. That's how it felt to Detective Inspector Patricia Eyethorne as she lay prone on the floorboards, at the top of the stairs between the walls of the narrow first-floor corridor. She viewed a possible way of escape some fifty feet away directly ahead of her; the window at the end cast a weak sunlit diagonal shadow half on the wall and half on the floor. Possible because not only was it on the first floor with a significant drop to the ground the other side, but from where she lay, she couldn't be sure if the wooden beads that separated the four glass panes would give way if she had to launch herself through it. But before she could reach that far she would have greater worries comprising of three doors; two on her left and one on the right of the corridor. She tentatively reached out her left hand to push against the wooden skirting board and the plastered wall above it to see how much resistance it would offer if she had to lean against it. A couple of prods with her outstretched finger told her that it was firm; at least this section was and there seemed no difference in the hue of it the rest of the way. She quickly returned her left hand to add support to her right one that held the pistol; elbows on the hard floor stabilised the gun perfectly, but her eyes now scanned the length of the ceiling above for any anomalies. Naturally squared-off corners where they should have been, all lit by a single light bulb more or less halfway down the length of the corridor, just beyond the first doorway. Tense though she was because she knew her adversary was somewhere ahead of her, she lay there analysing her five senses to see if she could detect anything out of the ordinary; anything that might betray their location. There were no vibrations, only a musty smell that went with a disused house, no sounds from either in or outside, and all she could taste was her own salty sweat. Which left sight as the only one of her five that was of any use. She took a deep breath and decided that the advice given to her regarding the bullet-proof vest was wrong; likewise for her smaller sized bra. Both of them restricted the easy movement that she was used to.

She decided to explore the nearest room on her left first. The door, a little more than ajar and some ten feet away, was hinged on the left and opened inwards. She shifted her body so that her right leg could gain better purchase to quickly rise to her feet, and in doing so her head moved with it. It was that small movement of her vision that made her spot the slightest of threads that hung down from the corridor light. Its reflective qualities made it easier to focus on because it was a little thicker than a normal web strand yet easily missed. At first glance it was a standard unshaded pear-shaped bulb held in a socket, suspended from a run-of-the-mill ceiling rose. The short cable that connected the two parts was cream-coloured with age and had the requisite number of random spiders' webs half-attached, but from the back of the bulb holder dangled a silver thread that terminated a couple of inches above the floorboards. It could have easily been mistaken as being part of a spider's web, but she couldn't see where the bottom of it would have attached to. And then she saw the counterpart. She twisted her head and lay her cheek on the floor so that her right eye was as flat as possible enabling her to look along the corridor's length at ant height. Just above where the strand terminated was the edge of a misplaced floorboard with a nail sticking out. Certainly it stuck up only a couple of millimetres and just enough to trip someone up, but then that may well have been a secondary purpose, because she suspected that the strand was really made of stainless steel and carried the same electric current that powered the light bulb. Whoever brushed against that thread would most likely be on the receiving end of two hundred and forty volts; especially if their foot was anywhere near the protruding nail.

She returned to her previous pose. Mindful that there was a time element, she quickly planned how she was going to safely check the first left-hand room and imagined the three paces it would take to reach the door. In her own mind she quickly went over her specific training on how to enter a room when one suspected that there was someone with a gun in it, and oddly enough, just the previous night she had gone to sleep imagining almost this exact scenario.

It was no good trying to stay quiet because if someone was waiting inside – the killer – they would hear you coming whatever you did, so speed was the most effective way to counter this. One should never pause to stand upright beside the door because it was the obvious place to be and if there were bullets fired in anticipation of where one would likely be standing, then that would be an excellent place to start. It was the other side of the doorway where one should be for two reasons. If the killer hiding inside was even of an amateurish standard, they would most likely have had time to work this one out and even if they hadn't, they might get a lucky shot off. And secondly, by passing the doorway they wouldn't know where you had stopped; even if they could see a passing shadow flitting by. In any case, one never stood upright next to a door, one always crouched below hip level. If the killer was determined to get off a lucky shot, or even had an automatic and was able to loose off several, because of the natural tendency for the gun barrel to rise in recoil after each shot, the line of 'stitching' would tend to rise. Starting at the door, by the time the 'stitching' reached where one was crouching, there was a very good chance that those bullets would miss above one's head. Oh, and holding the flat of the gun against one's temple to protect the eyes from splinters was also a very good idea. Once any firing had ceased, one would then be in the perfect position to kick open the door.

First, stamp not too loudly on the floor to simulate a falling body and then use the same foot against the door, not too close to the hinges otherwise it might

Chapter 1 - Today's Lesson

not open quickly enough. As one charged through the doorway, glance through the vertical gap between the hinges, maintain both hands on one's weapon, and bear it in the direction of the killer. Nine times out of ten they would be behind the door but one had to keep one's gun sweeping across the room in case there was more than one of them. If the room was clear, first check any large enough cupboards and all the while never stand directly in front of any door, and then look for any attic hatches. Lastly check the window, but this was the most dangerous part as one could not be anywhere else other than directly in the aperture to properly look out. Look for dust or freshly made scratches as evidence of recent passing, see if the handle moves easily and if so, push open the window as far as possible. Choose one corner of the opening and briefly show one's head. While one is waiting a couple of seconds, look round the room again to make sure nobody is creeping up on you, and then look out far enough to satisfy oneself that no one is outside.

Back to the doorway, crouch low and take a brief peek down the corridor – both ways. Now is the time to take stock of oneself but only for a few seconds. Pulse, perspiration, breathing; her mind started to cringe with what was coming next and she almost drew blood from where she was chewing her bottom lip. She was almost frantic with the situation and really wasn't sure if she could put up with this level of stress for much longer, but she closed her eyes for all of three seconds, put her fears to one side and carried on.

Move towards the next room, not forgetting the threat of the silver thread which she had to manoeuvre round. Repeat the process but with only two more rooms to go and with the knowledge that one's adversary will be in one of them puts pressure on one's nerves. This however cuts both ways as the enemy knows you are coming and is likely to be just that little bit more jumpy – and hopefully erratic.

As Patricia crossed the partially open doorway at a crouch, a series of thuds and the appearance of a line of holes confirmed where her killer was and that he was armed with a silenced machine pistol. She wasted no time and instinctively dived into the room, pointed her weapon in the area where the bullets emanated from and fired two shots. She adjusted her aim slightly and fired two more shots, this time hitting her target square on.

A gush of relief made her forget to sweep the rest of the room straight away and no sooner had she started to turn to see if there was anyone behind her, then a hand appeared over her shoulder, grabbed her gun and twisted it out of her grip. She immediately rolled backwards out through the doorway with the sole thought of removing herself from the line of sight of her assailant… and received a nasty belt to her ear from the electric thread.

"Aaargh. Bloody sodding fissthsrrrg, bleeding wire."

Then it swung back and gave her another healthy jolt to her head.

"Fuck off you poxy…" Then she realised that her left buttock was sitting atop of the nail and she felt and smelt the burning that went with it.

Chapter 1 - Today's Lesson

"Bastard bloody nail and you can bugger off too." She eyed the nail with anger and wished she had a hammer so that she could hit it back to where it rightfully belonged.

She stood up as her instructor appeared in the doorway which she had just unceremoniously launched herself through.

"That was good." Sarcasm pervaded through his quiet comment as he made her pistol safe by ejecting the magazine and catching the round from the chamber in mid-air.

Going back into the room, she shoved him to one side to see how many of her rubber bullets had found their target. She spun round and squared up to him. "Yes, that was rather good wasn't it?" She didn't need to look long at the machine and dummy that had fired above her, since all four of her shots had hit somewhere on the cardboard cut-out. "And don't start about not spotting you sooner." She forced herself to calm down a little before adding. "I'm not in the mood."

She went to leave but he grabbed her firmly by the wrist. "Well, this is part of it. We've now got to work on your temperament."

He was no taller than she was but somehow his hold on her was rock-like although pain-free. He repeated himself. "Temperament. Remember, you've got to control it even when you don't want to."

She looked into his steady eyes, explored her senses and did as she was told. He let go of her.

***

That was two days ago and now she was in a real life-or-death situation, only this time in a disused warehouse without the benefit of the walls of a corridor. At least there wouldn't be any sneaky wires to give her a shock. Or were there? It gave her an idea.

Having cornered her man at the far end probably over a hundred feet away, she lay behind a large rusty tool cabinet and recalled her training that had culminated two days previously. Despite the possibility of death, she felt no fear. She was beyond that stage. It is a state of mind that only exists once one has experienced that very real prospect. One is then at peace with oneself to such an extent that one can think with the greatest of clarity. Such was the mind frame of Patricia as she checked her pulse; it wasn't racing. She mentally put to one side how this situation had got out of control because it could wait until she had secured her target. Her predominant question right now was should she wait until support arrived or should she try to take him on by herself. She had her pistol but no vest. She knew he had some sort of gun as he had already loosed-off a series of shots at her as she had made her way behind the rusty box via the support pillars. That had established that his aim was pretty bad; but how much ammunition did he have left? Her Browning 9mm held thirteen, but she had no spares as her assignment hadn't warranted it.

Returning to her training she looked around the almost windowless, brick-built warehouse to see if there were any useful items, specifically looking for the snake of disconnected cables; and there they were, lying on

Chapter 1 - Today's Lesson

the ground no more than five feet away. She gingerly peered round the cabinet and saw that the snake wended its way in his general direction. She reckoned he must be behind the stack of old drums that had been left behind in the far corner because there was nowhere else to hide. The dim light that filtered down through the few openings in the roof didn't allow anything more than a general outline of the interior, and she couldn't be sure that he was behind those drums, but she had to assume he was; because there was nowhere else to hide. There didn't appear to be a rear exit either, so it had to be behind the drums.

She holstered her Browning, positioned herself and sprang the few feet, stretching out with her hands to reach the cables and then rolled back behind the shelter of the cabinet. In less than the five seconds that she had been exposed to his line of fire, she counted off three shots; none of which hit her, but one made a decent 'clang'. It wasn't a particularly thick cable but it was quite weighty and when she started to pull it, she had to brace both of her feet against the tool cabinet. The snake started to uncoil and she risked a glimpse round the side to see if what she was doing was having any effect, apart from disturbing several years of dust that had collected on it. The more she pulled through, the heavier it became and then she couldn't pull it any further. She sneaked a peek this time from the other side of the cabinet, and saw that when she tugged it, it disappeared under the stack of drums; perfect.

She assumed the position of the last man on the tug-of-war rope by coiling the cable around her body and jamming her feet against the base of the cabinet, then yanked it as hard as she could. Two things happened simultaneously. Certainly the cable moved as she intended but the cabinet also moved just enough to dump her on her bottom, but it was the noise that demanded her attention the most. By tugging violently on the cable and elevating it off the ground, it disturbed the stack of empty forty-gallon drums so that they clattered off each other and fell to the ground. There was now very little for the man to hide behind and they were still moving when her target loosed-off a couple of shots and started running towards her with the obvious intention of circling round behind the cabinet and shooting her at point-blank range.

She didn't panic or freeze but lined up her pistol and shot twice, all the while remembering that her instructor had told her to always shoot low.

The man screamed, collapsed mid-stride, creating his very own dust cloud that curled round his body as he heaped to the ground. He also let go of his own pistol which landed a few feet from Patricia who wasted no time in retrieving it. She then reversed away, leaned her back against the cabinet and, remembering her training, looked round to see if anyone else was in the cavernous building; there wasn't but she heard the sounds of a vehicle, no… two vehicles, pulling up outside. She initially assumed they were her support, but then a nasty idea crossed her mind. Suppose they were his support?

She looked closely at the man she had shot no more than a dozen feet away and decided that if he wasn't dead now, he soon would be. Ignoring him, she turned her attention to who was approaching. There were three of them starting to spread out through the entrance a couple of hundred feet away, and she spotted a fourth staying outside by the two cars. It was difficult to pick out their features as the light from the entranceway was behind them; perfect silhouettes. There was no way she could tell if they were friend or foe but it would be fatal to hide behind the cabinet and reveal herself at the last second, so she stood up and announced herself.

***

"You weren't supposed to engage and I expect he'll let you know how he feels about you in his own unique way."

Patricia compressed her lips as she followed the suited man along several corridors and down two flights of stairs. "Wait in there." He pointed at one particular door and without waiting to see if she entered, he turned and was gone.

It was a plain painted room with a thick-piled carpet without any other decoration; not even a picture and nowhere to hide a camera lens; well perhaps in the light which hung from the centre of the ceiling. There were several armchairs along the walls that reminded her of a well-appointed doctors' waiting room in the likes of Harley Street, but the thing that struck her most was the total lack of sound. It was as though it was insulated from the rest of the world. Not knowing how long she would have to wait, she chose one chair at random and was surprised to find that it was extremely comfortable. She closed her eyes and prepared her explanation of the day's events to whoever walked through the door to debrief her.

Once she had rehearsed, she found her mind wandering back to how she had come to work for one of the country's foremost security services. She had virtually fallen into the arms of the Diplomatic information Service (DiS) when she had sought out the assistance of Commander Gibbons. In finding the would-be assassin of Maurice 'Bloody' Hamilton MP just a few weeks ago, she'd identified the culprit and assassination method which had suitably impressed the head of the DiS to such an extent that… well… she was now working for him. She'd effectively given up her position of Detective Inspector with Thames Valley Police and was now just plain Inspector, but being an 'Inspector' with the DiS carried an awful lot more weight and gravitas than her previous position. She wondered for the umpteenth time if her OBE had anything to do with her appointment, but dismissed the idea once again as Gibbons was not the sort of man to take notice of letters after one's name; even if those letters were MP or even PM.

She had learned that the Diplomatic information Service existed primarily to protect political individuals and did exactly what it said on the side of the tin. Those individuals were not always foreign ambassadors or visiting dignitaries, but could include anyone deemed important, or even someone whose death on British soil might cause embarrassment to Her Majesty's

Government. From the outset, it had been instilled in her that the word 'diplomatic' was paramount when it came to describing their own existence as they ought to be neither seen nor heard. They weren't there to be bodyguards nor to 'babysit', but liaised with those who did such specialised service. In other words, the DiS was more of an intelligence agency who the public at large would never know about. Although they existed under the auspices of Special Branch, headed by Commander Gibbons, their remit was pretty autonomous in what they were allowed to do; subject to never being seen in public. They were there to gather information, sieve through what was often misinformation, highlight the salient issues and pass their suspicions onto their sister organisation; the Diplomatic Protection Squad whose job it was to be the bodyguards. It had been argued that the two ought to be melded into one agency, but this had been rebutted on the grounds that one could be highly intelligent and a brilliant investigator from a wheelchair, while quite the opposite was what was required to actually put oneself in harm's way. Quite often they needed to liaise with MI5 and 6 and whatever other relevant security service might be affected, which is where Commander Gibbons came in.

The last job Patricia wanted was to act as someone's bodyguard, and up until recently had been the job of Justin, her fiancé. Commander Gibbons had recognised her natural talent for investigating, hence her previous title of Detective Inspector. Officially she was still entitled to include the description of 'Detective' as she had only been subpoenaed.

She briefly opened one eye before resuming her ruminations. She considered the irony of the possibility of having to guard Maurice 'Bloody' Hamilton MP, when he was really the only person in the whole wide world who she would not shed a tear for, should some assassin's bullet find its mark. She smiled to herself thinking about how perfect her aim had been when she had kicked him in the balls and hoped that whenever he thought of her, a little twinge would remind him of her.

The door opened, Commander Gibbons closed it silently behind him before sitting down in a chair more or less opposite her and as he did so, she felt a few seconds of vibration. She deduced it was from one of the undergrounds which would have routed somewhere under their feet. For the first few seconds he did nothing but look at her, and it reminded her of their first meeting in his office when she had felt as though she had been under his microscope.

"How do you feel?" he asked.

At first she didn't understand the question because she felt perfectly alright, but one always had to think one, if not two, steps ahead with Gibbons. She hadn't expected such a basic question and stared back at him, trying to give herself time to work out why he was asking.

"Fine." She knew he didn't abide those who minced words. She kept a straight face.

He met her stare. "Hold your hands out straight."

She did as she was told, bending her arms slightly at the elbows to provide herself with a little support. She watched his eyes, inspecting her hands for a good ten seconds.

"OK."

She put her hands back on her lap and worked out that he was looking for a reaction.

"Your first and probably last kill and not even a shake. How do you account for that?"

In a flash she discarded making a smart response; Gibbons didn't have any sense of humour. She was about to say 'training' when she realised that that was not the answer he was looking for. He'd have worked that one out for himself. No. He was looking for a reason why she was not reacting to killing a fellow human being; most people would.

"I'm not sure I can accurately answer that. It didn't worry me at the time and it doesn't worry me now, but I suppose you can put it down to my stoic constitution."

His held a steady stare but it didn't unnerve her. "Do you think it might be because you were acting under orders and ergo the protection of this department?"

"That's irrelevant because if anyone tries to shoot me, I'll shoot back in self-defence."

"But what if he shot at you because of your provocation? This department's provocation." He paused. "If that was the case then you can no longer rely upon self-defence as an argument."

She knew she was being tested further and now being cornered. Two choices lay in front of her. She could either concede the point or continue arguing against it, but she suspected that she would probably lose the latter. She decided to attack the question. "Then what exactly are we doing here right now? You know I won't have an answer to that question and you know that the only justification is, as you say, 'following orders'. So no, I cannot simply rely upon the old excuse of 'following orders', I have to lay the responsibility at your feet."

"We all know that 'following orders' is the common euphemism used by soldiers when the fighting stops and we won't start debating the rights and wrongs of that now, otherwise we'll be here all night. What you must be very clear about is was it the right thing to do? This is the one question that you have to answer honestly, more to yourself than to me. If you get the answer wrong, then it'll eat you up until the end of your days and you'll be no use to me or this department a lot sooner than you can imagine. Whatever you tell me, or anyone else, only you have to live with your answer. Make sure you can do that."

He paused to let that sink in. "So, I'll ask you again, can you justify killing that person?"

She nibbled her bottom lip while thinking back to the warehouse. Undoubtedly she had done the right thing by shooting him; that was patently in self-defence. But what about his provocation point? "To answer that fully, I'd need to know about him. Who he was... what..."

Gibbons held his hand up and she stopped talking. "So now you want to be judge and jury as well as executioner, but I'm afraid to inform you that you can't have it both ways. Either you follow orders or you leave it up to us to decide. If you start asking questions, you'll end up in all sorts of trouble, so to make it simple for you I'll explain the basics and let you work the rest out later. You're easily capable of that."

He crossed his legs at ankle level before continuing. "If I were to tell you that he had been a rapist and child murderer on the run from Russia, you'd probably accept that. On the other hand, if I told you it was a case of mistaken identity and that he was really a family man from across the road who sold insurance, you might not accept that as it has he who was firing at you. But what if I told you he was one of ours and under orders only to fire back if threatened with capture? So now you have just three scenarios where there could quite easily be several others. Now take your reasoning another step and query if what I had told you was true. What if I had lied to you just to get the job done, eh? Then there's the possibility that whatever conclusions I came to were wrong and that whoever told me about the man had also lied. There's even the possibility that the man had been ordered to be killed or captured just to expose you. So now you're faced with the need to think about what you are doing while the man creeps up on you and puts a bullet in you head. You don't have the luxury of time in these instances, whatever principles you may have premeditated."

He could see the cogs turning.

"You either trust me to make the right decisions and follow my orders or crawl into a corner of your life and stay there. My advice is to leave it to your superiors to make the informed decisions, and you carry out our instructions. If you can live with that, then you have a future in the department, but if not..." He left the obvious consequences part of the equation unfinished.

The lack of sound in the room was intense as she considered the clear dilemma, but she eventually responded. "I think I can live with that."

Gibbons didn't actually smile but whatever she detected, it was positive. "In that case I can let you know a little more about this morning's goings-on."

They both shifted in their seats a little.

"Your brief this morning was a follow-up to your training as your instructor advised us that you were ready for such a procedure. Normally I would lay the blame for you being detected by your target squarely at your door but you'll be glad to learn that that was not the case in this instance, so don't berate yourself. It transpires that there were two of them. You were following one while the other was under surveillance by... another arm of the security services. It was they who erred and invertedly revealed you, which is why your target ran. Had you lost sight of him none of this would have been revealed to us, so it was rather fortunate that you found yourself in the position of having to act the way you did."

Patricia was grappling with his comments. Her first day on the job, first assignment, first for almost everything and despite screwing up, she was being given a pat on the back. "Am I allowed to ask why I was given the job of following him if there were others?"

"Fair question. OK. Firstly it was considered a very low-risk scenario. Following others is usually as safe as houses and a perfect way to start a novice off in a new job. We issue all our personnel with sidearms as a matter of course as it helps you to get used to wearing one. Just

Chapter 1 - Today's Lesson

as well we have that policy otherwise you might not still be here. Secondly, we needed to find out who this fellow was meeting, and that is where the errors began to creep in. Our friends from the other agency hadn't advised us that they were on the trail of the other chap and what we've gathered from the dead man's phone was that he was texted by his counterpart who he was supposed to be meeting. That happened about the same time as you made first contact; hence him ending up in that warehouse trying to lose you. Before you ask, yes it was I who sanctioned you for this as I thought you were ready for an easy task. Besides which, I need to weigh up who is suitable for what job."

He leaned forward a little. "I'm glad to say that I was right."

She stopped her gentle bottom-lip nibbling. "What happened to the man he was meeting and have we gained any insight into what they were passing?"

"Now, these are the sorts of questions one is legitimately allowed to ask, but it wouldn't have made any difference to what happened this morning, so I'm going to tell you because I'm handing this case over to you for further investigation. I'll furnish you with the official file, but in this job one has to learn to use one's nose as much as anything else and what I'm about to tell you is mainly conjecture, so don't go misconstruing it."

She nodded in automaton.

"I'll give you a brief outline before moving on. Bulgaria is part of the EU but as long as the European Commission's auditors refuse to sign-off on their accounts, they refuse to adopt the euro. Quite understandable really as there are billions of euros that have gone missing and can't be accounted for each year. Suspected slush funds and the like, and I gather that there's no French word equivalent to 'backhanders'. Laundry yes, but not backhanders. Pressure is currently being applied to the Bulgarian finance minister Kiril Hirov to change his mind and recommend adoption of the euro. He appears to be incorruptible and is one of several in his government who are staunchly against giving up their own currency. Quite logically, he approached us in the UK asking the best way of parrying the Europeans' demands. It all sounds perfectly fine on the surface, but believe me when I tell you that there are those who would stop at almost nothing to coerce the Bulgarians into adoption. The currency speculators of the world can be very persuasive when billions are concerned, but on the other hand the Russians appear to want the Bulgars to retain their levs, despite its exchange rate permanently being on the poor side. Hirov has a series of meetings with various finance ministers in 'neutral' London at the end of next week and will no doubt bring his own security detail. Meanwhile, before he arrives it's our job to expose those who may threaten the well-being of the visiting finance minister while he's on British soil. Once we have collated any relevant information, it will be passed onto our colleagues in the Diplomatic Protection Squad who can act appropriately."

Before continuing, he watched her for a moment to see if she was taking this all in. "When I say it's our job, it's now your job."

Chapter 1 - Today's Lesson

"My job?" The inflection and tone of her voice betrayed that she had not been expecting this.

"That's right. Your job. It's what you do in this department."

She was flabbergasted. She hadn't actually wondered what her role was to be in the Diplomatic information Service and had assumed, up to now, that she would be given orders which she would have to follow. Gibbons was putting her in a position where she would be neither giving nor taking orders; merely analysing. Her mind was working down two tracks at the same time; one as to her position within the Section, the other on the issue that Gibbons had just landed on her lap.

"Are you sure this is what you want me to do?"

"Certainly. You're the perfect person to tackle this." Before she could respond he added. "Think about it. Firstly you come from the perfect background of detective work, often with little more to go on than what you read from a file, and from your record you're very good at getting results. Secondly you're the only person in this department who has had any recent experience of Bulgarians… the chap you put an end to earlier today was Bulgarian. And that reminds me, I haven't told you what we think he was doing."

She held her breath waiting for him to reveal what it was. Instead he half held up his hand.

"No… I think we'll wait and see what conclusions you come up with. I don't want to be putting ideas into your mind, otherwise there's little point in having you on board, is there? If I tell you one thing, when you come up against a brick wall, you'll only revert to the notion I could have supplied you with."

Sarcasm was not her usual first reaction, but on this occasion she replied with just one word. "Thanks."

She didn't expect him to react and he didn't, other than by standing up. "You've got two days. Wait here and I'll get Tates to hand you the computer file... he's the chap who showed you down here."

As he turned and reached for the door handle, she enquired, "Will Tates be showing me where I'll be working?"

He stopped twisting the handle but turned to face her instead. "You don't know?"

It was clear from her blank look that she hadn't been told.

"Well, I suppose your acceleration into this world by today's actions has meant that you have been bypassed with essential information, so I'll fill you in myself. The rest you can glean from Tates. You're not working from here or anywhere near here. You work where and when you like, as do your contemporaries. All we do here is discover, accept or refuse, analyse, pass on information and on the very rare occasion take direct action." He could see her working it out but decided to help. "Think of this as the centre of a spider's web and the rest of the world is represented only by the limits of the outer reaches of that web. You can gather whatever information you want from anywhere on this web just so long as you tell me about it the instant you arrive at a firm conclusion." He decided to embellish a little more. "Officially our Section exists to gather information.

Unofficially we do whatever is required to find out that information because our Military Intelligence friends cannot as they are permanently being scrutinised by all and sundry. In bygone years a secret agent would be exactly that but nowadays you can almost look up your local spy on the internet and find out where he lives."

He lowered his voice to emphasise the next part. "We're the real invisible chaps who actually find out what's going on in the world." He lowered his head just a little and raised an eyebrow to emphasise his next point. "We're so far under the radar that nobody knows we're here and certainly nobody from the press. Clear?"

She sat unmoving, so he repeated himself with a firmer tone to his voice.

"Clear?"

"Clear."

"Ostensibly you now work under me for Special Branch as one of my investigators and that's what you tell anyone who asks. That and nothing else. But if I want you to bring me back the Dali Llama's girlfriend from Timbuktu for questioning, then you do it without being found out and without question."

He looked directly at her to see if what he had just said had been understood and when he saw the narrowing of her eyes he added, "Here endeth today's lesson."

He abruptly opened the door and left.

Chapter 2

A Prayer

Soap suds caught in her nose as she forgot to breathe out rather than in at the wrong moment. She sneezed into her bath water not caring that any mucus would remain, and then she laughed at herself because she recognised that she had been concentrating so much on what had gone on that day, that it had totally slipped her mind to attend to the more basic needs of her bodily functions; namely holding her breath when rinsing her hair underwater. At least the bubbles didn't taste too soapy.

Clean, she stretched out with closed eyes and revelled in the warm water. She'd normally have used the shower but today felt like a bath day, and besides, some of the nozzles in the shower head still needed descaling. She let her mind wander away from the day's events. Wiggling her toes to reach the end of the bath, she wondered who on earth would fit a bath this long. The first time she had got in it some weeks ago, she slipped all the way down akin to a new ship launching for the first time, except that she acted more like a submarine submerging; her toes desperately seeking out the long stop of the end of the bath. Now she knew why

Chapter 2 - A Prayer

the previous owner of the flat had installed the two-metre long steel bath as she used her lungs to keep her nostrils above water while the rest of her entire body infused the toasty warmth of the water. It was pure luxury. And that wasn't the only odd item about the flat not far from Maidenhead that she and Justin had moved into not so long ago. Why he ever sold it in such a hurry was still a mystery, but he had been most insistent that they completed on the sale by the end of that month. They could hardly refuse to meet his timetable because of the most reasonable price he'd been asking and he'd even thrown in a ten-year-old Mazda MX5 in the garage that went with the flat. They had assumed that the Antipodean had emigrated back to Australia and had had fun guessing how many girlfriends he'd be disappointing. It had been such a good idea them both giving up their separate rented places and buying their first flat together; not that they were married yet, only engaged. She decided to get to know the little sports car so sold her relatively boring Ford Mondeo. Even Justin decided on a change and traded up his Beamer for a newer and much faster M Sport model.

In a dream or maybe for real, she heard the front door closing which announced the arrival of Justin, and supper. He'd already told her that tonight's was to be a surprise and if last week's takeaway episode had been anything to go by, she most definitely had something to look forward to. He'd blindfolded her before feeding her morsels on the end of a small fork and she'd had to guess what it was from taste and texture alone. He'd set the biased rules so that with each wrong answer he would undo one button, and when there were no more buttons or zips, the article would be removed. He took his time until she was all but naked and just as he removed her blindfold he smeared a decent dollop of ice cream over her midriff and laughed at her shriek. Before it melted onto the carpet she stood up and vengefully ordered him to lick it off but inevitably some dribbled down onto her knickers, so they were dutifully licked as well.

It was a memorable evening that had satisfied their carnal lust but she found it hard to imagine that tonight's events were going to surpass last week's. Or perhaps they would. She decided that the temperature of the bath water was on the turn, so pulled the plug and got out and, drying herself, wondered what he'd be telling her about his day. Since Maurice 'Bloody' Hamilton MP, Secretary of State for Northern Ireland, had forced him out of the Diplomatic Protection Squad, specifically as one of his own bodyguards, Justin had created his own private intelligence agency; what the general public would refer to as a private detective agency if they had known about it. He didn't need to advertise because it was currently living off the back of an outstanding result in exposing a network of moles in the heart of the Civil Service arm of the British government and was enjoying exceptional quality of work from Her Majesty's Government. Word had gone round the corridors of power in Westminster that Justin was the perfect discreet investigator.

It hadn't been all his own work as Patricia had done more of the running than he had when they had

Chapter 2 - A Prayer

discovered the assassination plot against Hamilton. It had definitely been a pooled effort that had not only saved Hamilton's life, but also exposed those traitors that had been close to him. Patricia was not one to needle him about it, but did so on occasion just to see his reaction.

Dressed, she was about to go through to the living room when she stopped and considered if Justin was about to hit her with another game of 'strip takeaway', so as a bit of fun she turned and donned an extra cardigan with lots of fiddly buttons down the front. It was really too warm for another layer but it probably wouldn't stay on for too long; she hoped.

She tried to guess what delights he had bought with him by sniffing as she walked towards the kitchen, but there was no odour. No wafting smell of a curry, Chinese, fish and chips; nothing. He hadn't heard her so she crept up behind him and dug him sharply in the ribs, hoping for a knee-jerk reaction.

Nothing.

"I saw your reflection in the window."

"Owww." She was genuinely disappointed. "So, are you going to tell me what we're eating tonight or have I got to guess again?"

"No secrets tonight. It's sushi."

"Sushi!" she exclaimed. "That's wet fish, isn't it?"

He turned away from his countertop preparation. "Uncooked," he corrected. "And very healthy to boot."

"I'm not sure I've had sushi before." Apprehension was in the tone of her voice. "Not sure I'm going to like it."

"Oh, I'm sure you will. You like smoked salmon, don't you?"

She nodded.

"That's sushi. So are roll mops, cockles, muscles, whelks and several other day-to-day items that I know you've had in the past, so there's no need to turn your nose up at Japanese sushi. Now if you'll wait just a few minutes while I finish off here. On second thoughts, can you open that bottle of Macon in the fridge and get a couple of glasses?"

Perched on stools, they faced each other over the waist-high peninsular unit. There was only one large oval dish between them that Justin had prepared and she looked at him with a little awe as he described each in turn. "A word of warning. You may find the wasabi a bit on the hot side, so don't take more than a pinch. Here, add some soy sauce to the rice if you like. Spices it up nicely." He handed her a pair of chopsticks.

"Chopsticks! I'm hopeless with chopsticks. How am I supposed to pick up grains of rice with these pathetic twigs?"

"You'll get the hang of it. Hold 'em like this and watch me."

After her first effort, she removed her cardigan because she didn't want to drop any more food on it, despite making sure her mouth was over her side plate.

"What's this? Looks like an oyster," she said, pulling a bit of a face.

"That's because it is an oyster. A cherry oyster to be exact. Go on. Try swallowing it whole."

Chapter 2 - A Prayer

She picked up the shell and tipped it into her mouth and he watched her screw up her face as the slippery mollusc travelled down her throat. When she eventually opened her eyes and discovered that she was still alive, all she saw was Justin staring right at her with a big grin on his face. "Don't know if I like them or not."

"They're supposed to be good for the libido."

After a second's thought she responded, "You've always got an ulterior motive, haven't you?"

"You know the difference between oysters and kid's snot, don't you?"

"No. Go on."

"Kids won't eat oysters."

"Yuuurchhh."

"And for you next prize, try this one." He'd trapped a small, cubed piece of fish at the end of his chopsticks and offered it to her across the table.

"So what's this?" she asked, before she opened her mouth to accept the offering.

"That's what you've got to guess."

It had been in her mouth for a few seconds but it was evident that she was thoroughly enjoying it. "What a flavour. Ummm. Texture too. Wow. Go on then, what is it?"

"That was yellowfin tuna with rice."

It took them nearly an hour to devour the platter and towards the end she couldn't help asking Justin what he'd been doing that day.

"Funny you should ask, because I had to take this chap down the local martial arts centre and beat the crap out of him until he told me where I could buy the best sushi in town."

She decided to play along. "Did he tell you before you strangled him?"

"Naaah. Wong guy. But I did have a man from the Treasury asking me to see what I can find out about a certain metal trader. Deals in bullion in particular."

"I don't know much about bullion other than it's gold and comes in heavy ingots."

"That's most people's idea of bullion but in reality an ingot is made out of any metal. It's just the expensive stuff like gold or silver that people remember, but in this case it's platinum."

"Platinum. I don't think I've ever seen any platinum."

"Oh it's all around us and I'll bet you at least one of your friends will have a platinum ring or another piece of jewellery made out of it. Looks a bit like silver except it doesn't shine quite like it, but it's an awful lot more expensive due to its rarity."

"And how rare is that?"

"Well, gold's currently trading about £1,300 an ounce and silver a mere £20 or so, but platinum's nearly up to the level of gold at £900. Now that might well not sound like too much, I mean you and I could go out tomorrow and buy an ounce of gold just like that, but if you wanted a kilogram of the stuff, then that'll cost you."

"Save me the trouble. How much?"

"A kilo of platinum will set you back about thirty grand, and gold over forty."

Chapter 2 - A Prayer

She recoiled in surprise. "Wow. Now that's what I call expensive."

"I'd like to say that engagement ring you're wearing is platinum, but it's not. It's silver."

She naturally looked down at her ring, flicked it with her thumb so that it moved back and forth catching the light. She decided to have a dig at him.

"Cheapskate."

"Not at all." He'd been expecting such a retort. "It complements the rare amethyst perfectly." He risked a further comment. "I could always give it to someone else if you don't like it."

He blinked as she threw a few grains of rice in his direction.

"What's this bullion guy supposed to be doing to warrant the scrutiny of HM Treasury then?"

"Ummm, not sure yet but it looks like someone is passing on information from within to without; if you get my meaning."

"Insider dealing?"

"Something like that. I've only been at it for an afternoon so give me a chance. What about you? Anything exciting?"

She held her reactions in check just to see if she could, maintaining a level emotionless voice. "Well, what started out as a run-of-the-mill tailing job turned out to be a bit trickier than anyone imagined."

"Go on. I thought you were about to finish your training?"

"So did I, and one of those tests was to follow someone, only this time it was for real." She paused, trying to repel the emotion that she could feel welling up. "I had to shoot someone... the man I was trailing turned and tried to kill me."

Her slightly warbled tone betrayed her feelings enough for Justin to pause his nonchalant chopstick plate scraping. He wasn't sure how affected she was and decided to try the humorous approach first.

"I'll bet he was pissed off then."

"Justin... I killed him."

He wasn't certain how to react but put his chopsticks down anyway and reached out across the table with his hands to hold hers; they felt rather cold to his touch. "How do you feel?"

She half-laughed at his question. "That's the second time I've been asked that question today and to be perfectly honest I'm still not sure. Oh I know that may sound rather cold-hearted and perhaps I ought to have more empathy but I'm not about to have a nervous breakdown if that's what you're getting at."

"I'm not sure how I would react either, but you seem perfectly alright to me. I was only asking because I've heard stories about those who have gone through what you have and not come out of it as the same person. You see, it may take a day or two for it to sink in, so regardless of what those in London said, I'll always be here for you. Oh and by the way... it's OK to cry. Apparently it helps ease the guilt."

"I never said I felt guilty and it wasn't quite self-defence, but he did fire at me first, so that probably justifies my killing him. It was him or me. Simple as that."

Chapter 2 - A Prayer

Justin thought about it for a moment. "Did Commander Gibbons sanction both the operation and... your actions?"

"I doubt it's written down anywhere but he seemed quite satisfied that I had done the right thing."

"I'm sure he must have otherwise you'd be locked up in The Tower by now."

"Justin... I'd rather not talk about it anymore tonight... give me a chance to take it all in. OK?"

They stared at each other across the table but it was Justin who broke the spell. "Well, if you insist. Anyway, I was hoping to get your opinion on another matter."

"Go on."

Hanging onto her hands, he hesitated long enough so that it was clear that she was becoming concerned, but then he let his secret out. "Do you think you'll be able to help me make enough sandwiches for the cricket team this year?"

Chapter 3

Digging

As Justin sat down in his leather rotary chair behind his desk, he caught his shin on the left-hand filing cabinet that he still hadn't straightened out from weeks ago. He cursed as he shoved it so that it wouldn't be in the way again and immediately afterwards, rubbed his shin that was still smarting from Patricia's well-aimed kick the night before. She had eventually agreed to help him with the team's sandwiches after he pointed out her unfair reprisal. Unfair because it was she who had requested a change of subject.

His desktop screen came to life with its unusual strange ping-pong noise as he jiggled the mouse and he set about reading more reports. Bullion smuggling was becoming a thing of the past and he concluded that it was because of its bulk and weight, but related internet crime was on the increase. For some reason his mind kept wandering as he trawled through one article after another. This was his first real job since setting up his own detective agency with his sleeping partner Patricia and he wondered if he was going to be up to the challenge. Together they certainly worked out problems very well by bouncing ideas off each other, but with

Chapter 3 - Digging

Patricia now ensconced in her own demanding job, he was virtually on his own; except of a night-time when he would have the chance to catch up with his fiancée.

His mind kept drifting back to how efficiently they had worked as a team and ended up by saving Maurice 'Bloody' Hamilton's life by tracking down his assassins. That the MP had tried to rape Patricia and put them both in jail as part of his natural vengeful attitude was irrelevant. Had it not been for them, he would now be a deceased Member of Parliament, but by preventing his murder he was still the minister in charge of the Northern Ireland office and part of the Prime Minister's inner circle. A powerful man indeed. Hamilton had fired Justin from his position of being one of the many bodyguards in principle just because he was engaged to Patricia, but the word had gone round the corridors of power that Justin and Patricia were incorruptible, discreet and very good at getting results. After all, they had exposed a network of moles in the higher echelons of the Civil Service which had directly led to Justin being approached by a man from the Treasury.

His screen emitted another ping which helped him to re-focus. His chosen search engine had produced a list of countries that reflected the amount of platinum mined annually during the past twenty-five years and he couldn't help but raise an eyebrow when he came to Bulgaria's results. Next to nothing had been produced by that country since digital records began, and before that, the paper records had shown that apart from the minor pick-up from the manganese mine in the mountains of the Krumovgrad region in the south, there had been less than a ton of the raw material that had been exported. Until the year before last which showed an annual net export weight of over 200 tons.

He did a quick mental calculation but then reached for his phone and accessed the calculator. His mouth dropped open at the vast figure of £7 billion. His eyebrows knitted together, his eyes and fingers focusing on the keyboard and it didn't take him long to discover that this amounted to almost ten per cent of Bulgaria's GDP. The gross domestic product of each country normally varied by one or two percentage points each year; five per cent would be particularly healthy and anything over that was extremely unlikely. Economists around the world would be stunned in awe at the abrupt turnaround which would launch Bulgaria's standing significantly upwards in the eyes of the world's banks, as well as the IMF.

He did some more digging and discovered that the state-backed mining company had unearthed a vein of platinum in the south of the country, close to the border with Greece. Photographs of smiling yellow-helmeted figures standing under the belly of a massive excavator in an almost black crater attested to the fact. Reading down the page revealed that they were projecting further finds the more they dug, and that it really was leading to an economic boom in the south. A new town with spas, libraries, etc., had replaced the almost stone age rubble that had previously housed a few thousand miserable peasants, and in one photo, a group of particularly healthy individuals standing on the patio of the lido supposedly proved that this was indeed true.

Chapter 3 - Digging

While taking it all in, Justin simply didn't believe it. Nobody got that fit and healthy that quickly nor did money suddenly appear like that. He looked at the market price for platinum which showed a graph line akin to a drunk cyclist wending his way back home after a heavy session in the pub, but overall, the price had been rising for nearly three years. Zooming in on the graph line, he could see individual 'candles' showing the price either plummeting or launching at any given time. He presumed that somewhere in the world there would be experts examining this performance to see if there was any market manipulation, so he didn't bother trying to carry out his own analysis. Assuming that a certain amount of platinum ended up in the UK, a price would no doubt be brokered; which was why HM Treasury were asking questions. What puzzled him was why he should be asked to investigate when they could quite easily make their own enquiries. He automatically felt that he ought to be on his guard. Not just ask questions but ask himself why those questions were being asked and project theories to each answer. It was clear that with this amount of money around, it ought to come as no surprise that there would be criminal activity. And then it dawned on him. There would be a physical side to all of this as well, which was why he had been asked.

He groaned as he conjected the lengths those sorts of people would go to to protect their lucrative illegal income with bribery, corruption and all that went with it. He'd only spent a few hours on his first assignment and he was already beginning to feel out of his depth, but then on the other hand, perhaps there really was a newly discovered mine in Bulgaria. The only way of finding out was to actually go there and see for himself, but surely the people running the mine would have also thought of that and any visit was more likely to show that the mine was fully operational; even to an official visitor being shown round.

He reached for his phone to contact his Treasury man whom he had met only once before.

"Mr Thomas, Crawford here. Looking into this problem of yours, it looks like I'll need to go down there and see for myself, so I'll need official papers. I'll also need your chaps to pre-arrange matters for my visit but that would best be coming from the Trade and Industry Department. We don't want to alert them that we're investigating them, so an official visit from that government department would seem absolutely normal, especially if we're supposedly about to buy several tons of the stuff. Do you think this can be arranged at short notice?"

"Ahhh. I see what you're getting at. Leave it with me and I'll see what I can do. Any idea when you might want to go down there?"

"Anytime's fine by me, say a couple of days? And errr, perhaps I ought to have an assistant just to make it look a bit more official."

Silence at the other end of the phone, then. "OK, I don't see why not."

"Her name is Patricia Eyethorne."

"I thought it might be. Right then. I'll get straight on it."

Chapter 3 - Digging

"And one last thing… could you put me in touch with one of your metallurgists?"

"Consider it done."

"Thanks and bye."

Putting his phone back on the desk and leaning back in his chair he wondered how Patricia would take being offered a 'holiday' in Bulgaria. He chuckled to himself and almost sadistically looked forward to being slapped round the face when he told her of the real reason why they were going to Bulgaria.

His daydream was punctuated by his computer making another weird pinging noise and he reluctantly leaned forward and started another line of enquiry on the internet. Delving into the world of platinum mining, there was something at the back of his mind that refused to wake up and come to the front.

Chapter 4

More Digging

Despite Tates' boringingly suited appearance, he was actually a very forthcoming person; at least that's what it seemed like to Patricia as he went through some procedures.

"I must say that I'm a little surprised that you were asked to shadow someone without having come through me first. It must have been a very last-minute job." It was a comment and he didn't expect a reply, so carried on. "You must have fallen between two stools if you get my meaning; somewhere between training and inauguration, but then that's one of my jobs. Still, you're here now so we can finish you off."

His voice was easy to listen to and his manner a little condescending but there was a steely edge to some of the dos and don'ts; fortunately there weren't many of them. He finished up with the security protocols. "This voice-activated device plugs into any laptop or similar device but it only goes in one way. You have to push it in with your finger and thumb which also acts as a fingerprint detector so make sure you use the same ones each time." He paused to look at her. "Left or right." It was an obvious statement but she surmised

Chapter 4 - More Digging

that he must have got some enjoyment from stating the bleeding obvious. "Once activated you can access our comms team 24/7 but you'll need to use it every 48 hours otherwise it ceases to function, so don't worry about losing it. By the way, if someone should steal it and plug it in, there's some useless football or cricket scores to bore them to death."

She could see the logic of it as passwords and codes could be hacked whereas with this method, not only would her fingerprints be verified as she inserted what was essentially a dongle, but she would need to confirm that it was actually her by speaking.

"Goodbye for now then." He abruptly turned and disappeared through one of the doors which self-closed with a reassuring clunk.

Patricia was left holding her dongle which she now looked at a little more closely, trying to see the fingerprint detector parts, but it was black and smooth all over and no hint of what it might really be. From its shape, it might even be considered a form of jewellery, a black diamond even, and she made a note to buy a silver cord to thread through the loophole. She exited the building and headed for the nearest local market trader a short walk away on Embankment. By total contrast to what she had just been through, it was a bit of a relief to just stand by the wall that separated the path from the Thames and watch the multicoloured masses of tourists meandering this way and that in the shadow of Queen Elizabeth Tower that housed Big Ben. While she waited for the stall holder to finish ripping off a family of foreigners who had just bought a canvas union flag bag, her eyes skitted over the free-standing newspaper advertising frame depicting the headlines of yet another arson attack on an innocent magazine printers, and out of curiosity she took a few paces and saw that the reverse side announced that the firemen were going on strike again. How typically British she thought; not hypocritical, just British. She felt proud to be British among so many foreigners milling around her. She was a little nervous asking the stallholder to thread a loop of 'unbreakable' silver through the dongle, but five pounds and the same number of minutes later, she was on her way.

Outside of rush hour, it was easy enough to find a seat on the underground as it wended its way towards Earl's Court where she would have to change en route to Heathrow; that was where she had left her car. The train behaved in its usual way by buffeting the passengers around as it traversed the hundred-year-plus tracks, but nobody seemed disconcerted by the relatively violent lateral shove from the entire carriage. It wasn't until she changed onto the more modern Jubilee line that the ride became smoother, thus giving her more time to absorb what Tates had told her. It felt like she was now working for an underground agency and thinking back on all that had been said to her during the past twenty-four hours, that was exactly what it was.

Once through the door to their flat, she stripped off, showered, sat in the corner of a large chair, grabbed her coffee and laptop in that order, inserted the dongle and was about to try it out when she realised that she had nothing to report. Instead, she started to trawl through

Chapter 4 - More Digging

the history of Kiril Hirov and other government ministers and ended up learning more about the history of Bulgaria in as short a space of time than the whole of her entire life to date. The one thing that stood out over the past thousand years or so was that Bulgaria suffered being the filling in the sandwich between the Russians in the north and the Turks in the south. Stability prevailed under Ottoman rule for centuries right up to when the Russians took over but since the fall of the Berlin Wall in 1989, it had become a true democracy.

Links to Hirov, often irrelevant or tenuous at best, took up an inordinate amount of time, but in her thorough methodology she started to gain a picture of him and his extended family. Middle-aged, he had made plenty of enemies in reaching his governmental position but appeared to have substantial backing from not only his fellows but also from the populous in general. It seemed even money that he would be Bulgaria's premier at some time in the not-so-distant future.

Checking local newspapers whose translations left something to be desired, it seemed he had survived one assassination attempt several years ago but she gleaned that assassination was considered almost a national pastime in that part of the world. After all, it was just such an assassination in 1914 in the region that had led to the outbreak of the first world war.

She picked up on a small article from just a few years ago on the third page of *The Dneven* that hypothesised that mercenary Albanians were still active and disruptive. The nameless group were pro-Russian and it seemed that they purposefully had no leader and it therefore followed that there was no head to that particular snake; nothing to cut off. She followed related stories reported outside of Bulgaria and nearly missed a report on the second page of the Italian *La Repubblica* that provided a name. The article reported that a man going under the name of Otrino Tuvo had been admitted to hospital with burns to his hands and that the authorities had been trying to trace this young man as they thought he had been a witness to a serious traffic collision directly outside Sofia's main railway station. The reporter had theorised that the burns to the chap had been caused by his failed arson attack on the adjacent print works that same morning.

Normally she would have dismissed this report as unrelated but she was clutching at straws so followed her nose, oblivious of the length of time it was taking. Just about at the end of her patience and with another cup of coffee beckoning, she was about to get up when an iota of an idea came to her. She left her laptop, thinking about it while she got up, boiled the kettle, stretched, etc. Instead of sitting down, she leaned over and scrutinised the first of several pages and blinked at what it was telling her. A link at last, so she set her mug down on the coaster so as to enable both hands on the keyboard. One final search confirmed what she had been thinking and as though in celebration, she started to lightly nibble her bottom lip.

She ferreted around for her notepad and pen and started scribbling anything of relevance and all the while hoped she was not wasting her time.

Chapter 4 - More Digging

From her point of view there had been an inordinate number of unexplained arson events on magazine and minor newspaper offices throughout the region and particularly those with right-of-centre sympathies. Some had been as a result of a fire to an adjacent property which had somehow spread and some had been attributed to other factors, but the outcome was undeniably that physical political activity was forcing out those who did not support Russian interests. And then she discovered that those attacks had been pan-European and not necessarily incendiary on every occasion. A bus had crashed into publishing offices on two occasions, one in Warsaw, the other in Barcelona. Goats had ostensibly chewed through a gas pipe in an adjacent shop on the outskirts of Athens. The flames from a chip shop in south London had spread to next door's printing works, and so the stories went on. All apparently unconnected and nobody had noticed; up to now.

A second article mentioned the name of Otrino Tuvo and it took her several minutes to discover that there was someone who went under the name of Hana Otrino Tuvo born in Minsk but there was precious little else.

Collating what relevant information she had gathered into a sensible format, she plugged in her dongle, uploaded her pages as instructed, and asked the communication centre about Hana Otrino Tuvo. Just as she tapped the send button she frowned as she realised that his initials spelt HOT and smiled wryly at the acronym. It took no more than a few seconds before a digital dossier on Tuvo was displayed, and oh what a naughty boy he had been.

It was thought he had been born in Minsk and that his father may have been a policeman, but nothing was known about his mother. There was next to nothing known about this man right up to just a few years ago, and even then his dossier seemed to repeat the stories found in the local press. There was nothing to indicate where he had been, what he had been doing, etc., and unusually, all bar one exception, there were no photographs of him. Enlarging a group photograph that by the look of it had been taken by an official because it was an organised layout of some thirty men all dressed similarly, in the background there was what may have been a military base. The photograph's graininess didn't allow any meaningful facial features but the red circle showed a tall, slender, dark-haired man.

Everyone had had a photograph of themselves taken at some point or other in their lives, and everyone had school reports etc. available and, in the main, one could see what anyone looked like on the internet, but with this man it was as though he had been airbrushed from the human race. Only governmental spy agencies had the power to do such a comprehensive job and this immediately raised her suspicions. More notepad scribbling but this time accompanied by some eye-rubbing and it must have been the dulling of the background light that made her look at the time. She let out an expletive.

"Yurrrccchhh!"

Chapter 4 - More Digging

She'd just made her mind up to carry on until Justin arrived with their evening takeaway when the phone rang. It was him but all he had to say was, "A or B?"

She was about to ask him to repeat himself when she realised he was asking her what kind of food she preferred that night.

"A."

"Half an hour then. Bye."

Half an hour to keep digging and she decided to see if her link to the security computer was what she hoped it was by requesting if immigration had had a passport in HOT's name pass through anywhere. She left that program running and requested any video footage of the fire in south London which had engulfed the *South London Post*. She concluded that it was most likely arson because the event had occurred mid-week and well past midnight when only vagrants frequented the shop front recesses. The fire officer's report stated that while no accelerant had been used, he suspected that hot frying oil was unlikely to have found its way to near the front door and the air bricks that adjoined the printing works next door at the same time, but he couldn't prove it. She surmised that once the fingers of fire found their way into the print works where there would be even more flammable liquids, there was little chance of stopping the fire.

She started to go back through some of the others and a similar story emerged that nothing could be proven.

This HOT man was certainly no idiot.

The CCTV footage was night-grainy and from too far away to make out anything meaningful and by the time she had looked at that, she saw that her immigration query had drawn a blank; she already suspected the answer.

Stretching before she got up, she felt in need for something alcoholic rather than more coffee but the decision was taken out of her hands as she heard the front door of the flat bang open against the foot locker. He called out and she saw him disappear into the kitchen but nothing could disguise the unique waft of fish 'n' chips, and her heart instantly upped its pace with joy.

Being 'southerners', ketchup was called for rather than vinegar.

"Wally?" Justin dangled the green offensive-looking pickle between forefinger and thumb mid-way between them.

Without hesitation, she lunged forward and took a decent bite out of the gherkin, winced as the spices permeated her gills, grimaced and shuddered in happy reaction before chewing it into acceptable pieces. "Come on then mister know-it-all, why do they call it a wally?"

"You really did lack proper education, didn't you? Every decent schoolboy knows that one."

"I was never a schoolboy. Look. I've got lumpy bits in the right place." She thrust her ample bosom forwards.

"OK, OK. As far as I remember, it was because the man who started the firm back in the 1800s decided that when he'd packed the baby gherkins and put them in a tin, he'd save money by letting customers see what they were buying by putting them in a glass jar rather than having to put a label on the tin. His name was Walter, shortened to Wally."

"What? Simple as that?"

"The best explanations usually are, you should know that." He let her mull on that one while taking one of the last mouthfuls of battered cod. "Of course, there's always the rugby version of the truth."

She paused her own mastication, swallowed and washed it down with a swig of wine as it dawned on her that he was probably having her on again. It gave her time to consider how best to react. She did so enjoy his teasing but never seemed to be able to get one over on him. "OK then. What's the unofficial version?"

She almost regretted asking the second she had done so because of the wolfish grin that instantly appeared on his face.

"It's phallic."

Their eyes met across the countertop and try as she might to maintain a straight face, eventually a smile emerged followed by her blurting out a laugh.

"What's so funny?" he asked innocently.

She leaned back in her chair. "You don't even know, do you?"

"What?"

"Haaa, haaa. The way you're eating your wally. Haaa haaa. You've been sucking at it like a baby's dummy. Talk about phallic."

He paused with the gherkin half in his mouth with his lips wrapped round it and had to admit that he'd been enjoying the sensation of the knobbly obtrusions of the wally as it passed his lips.

She knew straight away how to counter. Leaning forwards, she moved his hand to one side, extracted it from his mouth, looked at it closely then seductively extended her tongue so that it licked and teased the end of it. She wasn't sure how long she could maintain this charade, so changed her grip on it with one hand while rubbing up and down with the other. The inference was unmistakable, and she chose her next moment for maximum effect. Stopping suddenly, she grabbed it firmly, violently squeezed and watched his reaction as it imploded. Without waiting to see what he would do, she yelled. "Bingo."

They only just made it to the bedroom without tripping over their clothes which they peeled off each other on the way, and it was a good twenty minutes later before either of them stirred from carnal satisfaction. Justin was the first to get out of bed and turned on the light. As he did he noticed a distinct mark on the white duvet cover. He peered at it closely. "You might want to look at this."

It was the serious tone in his voice that got her attention, so she reluctantly complied. Their heads were nearly touching as they both peered closely at the red stain that neither of them could remember being there before.

"Blood?" he queried.

Patricia changed angles by pushing Justin out of the way, sniffed at it and smeared a little on her forefinger. After a few seconds she sat upright. "I think I'd better examine you closely."

Chapter 4 - More Digging

"Me!" he exclaimed. "What makes you think it's me?"

"Just kneel down and splay your legs so as I can get a close look at your scrotum."

He paused, so she added. "I think I know what it might be."

With that worrying sensation, he complied and waited for her deliberations, but what came next really caught him out.

WALLOP. She had left a superb red weal of her handprint right in the centre of his buttock and he let out a tremendous 'arrrgggh' as he flopped forward onto the mattress. When he turned over to look up at her all he could see was her holding her hand up to her mouth and laughing uncontrollably.

"What was that all about?" he asked as he rubbed his rear end, but she couldn't stop laughing, so he flicked one of her nipples.

"OK, OK, OK, hang on a sec." But she continued to laugh, so he tweaked her other nipple hard enough to get her to calm down.

She pointed at the stain on the duvet cover.

"Well it's not my blood then is it." he commented.

Half laughing, she agreed. "No it's not, and it's not mine either."

"Well, who's is it?"

She had another bout of the giggles but he kept his patience until she calmed down enough. "It's ketchup."

It took him a couple of seconds to decide to teach her a lesson and he launched himself on her and ended up straddling her torso; this time their lovemaking didn't last quite as long.

Chapter 5

Of Metal

"Why the bloody hell do I want to go to Budapest? There are loads of other places I would rather visit and I don't think Buda-bloody-pest's even on my list. I'm not even sure where it is let alone how to get there. And do we need visas?"

"Oh OK then. I lied. We're off to Sofia."

"Where's that?

Justin could see that he could no longer palm this off as his idea of a working romantic weekend. He was going to tell her why on the plane but now ruefully accepted that he never ought to have tried; but he kept that one to himself.

They were still cuddling each other in bed, but now it seemed senseless to continue their gentle caresses.

"I've got a confession," he said rather sheepishly.

Ten minutes later with beers in hand and attired in their dressing gowns, they were both wandering around the living room furniture discussing what came next.

"Try not to trip over the dead fish and chips. We don't want any more ketchup stains."

Justin about turned and picked up the newspapers that it came in. "We can still carry on doing what we're doing while we're waiting for our official government visas to come through, and when we're there, there's bound to be an opportunity or two to do some sightseeing."

"Of course we can, and I'm thinking that it's not such a bad idea anyway."

Justin stopped mid-stride. "You don't?"

"Think about it. What would be more natural than a government employee taking his 'girlfriend' on a jolly as a perk of the job? I'll bet you most of the EEC employees do and I'll also bet that they'll be expecting some sort of bribery angle, so we'd better be prepared with some sort of scheme. Furthermore, and this may just be a coincidence, as I'm working on job that may or may not involve someone linked to Bulgaria, it'll give me the chance to get a flavour of the real people. When do you think we'll be going?"

"You've changed your tune, haven't you?"

"Oh, you know me. Easily persuaded. I even said yes to your proposal."

Justin didn't rise to the suggestion, but instead countered. "Ahhh, but I didn't say when, did I?"

"Just as well since we're probably going to be busy in Budapest for a few days." She stuck her tongue out him. "And anyway, it's going to have to be next year now 'cos we've run out of time to book the wedding venue we wanted for this summer."

***

On the western edge of Finsbury Square more or less in the centre of London's square mile lies the smart entrance to the Metal Exchange where, as one would expect from the description on the brass plaque, metals from around the world are traded. Anything metallic is bought and sold in commercial quantities from the plentiful and cheap iron ore that can be scraped off the surface in some parts of the world, to the rare and expensive mined uranium. Platinum is considered rather sought after and seldom does it take long for any quantity to remain available for long.

Upon giving his name to the concierge, Justin took the lift to the seventh and top floor and stepped out to face an extraordinary metal sculpture directly in front of him, backdropped by an equally extraordinary view of the business district of London. An eager receptionist ushered him along the glass-lined corridor to what was obviously one of the prime private offices on the top floor of the building.

"Justin Crawford is here to see you, Sir Neville."

Justin had guessed that a knight of the realm would either be a dashing figure of a man or a distinguished looking gentleman. The person holding out his hand in front of him was neither, nor could he be easily pigeon-holed.

"Can't quite get used to the 'Sir' bit so just call be Neville. Neville Chambers." He was dressed in grubby joggers, knackered sandals, and a moth-eaten t-shirt with a beanie hat of indeterminate colour on the floor. He sat down in a sumptuous leather armchair and

Chapter 5 - Of Metal

indicated for Justin to do likewise in a similar one a few feet away. It was really comfy.

"Hang on one tick. I've just got to make a note of something I should have done hours ago."

Justin watched a fit forty-something-year-old man as he wrote with an e-pen on a tablet and wondered how long ago he'd received his knighthood. In the New Year's honours list just gone maybe? Whatever, he was nothing like what he had pictured previously.

The e-pen bounced across the desk. "Now then, I gather from one of you government boys that you want to know something about platinum, so what can I tell you that you haven't already looked up on the internet? Umm."

The direct question caught Justin out. No 'how are you' or 'tea or coffee'. Other than his name, hardly any introduction at all. It must have shown on his face because before he could respond, Neville continued. "No, you certainly aren't a metal man are you, otherwise you'd have asked me by now. You see, the metal exchange is an extremely fast moving and particularly stressful market and there's usually no time for mamby-pandying around. Here we do deals in an instant and if you've ever seen 'The Ring' in action, you'd know what I mean." He looked at his watch. "In fact, come with me."

He rose and turned to a hanger behind him, donned a tie and jacket that disguised his tatty clothing, pressed a button on his desk and without waiting to see if he was being followed, strode off at a rapid pace, through the office door to the lift. By the time they reached it, the doors were opening. Once inside he commented, "Useful thing having a lift call button on your desk. Of course, not everyone has one, but as one of the top dogs, I get to be able to use it. Here we are."

The doors had hardly opened when a cacophony of sound filled the cabin and the volume increased ten-fold as they walked into 'The Ring'. This was the circular trading floor where dealers, clerks and their superiors all seemed to be shouting at one another, but nobody seemed to be referring to the extremely large set of screens at one end that displayed world-wide metal prices.

Justin followed Neville through the throng of frantic activity to one of the nine bays that encircled the arena and, all the while, tried unsuccessfully to comprehend what the myriad of voices were saying. Before he knew it, Neville was talking loudly in his right ear.

"Platinum's just coming to an end in a few seconds and it'll be tin next, but you can tell that there's a lot of demand because those three over there are still trying to fix the price."

They watched as the blood pressure of the three city gent types seemed to climb rapidly as did their gesticulations and voices. The sudden silence.

"That's it then." He glanced at the screen. "Fallen nearly 2% since yesterday. Come on."

In what seemed like the blink of an eye they were sitting in the chairs back in Neville's office.

"Now, I'll ask you again... what do you want to know?"

Chapter 5 - Of Metal

Having just seen how fast the metal market moved, Justin had a few questions he'd already prepared, but thought Neville might be able to provide a little more help if he knew a bit about the background. "In a couple of days, we'll be visiting a mine in the Krumovgrad region of Bulgaria and as a representative of the government's Trade and Industry Department I'll be trying to ascertain if it really is a platinum mine or not. What I need to know from you is how to tell the difference between platinum and other similar metals."

Neville cocked an eyebrow.

"Is it really platinum or some other mineral? As you already know, Bulgaria hasn't been known for platinum production and we want to make sure that this is the real source or if it is just a front for laundering money. And we certainly don't want to burn our own fingers." Justin added the last sentence as he felt it would be just the sort of comment a government official might say.

"Hmm. I see what you're getting at. You don't want to be paying extortionate amounts of HMG's cash if you're not receiving the real goods, and to boot, if you happen to come across some nefarious scheme, you may have the Bulgarians by the short and curlies and owing you a favour... Yes?"

"Yes. That's more or less it."

"I presume a certain quantity will be required by our military, and I therefore take it that our conversation here today is off the record."

"You're most preceptive."

Neville picked up his e-pen and tapped it a few times on the table. "Well, you're quite right to question the provenance of platinum coming out of Bulgaria and we too have been wondering how kosher it is." He ceased his twiddling of the e-pen. "In fact, we haven't heard from our own investigator for over a week now but I'm not too concerned as he has his own unique methods of finding out things that others can't. Err, it seems that our interests coincide and that being the case, I feel sure we can mutually benefit from your own input."

Justin mused that Neville was convinced that he worked for the Department of Trade and Industry, commonly referred to as the DTI, and that he really didn't know that he was pursuing a possible criminal investigation on behalf of HM Treasury. Still, he didn't want to compromise his own position and needed a fairly neutral response. "I'm certain my superiors at the DTI will be happy to advise you if they think it is in the public's interest." It was his way of passing the buck without upsetting Neville too much.

"In answer to your question, if you're going to go down a mineshaft, the first thing you'll notice is that there'll be plenty of gold and silver about. Simply put, that's because it all goes into a bloody hot melting pot and once all the other metals have been skimmed off the surface, all that is left is platinum at the bottom. Assuming they're going to try to convince you that it really is platinum that they're mining, they'll probably put some in your hand and it will probably be the real thing, but what you need to see is the skimming process and then look out for the residue at the bottom; that'll be 100% pure platinum. Get them to hand you some of that. Don't worry about it being warm, it won't hurt

Chapter 5 - Of Metal

you… unless it's too hot." He snorted in short laughter, but continued straight away. "Now, platinum's not magnetic so you can't check it like that, nor does it react to acids, but what it does react with is salt. See if you can't rub a little salt onto it and feel the smooth surface rough-up a little; it'll only last momentarily mind and then it'll fade almost instantly. Then smell your fingers which were rubbing the salt in and they ought to have a faint whiff of chlorine about them. If so, then it's real platinum, otherwise it might well be magnesium, or silver, or some other such metal."

"Any special type of salt?"

"Nooo. Bog standard table salt will do, but here's another pointer. Platinum's heavier than silver, about the same as gold but lighter than lead, so get yourself cognisant with weighing up lumps of these in your hand. I'll show you."

He got up, went over to a wall-mounted showcase cabinet, and retrieved a few lumps which he put on the table in front of Justin.

"Here, feel these and tell me which one's platinum." The five items were about the same size as a tennis ball but misshapen and in partial crystalline formation. He hefted each in turn and then compared two of them but apart from the colour there was no difference.

"This one."

"Very good. Most people would have gone for the one on your right as it's got a little more sheen to it, but platinum doesn't reflect or sparkle. So, you're now a qualified metallurgist." He beamed in jest.

"No other clues?"

"Umm not really. It's something one tends to get a feeling for over the years. Experience is something I cannot help you with."

"Can you help me with trying to locate your investigator?"

For a change, Neville's repartee wasn't quite as quick as it had been up to now so Justin took the opportunity to press home his aspiration. "For two reasons. One there's a good chance we're after the same thing, and two, if he's stuck on something, as a government official I may be able to open a door or two for him."

Neville somehow managed a mournful look as he responded, "There's only a couple of us who know who he is and what he does. You see, he's extremely good at delving into investors' dealings and smokes out the bogus ones so that we don't get taken for a ride. If I give you his details, you really must keep them to yourself otherwise his usefulness to us would most likely come to an end. It might also jeopardise his own life as there are some pretty nasty characters out there."

Realising the gravity of what Neville was portraying, Justin purposefully hesitated before responding. "I think you'll find that I'm very good at keeping secrets and perhaps you can imagine that as an industry official, I too have similar needs."

Neville retrieved his e-pen, tapped and dragged it across his tablet before spinning it around for Justin to look at. "Paul Wiltern has done us proud, saved us millions, and is well rewarded, but he does like his privacy. It's unlikely he'll even talk to you unless he gets the say-so from me or my other colleague, so when you're ready, get in touch with me and I'll give him the heads-up."

Justin looked at a headshot photo of a sad-looking man with a haircut that left one wanting to pay for him to visit the barbers again. "How tall is he?"

"Oh, a little less than six foot, and when I've met him he's been dressed in jeans and a gym-type sweatshirt, and before you ask, I haven't a clue about his nationality, but from his accent he must have lived in Yorkshire for part of his life. Economical with his words but always polite."

Justin scrolled down with his fingernail, made a note of his mobile number on his own phone and handed the tablet back to Neville. "Thanks. I'll keep this to myself," he reassured. "If I need to text you or him, I'll prefix all my messages with a 'B'; that way you'll know it really is me on the other end."

"Sounds sensible. If there's nothing else I can help you with?"

"No thanks, but if there is, I'll be in touch. Oh errr… what's your mobile by the way?"

Neville had obviously pressed another button because as Justin turned to go, the receptionist was already holding the door open for him.

***

Bloody metals made her feel like she was swotting for an exam at school again. In her thoroughness, Patricia had started to query Bulgaria's recent relative meteoric rise in financial standing in the eyes of the International

Monetary Fund and spotted that it was partly due to the recent discovery of platinum. Certainly some of this new-found wealth was attributable to their joining the EEC some years ago and in particular the influx of European money that had taken its time to filter through to the country's infrastructure. Yet by any standards, two plus two seemed to be adding up to five. It was all too easy to become distracted by surfing, but at least she was now wiser about platinum because of a couple of links to security sites. It seemed that platinum and crime went hand-in-hand these days.

All of a sudden she stopped at one website and the more she read the more her jaw dropped. Why had she never heard of OSCE before? After reading just one page she traipsed off to the kitchen to fetch another coffee, all the while mulling over what she had just read. She got to the end of the relevant parts of the document and started scribbling notes. The initials stood for the Organisation for Security and Co-operation in Europe and employed thousands of personnel drawn from countries around the world, mainly Europeans.

She mentally gave herself a slap trying to get to grips with the size and scope of this establishment that encompassed virtually every aspect of each European state. Security, politics, economics, human resources, military, education, migration; there was hardly a subject that wasn't included in its remit. Over three and a half thousand employees headquartered in Vienna making it the world's largest intergovernmental organisation. Looking harder she could see that it had in

Chapter 5 - Of Metal

fact been created by the UN in the mid-seventies but had grown to include anything that it considered relevant.

She groaned at the size of the website and realised it appeared to be yet another of those invisible, self-generating organisations that delighted in meddling with the day-to-day lives of the general populous of Europe. Somewhere else for her taxes to end up. She hovered the mouse over one section after another before she realised that what was available to the public on this website wasn't going to be of much help, so she posed a question to the Special Branch computer that she'd nicknamed Doris. It might well have been the same sort of Doris that Justin had used when he was protecting diplomats.

What a surprise she got when she entered the name of Hana Otrino Tuvo on the OSCE link. Her screen blanked out everything and went bright red. The only way of getting her laptop to do anything was to remove her security dongle and restart it. She was about to repeat her actions to pursue HOT in the hope that whatever she had done had been inadvertent when her mobile rang.

"Tates here. Gibbons wants to see you."

"It'll take me an hour to get there."

"I'll tell him." The line went dead.

She wondered if it was anything to do with what her laptop had done. No, not her laptop. What she had done on it. Or perhaps it was yesterday afternoon's report. Maybe… she stopped thinking about it and got herself ready to catch the train.

Emerging into daylight on Embankment, she passed the same market trader that she had bought her lanyard from and the A-board next to him proclaimed 'Thieves steal rail line'. She wondered how many of them it would take to steal a length of very heavy railway line and then somehow smuggle it away without anyone noticing. They had to be at least fifty feet, didn't they?

She was told to go up and wait in Gibbons' ante room but hardly had a chance to sit down before being told to go into his office. She'd been there once before when looking into Hamilton's assassin case and tried to remember if anything of significance had changed. The view overlooking the Thames certainly hadn't.

He indicated for her to sit in an average-looking armchair off to his left. "From what you've been up to of late, I presume you've fully recovered so won't waste any further time on that subject. I see you've bought your laptop. Good. I set you on a task and some forty-eight hours later you start alerting security systems that you had no right in trying to access. Would you mind explaining yourself?" he asked sarcastically.

So, it was the incursion that she'd made with her laptop and she'd expected a direct question. She had a direct answer ready. "Doing as ordered, Sir. Pursuing information about potential assassins which led me to make enquiries about a certain individual."

His even stare didn't unsettle her as he considered her reply. "Hana Otrino Tuvo?"

"I've shortened his name to HOT."

"What a coincidence, so have we."

"Then I'm on the right track then?"

Chapter 5 - Of Metal

"Unfortunately, or rather fortunately, yes you are, and so much so that we're not the only people who would like to interview him." He shifted in his seat a little. "You won't know this but certain parts of our security system are linked to Interpol and what you did through our linked-in system was to raise an enquiry alert beyond your level of security clearance."

She could see that he wanted to continue but interrupted anyway. "I was using our security system but not linking it to Interpol's. I was raising my queries through OSCE."

This time he raised an eyebrow. "And why do you think OSCE may have been able to help rather than Interpol?"

"I didn't but it was a natural progression in my lines of enquiries, and anyway, I'd probably come up against the same sort of brick wall even if I did."

"Well, you're quite right and I'm not about to admonish you for what you've done; in fact quite the opposite, but I just hope you haven't alerted our target."

"Alerted?"

"Yes. It'll come as no surprise to you that in every security service or police force there'll be an element of those who have chosen to line their own pockets rather than be content with their salaries. The OSCE as well as Interpol are no exceptions. By trying to tap into their information bank, you may have alerted HOT that he was under scrutiny, but I've since been assured by our own experts that this didn't happen. I'm told that our automatic blocker kicked in and I believe your laptop will have reflected this."

"The screen went red."

"That's what they told me as well, but to go red level you'd need the necessary passcodes."

"And I presume that by doing so it may warn HOT through his placed personnel in OSCE?"

"Correct. But we've other sources of information that you're not aware of, yet if I allowed you access, you may still tip him off. No, not by human hand but by automatic computer program." He paused to let her think this one through.

"You mean hackers?"

"Yes, hackers. However careful we try to be, these hackers are extremely good at inserting certain programs that automatically alert them, so while we utilise databases, we rely upon our good old-fashioned grey matter to work out what they're up to."

"And that's why you wanted me to find out for myself rather than guide me in this direction."

He nodded.

"In that case, what can you tell me about HOT?"

He opened one of his drawers and retrieved a red-coloured file. "I think you will find most of what you want to know in here and once you've read it, I'll fill in any gaps. There's not much so you can stay seated where you are while you read it."

There was little more to be added to what she already knew. It consisted of an extended list of other targeted addresses, again with no actual proof, but in a separate part of the folio it included people who had been murdered. All of those murdered had appeared to

Chapter 5 - Of Metal

have been political critics of Russian influences and they had not all been quiet murders either. It was suspected that HOT had been responsible, but they had been done in complete contrast to other assassinations where nerve agents had been used in the hope of death appearing to have been natural.

There was a recent report suggesting that messages to HOT may have been emanating from the city of Norilsk in northern Russia, and another adding that the encryption codes had been written in Cyrillic with Viatka variations. Whoever wrote that second report likened its obscurity to one similar to Welsh with a twist of Scottish cockney and almost impossible to fathom unless one had frequented that part of Russia.

Going on the principle of 'there's no smoke without fire', there was a link between Norilsk and HOT.

There were two columns on the next page headed 'possible target locations' and 'possible target people'. Kiril Hirov was listed.

Patricia looked up with surprised eyes at Gibbons. "Yes, Hirov's name's on that list and being just about the highest profile name, he's bound to have a go but our next questions are where and when. If HOT chooses London, then it'll be at the end of next week but he'll only have a three-day window. If his previous kills are anything to go by it's unlikely to happen during 'office hours' if you know what I mean. Not when the eyes of the world are on him via the news crews. More likely to happen on his way from the airport or at his hotel; that sort of scenario."

"From what you've added, I agree."

"Normally I wouldn't give a tinker's cuss if the man is killed outside of this country, but due to our previous involvement it seems that security UK has been given the lead by both Interpol and OSCE and I'll be damned if we can't nail this bastard before others do; particularly the DGSE." He saw a quizzical look on her face so added. "French external security to you."

"Why them?"

"Not now, that's another story. So what we have here is strong suspicion that HOT may strike at Hirov when he's in London away from his own country and if HOT is as good as he appears to be, then he'll probably arrive ahead of Hirov with his own team. Naturally they won't be travelling under their own passports, so we need to out-guess him as to how he gets here. Any thoughts?"

"I think you are more qualified to answer that yourself, Sir."

"Dammit, of course I am, but why do you think I'm asking you. Ummm?"

Patricia took a moment. "Ahhh, I see. You need a fresh mind on the matter."

"Correct."

She took another moment. "Staying away from main entry points where there's CCTV is certain, so either a small boat or a plane." Gibbons watched her as she thought the next part through. "The Channel is under too much scrutiny at the moment due to illegal immigrants, so I'd choose a plane; something small enough so that can be passed off as a day trip either

Chapter 5 - Of Metal

from France or Belgium. I know there's a myriad of private airfields dotted around the south of England and there's bugger all security. One only has to show your passport, forged or stolen in their case, to an untrained official and voila, you're in the UK. Plus you can unload your guns, bazookas, or whatever at your leisure."

"And how do you know all this?"

"A friend of mine flew us on a day trip to Le Touquet for lunch in his Piper, and as I've already said, security was a joke. One thing though… on returning to Redhill aerodrome I asked the man in the tower who took copies of our passports and he told us that they got forwarded to Immigration the following Monday, and that was on a Friday. If whoever does come across and gets their timing right, they could have three whole days to do whatever they want to do, then disappear back from whence they came before we knew they were ever here."

"I believe the checks are digital now so there's no delay."

"And who's going to check a backstreet aerodrome over a weekend when there are thousands of tourists passing through several airports and ports every hour?"

"The computer."

"And who's going to check the computer?"

"I see what you mean."

"Another thought's just occurred to me and bear with me as I'm thinking this through as I go along. I reckon that while HOT's team may come over by plane where the risk of being caught is pretty small, but nonetheless a risk, he's more likely to catch a regular flight. If we're correct in our assumption that his activities are supported by Russia, then he'll have legitimate documents under a different name and he'll be able to hire cars, check into hotels, and everything a normal tourist would do. He will of course be in disguise so won't be recognised even by our own smart cameras. And then he hops on the plane to go home when it's all over."

While she gently nibbled her bottom lip, for the next half minute Gibbons tried to find a flaw in her reasoning. "Boats are too risky so I'll go along with that. What you have just outlined is a scenario that we have already investigated and updated on a permanent basis and while we have contingency plans in place, we don't have the personnel to cover every airfield from Norfolk down to Dorset; there's hundreds of them plus a few unlicensed ones. It's a security nightmare."

"And I'll bet you HOT knows that from when he's visited previously, so he'll do it again. He may have bribed a local farmer to look the other way or utilise one of the many mothballed airfields."

Gibbons looked down at his desk for a moment. "Hirov's due here next Thursday and returning Sunday, so if your theory is correct, we can expect something Friday or Saturday. Being Tuesday now, that gives us over a week to find out what. Ordinarily more than enough time, but…" He left the sentence unfinished. He raised his finger to his mouth by placing his elbow on the desk in obvious contemplation. "I hear you're off to Sofia for three days with your fiancé."

Chapter 5 - Of Metal

Before she could say anything he moved his finger half towards her stopping her from speaking. "Don't worry. I know why and I approve."

"You do?" Surprise was total. She was expecting him to order her to cancel the trip and concentrate on HOT.

"I'm going to get Tates to give you the passcodes for red access so that you can continue your investigations on your laptop. It won't matter where in the world you are but tread carefully; I think you know what I mean. Besides which, I think Crawford could probably do with your extraordinary capabilities and insight, so you go and enjoy the flesh pots of Sofia." He looked at his expensive-looking watch. "Anything to add?" He gave her ten seconds.

"Any suspects in Interpol or OSCE?"

"Oh, several, but now's not the time to go into that. By the way, why did you try to access OSCE instead of Interpol? There's hardly a soul who's heard of OSCE; you hadn't."

"It was just a link I was following."

He looked at his watch. "Ummm. Time I was elsewhere. Goodbye."

Chapter 6

Sofia

Some capitals are overrun with pickpockets, others by gun or knife crime, and some by plain old thievery. On the other hand, in a few capitals around the world one could drop one's wallet in the street and it would be handed in with contents intact. Sofia's cosmopolitan mix of religious and ethnic groups is not that much different from most other European capital cities, but its chequered history has instilled the now indigenous populous to err on the cautious side. On the downside, families are born into the gang way of life that is one of the more prominent features, and those gangs excel at smuggling. On the other side of the coin, Sofia's universities are famed for their technological achievements and have created a culture of advancement in the nano-world. Unfortunately this includes a little more than their fair share of computer hackers.

Justin and Patricia sat on poorly painted aluminium chairs and looked out over the well-tended gardens from the atrium of The Grand Hotel while supping locally bottled lager; at least they were cold. They'd been met at Sofia airport by a minor ministry official who had rushed them through the diplomatic channels

Chapter 6 - Sofia

and dumped them at The Grand, telling them that they'd be collected in an hour. With little else to pass the time they actually began to relax, but it didn't last as they heard the unmistakeable clattering sound of officialdom approaching on the marble floor. Justin was better positioned to casually look to his left to see a neatly suited man complete with patent black leather shoes approaching; he stopped just short of them.

"Todor Yordan at your service," the youngish man announced with a smile and a musical inflection in his excellent English. He held out his hand to greet them, displaying white cuffs held together with gold cufflinks.

They both stood and shook hand in turn. "Will you join us for a drink?" asked Justin.

"I am afraid I cannot do that and I must ask you if you can both accompany me please. We have only one item on today's agenda and I will be happy to explain tomorrow's on the way."

"And where might we be going this afternoon?"

"You don't know?" There was a genuine look of surprise on his kindly looking face. "You weren't told?"

Shakes of heads followed.

"Tsk, tsk, tsk. I must have Gregor admonished, but come. We're off to see one of Sofia's greatest monuments and it has been closed an hour early just for you." He looked at his watch. "But it must reopen in time for prayers which is why I must ask you to come quickly."

They both looked at each other, left their half-finished drinks and went ahead of Todor's ushering hand. "Where are we going?"

"I will tell you in the car."

A chauffeur held open the rear door of a long limousine and once they were all seated inside, Todor continued much as a tour guide would do so. "The Alexander Nevsky Cathedral..."

On the way back they were told that the next day he would be accompanying them to the Chelo Tepe mine in the Krumovgrad region. It was about an hour's flight to the south, and could they please be ready to leave straight after breakfast at nine o'clock tomorrow morning. Would they like to borrow some suitable clothing and shoes as they would be going down the mine? Then tomorrow evening, could they please be appropriately dressed for dinner with his Minister at the National Palace of Culture.

Back in their room they both headed for the French windows that opened onto the balcony overlooking a pleasant tree-lined avenue that was wide enough to allow two-way traffic and a pair of tram lines. During the flight over, they had agreed to maintain their temporary personas, just in case they were overheard.

Keeping up the appearance was easy. "Well that was certainly worth it, but I wasn't expecting an exclusive tour with our own ministerial guide. Were you?" asked Patricia.

The only other people in the cathedral had been church wardens and the like as it had been closed to the public, solely for their benefit.

"First time for me too, but I can't see them doing the same for us back in St Paul's."

"They might if they thought we were going to confirm several million pounds worth of trade."

"Do you get the feeling we're being buttered up?"

"Yes. But that's why we're here isn't it? Keep us sweet so that we can put in a favourable recommendation to the chief."

"But only if the price is discounted enough."

"That's what we're getting paid for isn't it?" remarked Patricia, referring to whatever persuasive monies might be asked for as backhanders. They were both wondering if such an offer would be forthcoming at tomorrow night's dinner with the minister.

Their evening meal in the hotel's restaurant started off as a drab affair as there were only a few other diners in the spacious but elegantly decorated room. Virtually every knife and fork clatter echoed off the wallpapered walls and the comings and goings of the pair of waiters through the double-hinged swing door seemed to emphasise the lack of atmosphere. Only the comfortably well-off could afford the relatively high prices, but the food and local wine were rather good. A pair of well-dressed young ladies were their nearest neighbours two tables away, oblivious to their surroundings as they chatted. Patricia thought they could have been sisters on her couple of glances in their direction.

Once seated, Justin had spent the first minute or so trying to spot any microphones and when he explained as much to Patricia in guarded language, he received a sharp rap from her shoe on his shin; it didn't stop him being observant. When the main course arrived, the nearer of the two ladies turned to Patricia and in good English asked to borrow the salt and pepper caddy, explaining that their salt was too damp to let it sprinkle.

She half watched as the two ladies took their turn and then the first lady got up and returned the caddy and, with a smile, thanked them both.

It was only when Justin used the salt cellar herself that he noticed that there was a folded note neatly stuck to its underside, and was experienced enough not to falter or comment as he deftly retrieved it by tapping the cellar in an inverted position over his food. Not even Patricia noticed. He unscrewed the top to obtain an abnormal amount of salt which he poured onto his napkin, and thence into his pocket for use tomorrow.

Untrusting of the ex-communist state not to put them under surveillance, if they had hidden microphones then they probably had hidden cameras as well, so there was only one safe place to read the note. Once Patricia had joined him in the king-sized double bed, he covered them both with the duvet and told her to start giggling; it helped when he tickled her. Using the torch on his phone, he carefully unfolded the note so that they could both see it.

Temple of Martyrs tomo at midnight

He dug her in the ribs and she dug back causing them both to squirm and utter suitable noises; a perfectly natural thing to do for a young couple sharing a large bed under a giant duvet. He held his finger to his lips and she nodded in acknowledgement. He stuffed the very thin piece of paper into his mouth and began to chew, while Patricia used her fingernails on him to elicit an erection.

Chapter 7

The mine

The waiter told them that traditional Banista was made from pastry, eggs and cheese and was always offered to guests at breakfast but if they preferred something else…?

"Tasty," remarked Justin.

"So's the coffee but I wouldn't have too much of it otherwise you'll be looking for the toilet all day."

Justin looked at the side of her cup that showed how grainy it was and took her advice by drinking just half a cup. Patricia managed to pour some salt into a piece of toilet paper that she had bought from upstairs.

Just before 9 am the same chauffeured car pulled up outside and Todor hopped out, full of smiles and greetings, but this time he was dressed in far more casual gear. He didn't stop describing Sofia's landmarks all the way to the airport a short drive away. Again they were ushered very smoothly through the officialdom that pervades through the airports of the world to a waiting twin-engined executive turboprop.

Once they were airborne, Todor continued his monologue. "It won't take us long so I'd better tell you a bit about our new mine. After all, that's why you're here, isn't it?"

A pretty stewardess presented them with a tray of sparkling water and a bowl of peanuts.

"Everyone's heard of our new major mine at Ada Tepe where we extract a good quantity of gold and silver, ahhh... with a little help from a Canadian firm, but few have heard of Little Tepe geologically next door. Although in the same valley, it's the other end of the village of Dazhdovnik and we don't advertise its whereabouts to everyone. Platinum's becoming more and more useful for military purposes so we maintain a high level of security there because we don't want everybody knowing where it is."

Justin started asking questions which were glibly answered and then decided to probe a little deeper.

"Who discovered it?"

"Who? I don't know his name but we're constantly looking for more minerals."

"Would it have been the same Canadians who helped you with Ada Tepe?"

"Oh no no no. This is strictly our own national enterprise. No foreign input on this one."

"So that you reap all the profit," observed Justin.

"The price is perfect for those of us who know how to do business." With a knowing smile, he rubbed his forefinger and thumb together.

It was indicators such as this that Justin needed to help him paint an accurate picture, but he reserved judgement until he could actually see mining in operation. Todor's gesticulation when it came to money left little doubt in his mind that there was bribery at the heart of whatever operation they had going.

Chapter 7 - The mine

Todor continued to rattle off facts, obviously memorised to satisfy the usual enquiries before the plane began to descend, and all the while Justin tried to appraise the smooth-talking man whose job it was to escort them. Mid-forties, well-built without any excess fat, a swarthy-looking face but clean-shaven except for the almost obligatory moustache that was so popular in that part of eastern Europe. Justin was not expert enough at facial expressions to be able to assess if honesty or subterfuge was at the heart of what was being said, but he got the impression that Todor was being rather guarded in what he said. And was what he said constrained by himself or by what his masters had told him to say? One thing that was crystal clear was that Todor must have spent a decent amount of time in England to attain that level of command of the English language, and his accent was very much Oxford. Justin asked him about it.

"My father was one of the heroes founding Bulgaria soon after the end of the second world war and apparently met my mother when the British embassy was inaugurated soon after. Sadly my father was executed in the Stalinist purges of the 1950s but she managed to smuggle me back to her family home in Cheltenham without getting caught. I was her only son and she insisted that I be bought up to be a proper English gentleman. Unfortunately she was consumed by tuberculosis halfway through my education but had left ample funds for me to complete my education, so I ended up at Oxford with a First in languages." His smile was genuine. "And now you see me as your most humble guide." He dipped his head a little.

Although the concrete runway was smooth and well maintained, the terminal building looked like it belonged to a bygone era; single storey with a metal railing on the roof and what looked like a wooden radio shack perched on top of it. A crude metal tower with a few whip aerials revealed its modern side but adjacent to the main building was a smelly cow byre; they were downwind of it.

Todor pointed them in the direction of a newish Range Rover and waiting driver and as they got in, they heard the sound of cattle coming from the byre.

Justin couldn't help commenting, "Seems like some of the villagers still prefer to work the fields rather than down the mines."

"We didn't feel the need to dislodge an entire village and anyway, it's still a strong tradition to raise cattle in Bulgaria." He pointed across the road. "Over there is a pig farm and I think you will be surprised how well our chefs can cook. You'll find out this evening."

"You must tell me more about the locals and villages round her. It looks lovely countryside." It was Patricia's turn.

"I'd love to but that's more of a job for one of our local tourist guides and I'll gladly put you in touch with one of them on another occasion. I'm more of an expert in our capital, so I wouldn't be of much help down here."

The way Todor managed to change the subject when asked any number of questions was beginning to irk Justin. He knew it was a trait of an evasive person but he didn't let his feelings show.

Chapter 7 - The mine

The choice of a Range Rover became clear when after a couple of miles, the driver took a turn onto a gravel road and straight away had to stop at a manned barrier. The plain-clothed guard only glanced at the car before leaning on the counterweight to raise the red and white pole. The driver clearly enjoyed his job as he hurtled up the incline and round the hairpin bends, occasionally throwing them from side to side. Justin knew from previously studying maps of the area that they might well climb to over a thousand metres but at the speed they were going, it wouldn't take long. The driver braked suddenly and dived off down a smaller track and they all instinctively, but unnecessarily, ducked to avoid the overhanging branches of the pine trees. They came to a stop in front of a pair of heavy wire gates and this time there were several armed guards in military uniforms; one stood by a small guard hut with what looked like a Dobermann on the end of a short leash. A tall wire mesh fence topped with barbed wire extended as far as could be seen each side of the gates and a pair of tall poles with lights and cameras completed the security set-up.

"You see, I told you it was a secure mine. Only officials… and of course those invited along with them will get past this gate." He looked over his shoulder at them and smiled before producing a small pass from inside his pocket to show to the guard standing by his door, but already one of the others was opening one side of the gate.

Rounding the slight bend directly ahead of them, they could see that they were about to drive into a cave but it turned out to be the entrance of a tunnel that descended gently for a quarter of a mile or so. When they did stop, it was in an opening that had been enlarged to contain several rooms cut into the rock but a little away from them was an industrial lift. To Justin and Patricia, it was straight out of a baddie's lair in a science fiction film and even the lighting had an eerie feel about it.

"Where's the organ?" commented Justin as they got out and looked round in awe.

"What?"

"I said where's the organ?" he repeated but when she still looked nonplussed he added. "In a lair like this there's always someone playing a church organ in the corner and it's usually a vampire such as Christopher Lee. You know... toccata and fugue echoing off the walls."

"Trust you to think of that one."

"Yes, but you've got to admit it would fit in nicely here."

Todor finished his brief discussion with one particular man and came walking over to them followed by another subordinate who carried two yellow hard hats and a clutch full of bandanas. "Now we go down, yes?"

"How deep are we going?"

"Oh, about three or four hundred metres and takes just a couple of minutes. Follow me please."

The cage door was held open then closed for the three of them by the subordinate who got in with them and operated the lever that started the descent. The first

Chapter 7 - The mine

thing that they noticed was the updraught of air which became warmer as they descended. Then there was tangible dust in the atmosphere which they could feel on their teeth. Arriving at the bottom with a jolt, they smelt machinery – or rather the grease and oil that kept it in working order – and stepping out onto firm rock, felt a slight crunch of grit underfoot.

"Unique, isn't it?" Todor had started his narrative again. "It's an experience just feeling the air around you, but to those who work down here, it's like coming home." He stopped his walk along the narrow roughly hewn corridor, rubbed the palm of his hand against the rock and smelt it. He looked at them. "Try it. Feel it." They did as they were told but couldn't decide what he was getting at, despite mimicking him.

Walking through the tunnel reminded them both of the London Underground and they could even feel the rumble of wheels on track, but one difference was that it lacked the sudden rush of air in one direction or another that a train would cause. This airflow was even. Strung light bulbs revealed the occasional rock protruding from the floor, walls and ceiling and although fairly straight, they felt that they were descending and after several hundred metres, felt as well as heard that they were nearing the end due to the rumbles and vibrations. On a particularly badly lit part, the passage took a sharp turn to the right. Todor held back what looked like a very heavy curtain and as they squeezed passed him, found themselves in a much wider tunnel with rail tracks directly in front of them. "The curtain helps keep the dust down as otherwise nobody would be able to breathe properly."

They could see what he meant as from the weakly lit walls they could again see and feel grit in the air.

"About once an hour a purpose-made electric train passes and the attached wagons are laden with ore that is then taken to the surface for processing. That's where we extract not only platinum but also any other precious metals."

They looked down the tunnel towards the business end and could hear drilling and other such noises. Justin was the first to ask and motioned with his hand. "Can we see the ore being mined?"

"I'm afraid not as it's far too dangerous. We've had a number of cave-ins lately as the consistency of the rock varies from one seam to another. The seam we're mining right now is particularly rich in platinum but the rock from which it comes is rather unstable. Just think what would happen if such a cave-in should occur while we were taking a look." He saw the obvious chagrin on their faces, but continued. "What I can show you is where the wagons off-load in the smelting chamber; this way please."

They began to walk in the opposite direction and as they did so, the train with empty and noisy wagons emerged towards them in the dusty gloom. They stood against the walls while it passed and in its wake followed a cloud of dusty grit. They automatically adjusted their bandanas to cover their mouths and noses, but it was some time before the air cleared enough to allow them to breathe near normally. As the noise dissipated into the distance Todor commented, "I told you it would be dusty. Not too far now." He set off at a quicker pace and all of a sudden they came across the area where the ore was unloaded into big skip-shaped bins that were hoisted up the long shaft by thick cables. They stood at the entrance to this unusual chamber watching the automation of it all and what struck Justin was that there were no personnel on duty, and he asked Todor about it. "All automated at this end because you can see how unhealthy the dust would make it. There's only one man in a sealed cabin about halfway up and his one and only job is to operate the kill switch in case something goes wrong." He pointed up the vertical shaft to where a partially glazed cabin stuck out. "The ore gets lifted from here up to the distribution chamber and from there onto smelting. We can go and see that once you've had enough down here."

Patricia and Justin stayed long enough to take in as much as they thought they could remember and neither of them even thought of producing a camera as they suspected Todor would be extremely unhappy. Being like-minded, as they turned to leave Patricia feigned a stumble against the wall and Justin angled his phone half-out of his pocket enough to take a couple of snaps. Being briefly distracted, Todor's eyes went to Patricia but were back on Justin in a flash; a move that wasn't lost on Justin.

They retraced their route along the tracks, through the heavy curtain and into the lift, but it was with a sense relief that they stepped out into cooler air at the top; there was none of that sub-conscious claustrophobic feeling.

Todor led them to the waiting Range Rover without giving them the chance to ask any questions, but once the last door was shut, he turned round in the front seat, smiled his usual smile that was starting to become a bit condescending and asked, "No ill side effects from the dust?"

The mere mention of dust bought on a coughing fit from Patricia. "No, not really." She swallowed a lump of phlegm.

"Good. Now we go to see the smelting process. You'll have noticed that we weren't able to follow the ore up the shaft for obvious reasons, but you'll be able to see it emerge at the top when we drive round."

Their driver surged out of the cave entrance with his familiar zest and into the sun-washed pine forest, the wire gate already open by a saluting guard as they shot past and onto the wider track. It took nearly fifteen minutes even at that speed as they went through a ford, climbed another hill and crossed over a ravine on a rickety looking wooden bridge. Todor explained that the lorries that took the reduced ore from there, down the mountain and then on to the next process, took a more substantial route. "Sometimes the heavy rains bring on a landslide or perhaps a few trees here and there need to be cleared away after a storm, and in the winter, well, perhaps you can imagine how icy it can become, but we manage. Got to keep the lifeblood flowing, eh?" He turned back to face forward and managed to brace himself just before the driver slewed them sideways and onto a much wider well-graded track.

They emerged from the trees and their approach to another gated compound, complete with guards and similar security measures, was surprisingly a little

Chapter 7 - The mine

more sedate that the last. Nevertheless, the inspection of passes was thorough and they were not allowed to proceed until there was a nod from the sentry post. As they parked next to a corrugated two-storey building, the door opened and out strode an officer. He didn't need to put his hands on his hips but otherwise from his stance he could well have been the man in overall charge of the site. Todor was out of the car and speaking to the officer before the others had hardly set foot on the gravelly ground, and as they approached the pair of officials could hear that the tone of conversation seemed strained. Neither Justin nor Patricia spoke Bulgarian with its superfluous use of harsh constantans, but even so there seemed to be terseness in the air. They had to wait until the exchange came to a conclusion before Todor stood to one side and turned to them, smile at the ready. "Major Hovalich is in command of this mine and it seems that our ministry did not tell him of our visit today, but he says you can be shown round only if we are accompanied by one of his sergeants. Here, let me introduce you."

It was clear that the major was disgruntled as they perfunctorily shook hands; he turned away and retreated back into the building as soon as it was over. They waited unaccompanied a good ten minutes in the warm sunshine listening to the background clank of machinery before the sergeant appeared from another building across the spacious compound and indicated that they should follow him into a much larger, newer looking building a couple of hundred yards away. Patricia got the impression that he had dressed hurriedly as one of his shirt tails was hanging out, and both of them made a note that there were no introductions as though the sergeant was used to this sort of thing. He pointed this out to Todor.

"Oh don't worry about him. He and I are used to each other from other visitors. He's just our chaperone."

"A bit like you are our chaperone," commented Patricia.

This provoked a sharp look from Todor. "I would like to think that I am a little more than just your chaperone. I am here not just to answer any questions you may have but also to guide you through those tiresome avenues of officialdom." His smile returned in an instant. "After all, you're here to do business and I am here to help you do business. After you."

They went from light to dark through the wide metal door being held open by the sergeant and instantly returned to a world of grit and dust, but they weren't offered any bandanas.

Todor started his oration much like a tour guide would do on a bus and initially pointed off to their right. "Over there in the distance you can see the lorries taking the final smelt down to the valley for further refining, but we're going down there." The sergeant had overtaken them and was leading them through a narrowing of the walls towards the loudest noise. They could smell the ore and feel it on their skin and as they neared a raised platform, felt a significant rise in the temperature. In file, climbing some twenty steps took them onto a stillaged walkway from where they could see the skip-like wagons reaching the top of their lift

Chapter 7 - The mine

and being tilted so that the ore cascaded down into a giant furnace.

Todor pointed out that they were the same wagons that they had seen in the lower chamber and that over five hundred tons of ore was smelted every day. He let them stay there for as long as their eyes didn't smart, about five minutes, before continuing their tour along the walkway and down another set of steps. "Over here are the separation and cooling pits which extend outside for obvious reasons."

They all caught the whiff of the rotten-egg smell of sulphur as they passed one pit, an acidic taste of another, and so on until Todor stopped them at the penultimate pit. "This is one of the platinum coolers. And once the temperature has dropped to below 50 degrees, the conveyor belt takes it over there and into the lorries."

The pit was about twenty metres across and the earth walls only about a metre high allowing them to see directly into it. Patricia remarked later that it reminded her of particularly dirty washing-up water while Justin likened it to the scum on top of a communal rugby club bath after the team had exited.

"I wouldn't put my hand into that if I were you. It's rather toxic in this state," Todor announced. Justin noted where the sergeant was, looked at Patricia, faintly nodded their pre-arranged signal and waited a moment.

Patricia approached Todor, initially blocking his view of Justin as much as she could, pointed at the last pit and asked if she could see in it, then began walking off towards it. Naturally Todor followed after her. Justin had noted that the sergeant wouldn't see what he was doing unless he turned round, so he bent over and retrieved a stone-sized lump of slag and a few gravelly bits and deftly put them in his pocket. After looking at an identical pit, they followed the crunchy path beside the V-shaped conveyor belt for quite a way and stopped at an unfenced edge where gravity would take over from the belt to deliver its load into a lorry that would be positioned directly underneath. There were no waiting lorries, but they could tell that one had just departed from the amount of dust that hung in the air.

"Well that's about it," announced Todor. "Before I ask you if you have any questions, may I suggest we start making out way back to the car?" He held his arm out uphill.

During the ten-minute walk back uphill they both asked pertinent questions which were glibly answered, then waited by the Range Rover for Todor who followed the sergeant into the administration building.

"Well that was instructive, but I really need a shower," commented Patricia.

"Me too, but let's talk through it later when we've had a chance to digest it all."

She looked at him and raised an eyebrow. Casually looking around, Justin pulled his hand from his pocket and rubbed it against his nose as though scratching an itch.

She looked at his pocket that held the stone, stepped forward so that she was nearly touching him and with a wicked grin said, "I see you're pleased to see me."

At first, he didn't understand, then he casually put

Chapter 7 - The mine

his hand back in his pocket to disguise the bump. "I'm always pleased to see you."

"Well then, I'd better find myself a decent-sized stone, hadn't I?"

"Oh I think you'll find that mine reacts when tended to nicely."

"Who said anything about being nice?" Very slowly and gently she pushed her knee into his groin area so that he instinctively moved his hips backwards a touch.

"You know, there are other ways to elicit the kind of reaction you're looking for."

"I know. But I'm just trying to even up the lumps in your pockets," she said seductively, standing nose tip to nose tip.

"How professional of you."

Out of the corner of her eye she saw Todor emerge, so disengaged. Within a minute their necks were jerked backwards as their driver demonstrated his car-handling skills again. Once in the air on their return leg Justin asked how the final product was forwarded after refining.

"Oh that's the easy part. If it's a small quantity we air freight it but if it's a bulk order then it goes by road to the port of Burgas on the Black Sea and shipped to wherever the client so wishes. It's all very straight forward." He leaned over. "If you look out of the window you can see just Burgas over there." They both did.

"And how about payment?" asked Justin.

Todor waited until the hostess was out of earshot.

"That is what you will be discussing with my minister tonight." He looked at his watch. "I see we are a little ahead of schedule but the limousine will collect you at eight this evening."

"Will you be joining us?"

Todor's smile wavered a little. "Yes I will be there but in my other capacity and unable to escort you."

"And what is your other capacity?"

"That I will let you discover for yourselves tonight."

Chapter 8

Culture

They were stunned. Stunned at the grandeur of the National Palace of Culture as they ascended the preformed wide steps that led to the yawning glazed entrance to the magnificent building. It was a tall building that they had seen from their hotel balcony and because of its size, assumed that it must have been the centre of government; but no.

"We could have walked here quicker," remarked Patricia. The limousine had taken them the long way round so that they had approached the palace via the excessively wide water-featured boulevard complete with fountains.

"Yes, but we wouldn't have been able to take in the sights."

It may have been the dusk with the twinkle of the evening lights that brought out the best of Sofia, but the underwater flood lights certainly highlighted the approach to the magnificent modern palace. They turned at the top of the numerous steps to look back down the series of rectangular pools flanked by mature trees that receded into the distance.

"Wow. I wasn't expecting this."

"Neither was I."

"Well let's go and see if the inside matches the outside." He was eyeing up the vast atrium through a series of glass doors and could see a few people milling about not far from the reception desk. "I wonder where we go?"

Ten minutes later, one lift, a leisurely stroll down a couple of wide corridors and a brief stop-off at a brilliantly lit display cabinet containing a baby woolly mammoth in an airy foyer bought them to a pair of doors. A matching pair of smiling usherettes each side handed out slips of paper designating the guest seating in the medium-sized theatre and as they took their seats, Todor joined them in an adjacent one, dressed in a military uniform. There was no chance to ask him as the light dimmed, as did the whispered conversations, leaving just one spotlight centre stage.

A superb performance by a solo female singer backed by recorded music, closed with a standing ovation and although it had lasted over three-quarters of an hour, it felt like only a few minutes had passed. Once through the theatre's doors and out into the spacious corridor, at his beckoning they followed Todor in the opposite direction to most of the leaving crowd, and got into the airless silence of a lift.

"That was exquisite," remarked Patricia as Justin nodded and 'ummed' in approval of her choice of comment to Todor.

"She's touring at the moment but I'll be surprised if you know who she is."

Chapter 8 - Culture

The pair looked at each other in surrender but it was Patricia who conceded that they didn't.

"Even if I tell you her name you still won't know."

They all exited the lift and followed Todor down another well-lit corridor. "Tolkyn Zabirova," he announced with one of his smiles as he opened one side of a pair of doors. They were none the wiser but didn't have an opportunity to ask further because they had clearly arrived.

The room was tiny by comparison to the others in the palace but large enough for the circular dining table that was set for half a dozen guests. The spare space was taken up by a mobile bar, next to which stood an elegantly dressed middle-aged couple and a younger man.

Todor had to raise his voice a bit over the piped music. "Let me introduce you to our economics minister Georgu Bayev and his lovely wife Violeta; this is Hana, the minister's personal aide." Justin wondered if he detected a slight inflection in Todor's voice as he indicated Hana with his arm, but didn't have time to think about it because he needed to concentrate on the first-contact protocols of shaking hands and the politeness that went with them. While irrelevant chatter ensued, Hana acted as barman to the group by handing out shot glasses of Rakia on a silver tray, and on cue from Georgu they downed the potent liqueur. Straight away, five of them sat down at the table while Hana popped his head outside of a door at the opposite end of the room before joining them.

Six waiters, one for each of them, appeared with prepared plates before disappearing back through the single door.

It was now clear that neither Georgu or his wife spoke much English and Justin assumed that that was why Hana was present, but it turned out that it was Todor's job. Between mouthfuls of what looked like mini dumplings, Georgu chatted away while Todor did his best to keep up.

"He apologises for the hurried meal, but they have to fly to Strasbourg later tonight to attend a European economic summit which starts tomorrow and he has a pre-arranged meeting with other officials before that. He says you are both welcome and asks if you enjoyed the performance."

They both nodded, assented and thanked through Todor, and Justin added that he thought he had heard that same performance elsewhere but couldn't place it, despite being told her name earlier.

This bought smiles from the Bulgarians around the table and after a few words from Georgu's wife, Todor asked, "Have you ever seen the film *The Fifth Element?*"

Justin immediately clicked but Patricia hadn't heard of it.

Todor continued, "The singer you heard tonight is the same singer who appeared in the film, and Tolkyn Zabirova is currently on her European tour. While we think we have the best auditorium this side of the Atlantic, we were still very lucky to be able to hear her in person."

Georgu chatted to Todor as he translated. "He would like to have claimed responsibility for her being here tonight but cannot as it was his friend and colleague, the minister of culture who arranged it."

While the light-hearted conversation had been taking place, Hana had initiated the passing round of a bottle of wine with his white-gloved hands, and now rang a small table-mounted bell. The same six waiters appeared, removed the plates, finished or not, then returned pushing a trolley containing a bubbling iron dish; it instantly smelt wonderful. With six dished bowls served out in front of them and the waiters retreated behind their door, Todor took his cue from Georgu and addressed Justin.

"My minister asks can you please indicate what it is that your government wants in the way of the platinum from our new mine, but let me explain a little first. There is naturally a high demand for this precious metal which also commands a high price and while he does not have direct control over that price, he does have influence to a certain extent." Todor paused while Georgu spoke. "The price is likely to vary depending upon market factors beyond his control and he asks if you understand this." He paused then added, "Other factors include quantities and frequencies but you must understand that it may depend upon how quickly it can be mined."

"Please ask the minister if he thinks the mine could manage up to, say, two metric tonnes each month."

Once Todor had confirmed the amount with Justin, he translated. It wasn't so much a look of surprise that came across Georgu's face; more like one of pleasure.

"He says that he would be delighted to be able to fill your order providing the mine could keep up. He says that they have many other orders and contracts to fill and he hopes that if there was ever a shortage, that your government may like to be prioritised." He paused while Georgu carried on talking. "In the unlikely event of a shortage, a priority fee would certainly ensure a continuity of supply over others." Again he waited to catch up with Georgu. "The tedious task of obtaining the correct export licences could be expedited if there was a system in place for such and he would be pleased to waiver some of the usual fees if that system meant that you were to volunteer to be our contact with the UK."

Justin had been expecting some sort of kick-back but not quite this blatantly put and it nearly caught him out. He genuinely had to stall for time to think. He could hardly ask them to 'hang-on a mo' while he conferred with Patricia, and nor could he stall for too long, so he fiddled with his spoon in contemplation. If he showed any indication of weakness or overplayed his hand, it would surely raise their suspicions of sincerity. Effectively on offer was the chance to secure a reliable monthly delivery of platinum at a price set by Georgu but on top of that, a bribery fee to ensure that reliability. All of this on top of an initial 'export' fee that would no doubt end up in Georgu's, Todor's and Hana's hands. He considered that if he agreed to their terms then he may be opening up a can of worms, but if he declined as a proper English diplomat may well have done, then that would be the end of the matter; he and Patricia would be sent on their way without ever being able to discover what exactly was going on. Even worse, by declining the offer he would probably 'queer the pitch' for anyone following after him.

Justin looked directly at the minister and asked Todor to officiate. "Please advise the minister that I am sure we can come to some amicable arrangement where both parties are content, but I have to warn him that I will need to ratify this with my minister back in London." As Todor translated the last part he saw Georgu frown a little, so added, "I am afraid I will have to obtain our own government's approval for an international transaction of this scale as I don't have that kind of spare cash myself." His small joke was not lost and the frown was replaced with a half-smile.

"My minister understands but asks that such dealings be kept to a minimum for obvious reasons… we don't want competitors interrupting our arrangements."

"Then we understand each other perfectly." Justin raised his glass in salute to Georgu who responded with a similar gesture and started talking again.

"He says that you and I can work out the initial details but should we encounter any problems, then Hana will be available to assist also."

Justin had to ask, "Does Hana speak English at all?"

"I speak English very bad." Hana's speech and accent were all out of kilter. It was as though his tongue was tied to the roof of his mouth and the words emanated from his throat in a Slavic kind of way with the emphasis on the consonants. His lips hardly moved but his facial expression said almost as much about what he was trying to say, especially his eyes.

"In that case, we'll be glad to liaise through Todor," Justin contributed smoothly before anyone else had a chance to pass comment and even Georgu paused as he was about to speak.

Georgu looked at his watch. "He understands that you are returning to the UK tomorrow evening and hopes that you and I can resolve the initial issues before you leave… he adds that he can recommend an excellent restaurant for lunch owned by his cousin and that you are welcome to enjoy its menu at his expense. Now he has to leave and he bids you farewell."

They all rose at the same time as Georgu but before he turned to go Justin replied that they were grateful for his hospitality.

Now that Georgu, his wife and Hana had left, the room seemed to have grown in size. None of them considered retaking their places at the table.

"Is he always this busy?" asked Patricia

"Oh our minister has many obligations but I think he enjoyed meeting you both tonight despite his tight schedule, because he's not always that polite."

"I'm glad we didn't disappoint him, but tell me, how come you're dressed in uniform?" Justin looked briefly at Patricia. "Neither of us thought you were connected with the military and I'm afraid I am not up with rank insignia."

"I did tell you earlier that you would find out tonight. It often pays to wrong-foot one's opposite number and in this case, yourselves. I suspect you thought I was just a lowly chaperone and as such, you might have divulged information that you would have otherwise withheld from someone such as myself. However, I am pleased to say that you passed with flying colours but I was obliged to display my true colours in public as well as in the presence of our economics minister."

"That's a relief to hear, but please do tell us what your official position is," Patricia asked.

"I am a major in our State Intelligence Agency. For example I am someone who looks out for criminals posing as salesmen trying to obtain an illegal advantage in our country and yes, I am also on the lookout for spies who would steal from us. Security is very important to us when it comes to something as valuable as platinum and any stranger we come across who shows interest in our dealings must be investigated. You both rate some interest as we have not had someone from the UK before nor someone trying to buy rather than sell; hence the interest." His fixed smile was back on his face. "I do hope you will forgive my earlier subterfuge."

"I'll only forgive you if we can sort out a few details before we leave tomorrow, and are these the sort of things we can do over lunch?"

"Oh no certainly not. The Tenebris may be owned by the minister's cousin but I wouldn't trust the walls not to listen in on our conversation. No. You must come to my office at, shall we say, 11 o'clock tomorrow morning. I'll send the car. When we have concluded our formalities then you can enjoy lunch but I am afraid I will not be joining you for that as I already have an appointment elsewhere. What I can offer you is a nightcap before your car returns you to the hotel tonight."

Knowing that they had a mystery appointment, Patricia took a small step forward as Todor was about to turn around. "Please don't take it as an offence but it's been a long day and I'd rather take a walk back to our hotel. I feel as though I need to walk off what we've just eaten."

"As you wish, but I'll walk you to the front entrance and if you take my advice, you'll stay on the lit streets."

"Is there a mugging problem here then?"

"It's not so much as a mugging problem but that too does exist to a small extent. No, it's the packs of feral dogs that nobody really wants to deal with and we don't want you going down with rabies, do we?"

Once at the top of the steps Todor wished them a good night and after speaking with the driver of their designated car, watched him being driven away in his own limousine.

"What do you think?" asked Patricia.

"I think we need to take an evening stroll and work off those stodgy dumplings. That looks interesting so let's head in that direction first."

Chapter 9

Martyrs

It was only when they had reached the bottom of the steps that Justin commented that eavesdropping would have been far too easy at the top of the steps, but more difficult as they walked. His comments were appreciated by Patricia who added, "Aren't we a little too early for a midnight liaison?"

"Only a little, which is why we're taking the long way round. Whoever it is who might be meeting us ought to be doing a decent job by watching the area prior to midnight and anyway, there's nothing wrong in taking one's intended on an amorous stroll through the capital's main attraction. It means we too can see if anyone is loitering in the shadows."

"Just don't get too frisky. It feels like it might rain."

They walked on a few leisurely paces before Justin piped up. "Well I don't mind if you don't." He got an elbow in the ribs.

Hand in hand and with the sounds of the city all around them but well in the background, it took them some twenty minutes to make their way round through the well-tended grounds of the vast auditorium. The direct line to their rendezvous point for any normal person would have taken less than three minutes but despite the threat of rain in the air, to any onlooker they were just another couple enjoying each other's company. Trees started to edge in on the pathways as they approached the Temple of Martyrs. From their internet search, they both recognised the small stone structure that seemed as though there was hardly any room for anyone inside, and they had learned that it was more of a monument to oppressed citizens as opposed to a religious centre.

They were both on alert for anything out of place and it was Patricia who spotted two people first. "Shall we go and sit down on one of those benches near that couple?" she half whispered in his ear.

They got a small shock when they did sit down and saw who was already there. The same 'sisters' from yesterday evening's restaurant were acting as lovers would, and as far as anyone could tell in the half-light, they were actually lovers.

Justin more than Patricia appreciated the location of the clandestine meeting as line of sight from two sides was all but impossible because to their left was a stone wall some six-foot high and in front of them, the Martyrs Temple. Almost directly behind their seat was the palace about two hundred yards away and anyone attempting to listen in or see what they were up to would instantly be seen in the refracted light from the water features. Off to their right was a series of intermittently spaced saplings in full-leaf which would have a disastrous effect on any listening device.

Chapter 9 - Martyrs

Without pre-arranged passwords or other such arrangements, Patricia and Justin sat quietly pretending not to look in the direction of the sisters, but all of a sudden one of them got up and took the few steps to stand right in front of them. "Have you got a light please? I think mine's just run out." She flicked the cheap lighter so that sparks flew out of it.

They both looked up to see an unlit cigarette hanging from her mouth, recognising it as an obvious cue. Neither of them smoked and it took Justin a few seconds to realise he would need to give an appropriate response.

"I'm sorry but neither of us smoke and we haven't got a light. Here, let me have a go."

The girl held out her hand with the lighter and as Justin went to take it from her, saw that there were two lighters; one hidden behind the other. No fast movements but a sure and steady handover of both items, one falling into his lap while he flicked the other so that the gas ignited. "It's all in the wrist action," was all he could think of as he handed the lighter back to the girl.

"I know what you mean. Thank you." She turned to walk back towards her friend who rose at her approach and they both sauntered off, hand in hand, behind the small temple and out of sight.

Rather than look at the memory stick shaped as a lighter, Justin manoeuvred himself so that he could surreptitiously put it in his pocket, made all the easier by them both standing. After a genuine kiss and a cuddle, they headed off in the direction of The Grand a few minutes' walk away.

"I'll bet I know something you don't," remarked Patricia as they approached the edge of the park.

"Go on."

"That temple marked the birthplace of three martyrs in particular. Now what three martyrs can you think of that might fit the bill?"

"I really don't know but I do know you'll take great delight in telling me."

She broke away from him with a playful skip. "Then I'm not telling you until you try harder."

It wasn't until they were in the lift at The Grand that she did tell him. "Saint Sofia had three daughters and she named them Faith, Hope and Charity, hence the temple in their honour more than the oppressed."

"So which one would you like to be tonight, just so that I know who I'm giving to?"

With a wicked look on her face she replied, "All three would be nice, but leave Hope until last."

Chapter 10

Nuts

Sex was foremost on their minds as they opened the door to their room, but Justin also wanted to find out what was on that memory stick as soon as he could. It would have to wait due to his physical condition as Patricia peeled off his shirt. During their stroll through the palace grounds, he'd come to the conclusion that with the revelation of Todor's intelligence status came the probability that they were probably being spied on. Certainly he'd been quite right to have been circumspect earlier, but now that Todor had let them know who he was, he was giving them a message. That message was *I'm watching you*. At some point of their undressing in the dark, he managed to sneak the memory stick and her laptop under the bedclothes and then he forgot about them until their first session was all over.

When amorous couples start looking at laptops under the bedsheets at two o'clock in the morning, it's usually to improve their sex lives, but it was quite the opposite in this case. Nor was it a video, only sound. Having to keep the volume right down meant that they needed to listen to some passages twice. Justin had to assume that the man speaking was the contact he'd been given in London by Sir Neville; he'd even started off his narration by stating that this was *B for Baker*. The security check that Justin had suggested tied in so he had no reason to doubt its authenticity.

Justin whispered in her ear. "Let's sleep on this and discuss it somewhere easier in the morning."

"Done. But why waste valuable sleeping time?" Her hand crept up his inner thigh.

"At least let me close this down," he gasped as she grasped.

Not too long after their marathon of sensual ecstasy ended, Patricia inserted her own dongle into the laptop; she needed to check-in anyway. It was not so much to report her findings which she did as a matter of course, but it was to see if there was any reference to Todor. Her logic told her that any high-ranking official in a country's military intelligence service at least ought to be listed, but if not, she would be happy to add his name to the list. There wasn't much on Todor Yordan other than the usual date, place of birth, parents, etc., but what did send a shiver down her spine was that he was listed as being the highest-ranking officer in charge of Bulgaria's 'internal police'. The last entry made into the electronic dossier was some two years ago by a DiS operative and stated that although their secret police had been forced to be disbanded by pressure from within the European community, it was natural that a replacement organisation should take its place. The out-of-date communist regime was too brutal in the eyes of today's society of integrated cooperation between EEC

Chapter 10 - Nuts

countries and therefore had to go. Not very much was known about ComDos which had appeared upon the demise of the old regime but it was apparently headed by Colonel Todor Yordan.

"The bastard lied," she whispered to Justin who was lying on his back, half trying to get to sleep.

"About what?"

"He's not just any old major. He's the bloody Colonel in charge of the whole of Bulgaria's secret service."

"Well, we have been in elevated company tonight, haven't we?"

"Don't be so flippant, this is serious."

"I know, but there's not a lot we can do about it under the duvet right now, is there?"

"Let me finish."

***

They hardly noticed what they ate for breakfast, nor that it was a rushed affair with half finished coffee cups and bread still left on plates.

They wandered haphazardly through the half-paved gardens adjacent to the hotel apparently in no particular direction, but chose their paths so that they could surreptitiously see if there were any observers lurking. Their initial chat was about the inconsequential aspects of life such as the rain that had recently stopped and how it bought out a fresh aroma from the verdant surroundings. It wasn't a big park but all four sides were abutted by busy roads with plenty of traffic noises, so they chose to walk along those paths where possible, thus making it very difficult for any electronic listening devices to catch their conversation.

"We're agreed then. The whole thing's a scam, but to what end?" Patricia was the first to say out loud what they were both thinking. "What's the point in them trying to convince us that it's a working mine? They don't produce anything but they can sell it, so where's the platinum coming from?"

"Hang on a tick. Let's retain a bit of scientism as Sir Neville's chap's report may not be the truth. OK, I accept that I too believed what he said but let's ask ourselves at the end if what we conclude is accurate."

"No stone unturned, eh?"

"That'll be our final stone so in the meantime we have to assume that his report is accurate. It all fits but let's go through it step by step."

They made a U-turn as they neared the end of a path.

Justin started off. "Just because he started his report with the words *'It's a sham'* automatically sets one's mind assuming that it is, so we need to question each part. He said that there is only one mine and that that was leased to and run by a Canadian corporation. I can quite easily believe that because now that I think of it, the route that Todor's driver took us was really round the other side of the mountain, not a separate mountain."

"You asked me to question everything, which I do anyway, so I now ask you are you 100% sure in your own mind that it could have been just one mine?"

"Look at it this way. Our initial encounter with proper security wasn't until we visited the gateway to

Chapter 10 - Nuts

the first mine and those soldiers looked real enough to me. But someone in Todor's position could quite easily have ordered a company of soldiers to make themselves look like they were on guard duty. He could also rustle up a decent set of gates, a dog patrol and a few hundred yards of fencing, all to make it look like it was government run. And then there was that tricky underground passageway with the heavy curtain at the end of it. That we emerged halfway along the train tracks doesn't necessarily mean that it belongs to a different mine."

"So that's not conclusive, is it." It was a statement from Patricia rather than a question.

"No, it's not conclusive but it's certainly an indicator. It must cost a small fortune to create an underground train tunnel of that size that far underground and I wonder how many other train tracks there might be down there. I'd say just the one, wouldn't you?"

No comment from Patricia, so he carried on. "I have to admit that the vertical shaft was real enough and there was no doubting that the ore being raised up in those skip-like bins was the same ore as we saw being delivered at the top. Same shaft."

"Even if we could have actually seen the ore being mined…"

"I know what you're going to say and you're quite right. There'd be no way of verifying if it was the same that ended upstairs, and anyway we don't know the difference between ore, gold, silver, platinum, iron or whatever. You see what I'm getting at. Todor was trying to convince us that there were two separate mines while in reality, it was just one mine accessed from two different parts of the same mountain."

"Explain further." Patricia was being awkward trying to find fault in his logic.

"Hey, looks like another park over there. Let's take a wander."

They crossed the busy road at a set of lights and continued their perambulations.

"Did you see the look on the face of the commander of the second mine entrance? He looked mightily upset to me and I reckon that Todor shows potential customers round from time to time and that poor chap had just had his lunch or woman disturbed. Somehow, the second part seemed much more official than the first. Not underground. Out in the open. Nothing nefarious going on. How did it strike you?"

"I think you're right. The security of the second mine was probably guarded by the local militia, while the first was a sub-branch of Todor's security department. That sergeant was genuine though. Hey, did you manage to smell that lump you picked up off the ground and have you still got it?"

"It's on the dresser back in the room in plain view. No point in hiding it since if someone does find it, we can say we wanted a memento. We can get it analysed back home. And anyway, I picked up two pieces. One in the open, the other in one of my shoes."

"What do we do now?" she asked.

"Fancy an ice cream?" They stopped at a stall. "Nuts?" He pointed at a punnet of finely ground bits of gravel that looked like nuts.

Chapter 10 - Nuts

They started sauntering back the way they had come and it was Patricia who answered her own question from a few minutes earlier. "Ask yourself this. If your contact hadn't alerted us to the fact that this might be some sort of scam, would we have suspected anything and would we be having this conversation right now?"

Justin stopped and Patricia stopped with him. "Probably not."

"Who is this guy or shouldn't I ask?"

"You shouldn't ask."

"From the way he put his message across, I'm guessing he's actually been inside the mine, but he didn't say so did he."

"No he didn't, but I'd have to listen to it again to make my mind up."

They re-crossed the road and into the gardens.

"If they are running a scam, it would need to be extremely well thought out," Patricia concluded.

"You've seen for yourself the lengths they are going to to disguise what's going on, but the price of platinum must surely make it very worthwhile."

"Now that we know what we think we know, we're going to have to be extra careful when we meet Todor in an hour's time." She looked at her watch. "Make that half an hour."

"We'll just have to put those kind of thoughts to the back of our minds and concentrate on being eager trade and industry representatives of Her Majesty's Government. I've had enough." He shoved his ice cream into a passing bin.

***

"No wonder civil servants get paid their vast salaries," commented Patricia in hushed tones as a translator droned on as he recited from the pages of a bound document. "If I weren't standing, I'd be falling asleep."

"This is obviously how they do things in Bulgaria but I doubt falling asleep is on their agenda."

"God this is so boring. All they need to do is hand it to us so that we can pass it on. I mean, it's not as though you and I are entitled to sign on behalf of HMG, are we. That's a job for the ambassador, isn't it?"

Drone. Drone. Drone.

"Do you think this is how they fill up their mornings until lunchtime?"

They were hoping that they were over halfway through the proceedings when Todor appeared through a tall door that was opened for him. "Good morning, good morning." He was dressed in full military uniform and indeed commanded the attention his rank deserved.

The droner and translator paused their monotonous recital.

"Sorry I'm late but I was unavoidably detained." He stood by the droner, plucked the document out of his hands and cast it on the ornate table off to one side. "I think we can dispense with the reading of the articles of trade as I suspect you will need to present them to your department chief anyway." He rattled off a few orders and the minions departed leaving himself, Justin and Patricia standing in the middle of the otherwise

Chapter 10 - Nuts

empty room. He sauntered over to the window. "I've been told that one can see thirty-one churches from here, fortunately most of them are Christian, but there are a few who follow Allah, some the Catholic faith and others just gipsies who follow their own noses. Taken all together it makes for a mixed and integrated society and as we all know, it takes those many facets to make up a complete picture." He turned to face them. "Right now I do not have a complete picture as it is missing a couple of pieces." He paused to see if there was any reaction from the English couple standing in front of him. "You are both of those missing pieces."

Justin and Patricia looked at each other and kept very blank faces but eventually Patricia opened her mouth to try to say something that would relieve the tension that was building.

Justin beat her to it. "I presume you are referring to our forthcoming arrangement… and some sort of commitment…?"

"Certainly, because so far you have seen how we operate and what's on offer, whereas I have nothing from you. You have seen our mine and how it works closer than anybody else has. You have seen the different methods of transportation on offer. You have met with our minister who you now know wishes to complete on our arrangement, but what you do not know yet is how much all this will cost."

It came as no surprise to either of them that he spoke with complete confidence as they now knew who he was. They were wary of the amount of power at his fingertips while in Bulgaria and needed to be extremely careful. One slip may result in their being thrown into Sofia's deepest dungeon.

"What are you proposing?" Justin decided not to add that any arrangement would need to be ratified back in London. That went without saying, but to have actually said it to Todor's face may have been construed as an insult.

"That, my friend, depends on how much you would be ordering but in any case, I think an advance contribution of half a million euros would show good faith."

Justin didn't have to pretend to consider it as he'd already made his mind up that whatever figure Todor came up with, would need to be negotiated. This was clearly the bribery part of the equation and had no bearing on what the price of platinum might be at a later date. "Sounds about right to me, but may I suggest it be made in two stages... so as not to attract too many questions?"

"Very wise." Out of his pocket he pulled a postcard face up showing one of Sofia's churches. "You will find all that you need on the back without having to pray in this magnificent structure. After all, you've already visited it. I showed you round it two days ago. It's the Alexander Nevsky Cathedral. Just in case someone asks you about it."

"How very thoughtful of you but we'll need something a little more substantial than a postcard to present to those in London who doggedly insist on correct documentation." Justin showed it to Patricia and

Chapter 10 - Nuts

they both noticed that there were several alphanumeric lines neatly written on it.

"I don't think that will be much of a problem because that document that was being read out to you just now is for the benefit of officials. EEC compliant and 'above board' I believe is the correct terminology." His eager smile had returned but they both knew how hollow it probably was. The mere fact that he had shown them round the Nevsky Cathedral previously and now had a postcard of it, demonstrated just how efficiently and deviously he had planned; which made him someone to be feared if it came to the crunch.

Todor looked at his watch. "I am needed elsewhere shortly so sadly I must wish you farewell. Do not worry about a taxi to the airport as Gregor will be your chauffeur for the rest of the day. I still recommend The Tenebris for lunch as you have ample time to enjoy its delights, but do watch out for eavesdroppers."

He turned firstly to Patricia. "These last two days have been enhanced by your beautiful presence." He took her hand and kissed it in the old-fashioned way by bowing his head and he then held out his hand out to Justin. "I look forward to our next meeting with great anticipation." He abruptly left, leaving the pair of them standing in the bay of the window overlooking the city centre.

"He must have something else terribly important to leave us like this," remarked Patricia.

"We all have our priorities so let's return to The Grand and get ready for lunch," he beamed sarcastically.

As they walked over to one of the entrance doors, an official appeared with a briefcase and with broken

English, presented it to Justin. "This is you paper for you government. Please to take it."

They didn't dare talk about Todor's implications while on Bulgarian soil, nor at the airports, nor in the aircraft and not even the taxi back in the UK; such was their suspicion of being overheard. It was nearly eight o'clock by the time they dumped their stuff down in their flat and Justin said just one thing.

"Pub?"

"Pub."

"For some reason I really fancy a Guinness."

Patricia tasted her tongue for a couple of seconds. "You know what… I fancy a Guinness too. Nothing to eat though as I'm still full from lunch."

Todor's suggestion had indeed been superb, and the owner had clearly been warned of their arrival as they enjoyed just about the best positioned table in the restaurant.

Fifteen minutes later and each with a Guinness in hand they managed to get a window seat overlooking the Thames at Boulters Lock. It was another iconic view. Overlooking the pretty weir and with a bridge in the background, they watched a flotilla of ducks paddling in and out of the reed beds. A pair of elegant swans floated nearer the far bank, and all the while the gentle sound of water trickling by.

Establishing that their nearest diners were merely tourists, they began to relax and bend their minds to their experiences over the past few days.

"Must be some big sporting event on telly as it's not too busy." He casually looked around.

Chapter 10 - Nuts

"Nah. Tourists have all but bedded down in their little B&Bs for the night and it's too early for the local crooks yet. Too light outside."

"Once your manor, always your manor. Do you think anyone might recognise you here?"

"If they do, they'll give this place a wide enough berth until we leave. Here, talking of crooks." She produced Todor's postcard. "I've been looking at his hieroglyphics. Apart from his mobile number which is quite obvious, the rest are bank account numbers etc." She offered it to him to have a closer look. "Took me less than one minute to figure out that those letters and numbers are bank account details; backwards."

Justin frowned as he too deciphered. "Ummm. Doesn't look like a British bank number as they all start with 'GB'. I'll check it out when we get back to the flat."

"Was that what we were expecting? Half a million euros?"

"Why not? I wouldn't have been surprised if it were a million. Remember, these chaps are playing for big stakes at government level and sums like that are commonplace when it comes to contracts. Slush funds are there to persuade officials to sign-off on paperwork. Just look at the amount of money surrounding football these days and that's just a sport, not even commerce. A player transfer between clubs can quite easily attract ten million or more, and not only does the agent receive his commission, but the player receives an amount also. The authorities have always known what was going on but couldn't control it so decided to legalise it. We have a similar situation here except what Todor and gang are doing is strictly underhand, but if the government wants a commodity such as platinum badly enough, they would be willing to pay the 'agent' their commission."

"So now that you know what you know, how's that going to help your quest to find out who's manipulating the platinum market from the inside?"

"Not sure yet, but something's out of kilter with Todor's lot and I haven't had time enough to figure it out. It wouldn't surprise me to discover that he and Bayev were somehow involved. Instigators even. I'll sleep on it and hopefully something might gel in the morning."

"Those two girls who seemed to know our whereabouts were obviously connected to your inside man, and if he's half-decent at his job they'll have just been the cut-outs you mentioned. Seemed well trained though," Patricia observed.

"Yes, I wondered if they had been a plant by Todor to give us misleading information, but dismissed that as there's nothing for him to gain by alerting us to his subterfuge, so yes, I reckon they were from my contact. That reminds me, I need to get in touch with Sir Neville and see if he's heard anything. Oh and by the way, you know that piece of stone I left on the sideboard in our room? Did you notice that when we packed our bags that it was gone?"

"I assumed you had already packed it."

"Wrong. It was taken."

Patricia closed her eyes to help imagine the scene. "I did notice that the room had been attended to by the chambermaid. You know, beds made, bins emptied

Chapter 10 - Nuts

towels tidied, etc. She could have thought it just another piece of stone and junked it."

"She could have, but somehow I doubt it. Anyway, I've still got that second piece and if Sir Neville wants to retain his reputation, he won't need to send it off to the lab for analysis."

"Listen, I really need to catch up on my end of things or Gibbons will start wondering what I've been up to, so tomorrow I'll leave you to your side of things." She paused before disclosing what was on her mind to Justin. "I was rather intrigued by Bayev's chap, Hana, and like you I haven't had a chance to figure him out yet. Bodyguard, do you reckon?"

"Yeah, he certainly looked the type, and his services were offered if we encountered any problems. What one might call a troubleshooter."

"Or a strong-arm man?"

"Not the kind of person one would normally introduce to accredited trade personnel such as us, but as they're on the make then a person such as Hana would doubtless have his uses. Especially in Eastern Europe."

"I don't usually believe in coincidences but in this instance a character of Hana's abilities might very well be the one and the same that's supposedly connected with… shall we say… unconnected accidents."

"I reckon he was asked along to show us that we were dealing with someone who wouldn't want to be double-crossed. Think about it. Suppose we kept that half a million for ourselves instead of passing it onto Messrs Bayev and Todor, it wouldn't take much for Hana to be dispatched in our direction to find out where

131

it had gone, would it? Bodyguard to Bayev he might be, but he could well be his enforcer." He paused to take another swig. "I've just had a nasty thought... I'll bet that if he's despatched by Bayev he'll be travelling on a diplomatic passport."

"Oh shit. Of course. Bollocks. If only I could have taken a photo of him." Her colourful expletives drew a glance from the couple at the adjacent table.

"You'd probably have been lynched there and then. No, correction. We'd have both been lynched."

She was about to say 'bugger' when she remembered the nearby couple, so mouthed the 'F' word instead.

Justin continued rhetorically. "I presume you can arrange a photofit artist, because once we have that, we can identify him at whatever airport he comes into and then put a name to him."

Patricia thought about this for a moment. "And what if he travels under different names each time? We won't see him coming."

"No we won't but at least we'll know when he's in the country from what the cameras pick up and if he ends up in London we can most likely track him and correlate any misdeeds. I'm going for another Guinness. Want one?"

"Half'll do me fine."

While Justin waited at the bar counter, Patricia rested her chin on her hands and stared out of the wide window at the typical English pastoral scene and half-wondered what it would be like to be as free of worries as the ducks. It was a relaxing scene that transposed itself into her mind and distracted her from concentrating on

Chapter 10 - Nuts

their experiences from the past few days. Perhaps it was the Guinness. Perhaps she was plain old tired. Whatever it was it freed up her mind of worries and left the rest of her subconscious to mull on what they had just been talking about.

She was nearing a conclusion when Justin returned. "They've run out of Guinness so what else do you fancy?"

She looked up at him for a moment. "Quite honestly I fancy going back home and getting a good night's kip."

Chapter 11

Collaboration

Each ensconced in their own worlds, they passed like ships in the night and it wasn't even six o'clock in the morning yet. Complete with an oversized cup of tea, Patricia reclined on the sofa with her laptop balanced comfortably on her thighs, while Justin threw a 'see-you-later' over his shoulder in her general direction on his way out.

Justin's comments regarding Hana yesterday evening had her thinking that it surely was too much of a coincidence, so she looked up the name 'Hana' on Google and found that it was a rare name in that part of the world. She recalled her digging from a few days ago and retrieved the grainy group photograph she had found, but it was of such poor quality she couldn't even guess if it was one and the same man.

She messaged Tates to arrange for a photofit artist as that was going to be the only way she was going to make headway on identification, and then carried on with digging into suspicious events across Europe. She recognised that her bias was that the Sofia Hana and HOT were one and the same person, so tried to counter that by presuming that they weren't when she

Chapter 11 - Collaboration

linked various events together. Trying to play the devil's advocate. The scant information available didn't prove or disprove whichever stance she took, so she decided that if she could find just three occasions where there was some mention of Hana in whatever guise, then she could be almost certain in her own mind, regardless of actual proof. Three occurrences would mean that coincidence was no longer a factor. Furthermore, if HOT/Hana was the perpetrator, then by inference that made Bayev and Todor not just involved, but architects of a whole series of crimes.

The link… where was the link that proved Hana was HOT? She returned to the report from *La Repubblica* and noted the name of the Italian correspondent who had written the article and rang the newspaper.

The female receptionist on the other end of the phone was sorry to say that Signor Antello Fraschini no longer submitted articles for their paper, but was unable to say why due to company policy. After a few minutes of condescending diplomatic chat, it was revealed that their correspondent had unfortunately died in a boating accident last year, and Patricia was directed to the online report in their own newspaper.

She swore at her laptop for the first time as it was reluctant to go into translate mode straight away, and she left it thinking about how to do that while she went and made herself a slice of hot, buttered toast with a thin spread of marmite. No sooner had she sat down than she swore again as she had forgotten her hot cup of tea in the kitchen, but by the time she had settled down, at least the English version was available. She scrolled through the pages and didn't need to look further than page four where there was the article about the demise of their beloved and loyal correspondent Antello Fraschini. Skimming his family aspect, a neighbouring boatowner who moored his small boat in the sleepy port of Talamone adjacent to Antello's stated that they often went out to sea in tandem to enjoy early morning fishing. On that particular day, the sea had been as flat as a millpond but the tranquillity of the early morning had been shattered when his small motor boat had inexplicably exploded as he had tried to start the outboard motor. The neighbour hypothesised that Antello must have left the valve to a gas cannister open, and by pulling the starter of the outboard had sparked the gas that had settled into the bottom of the boat. The report concluded that the Pubblico Ufficiale had declared the event the equivalent of death by misadventure. A blameless and unfortunate occurrence.

She didn't really want to go ploughing into the Italian system of filing deaths but felt she just had to in order to put her mind at ease, so started to track down the 'Ufficiale' concerned and found that it fell in the provincial jurisdiction of Florence. Looking at her screen to check the time, instead decided that she had better wait another couple of hours despite the continent being an hour ahead.

Trying to find another angle to discover if there was anything at all on Hana, she wondered how long he might have been Bayev's right-hand man and unsurprisingly had no luck on that front as it wasn't exactly the sort of thing one would advertise; anywhere.

Chapter 11 - Collaboration

However, when she cross-checked her notepad, she found that the start of those unattributed arson events coincided more or less to when Bayev came to power. It was nothing remotely concrete but there it was again; another unattributable abnormality.

She plugged in her dongle, connected with the main database and typed questions about gangs operating in Eastern Europe; what affiliations and who likely bankrollers were, among other spurious connections. She didn't feel as though she was violating any security rules since this was her remit as demanded by Commander Gibbons. And why could it not be HOT who might be Hirov's assassin, if indeed there was to be an assassination attempt? She hypothesised that not only was HOT perfectly capable of carrying out such an operation but if indeed his paymaster was Bayev, then it followed that money would be the prime motivation. As Bulgaria's finance minister, Hirov would be number one target if Russia had resurrected her designs again, and naturally there would be no easy loose ends to be found.

The one indisputable coincidence – and surely it was just a coincidence – was that she had had a chance to meet Hana/HOT, Bayev and Todor all at the same time. She closed her eyes and pictured their last meeting but it wasn't accurate enough to come to any conclusion. She tried to see the features on Hana's face as she would need the smallest of details when she met with the photofit artist. She considered that her memory was pretty good when it came to recalling details of a crime scene, but that probably only came about because she would have been looking for clues and concentrating on the subject at hand. At that time, she hadn't prepared herself mentally to contemplate that scenario and certainly not to have come face to face with Hana, possibly. No probably.

Oh for one of those legendary photographic memories that certain people possessed! She closed her eyes and relaxed as she pictured the scene. She didn't realise it but she frowned as she visualised them walking into the room where they had been introduced to Bayev and his wife. Hana had produced a silver drinks tray between the four of them and as he leaned forward slightly, she saw it. Hana had a small piece of silver jewellery pierced through his left ear. She tried tilting her head sideways to see if his right ear had a similar piercing, but it eluded her. The left one would have to do, so she recalled her vision and tried to concentrate on the shape of the earring; it wasn't round that was for sure but she couldn't quite focus on all of it at the same time. Small it may have been but it was as though it was deflecting her attention. She gave up and opened her eyes and immediately made a note on her pad. Perhaps it would come to her.

She turned her attention to contacting the Pubblico Ufficiale in Florence and discovered it was a woman called Carmen da Rosa from the easily accessed Italian webpage. She tilted her head while looking at the photograph and decided she was far too young and pretty to hold such an important office. Had that been in England, there might just be an ugly mugshot of a grumpy old man on the verge of retirement, or a prim-

Chapter 11 - Collaboration

looking woman with the beginnings of a moustache; not this filly showing off her perfect set of sparkling white teeth through a classic broad smile. She dialled the number through her computer and while she waited to be put through, took the opportunity to look at Carmen's public profile. She discovered that her father was a well-off industrialist whose family now made extruded plastics almost exclusively for European medicinal institutions. As a wealthy man, he would have been able to influence those in the right circles to provide his daughter with a prominent position, almost straight from university; now possibly the youngest Pubblico Ufficiale in Italy. She was just wondering why Carmen, with her beauty and curvaceous body, had chosen a fairly boring governmental position rather than spend her time among the rich and famous, when the background hold music stopped.

"Carmen de Rosa speaking. I believe I am addressing Inspector Eyethorne?"

Patricia was taken aback as she was expecting an average level of English accompanied by a heavy Italian accent, but instead it was perfectly inflected English. It put her on the back foot and she automatically tried to emulate the Queen's English; she winced as she did so a bit too thickly.

"Yes, this is Inspector Eyethorne." She quickly reverted back to her normal voice before it gave her away. "As this is an unofficial request you will need to refer to me as Inspector Eyethorne but please call me Patricia."

"Carmen."

She relaxed a little and explained that she had been tasked to follow up some loose ends.

"But why are you interested in Signor Antello Fraschini because from my files here all I can see is that he was a well-known journalist who wrote articles for *La Repubblica*. There's nothing here to say that he had any correspondence with the UK."

Patricia had been in two minds whether or not to tell Camren the real reason, or to make up some sort of story, as the last thing she wanted was for news of her enquiries reaching back to Hana. She decided on the spur of the moment to disclose the real reason, quite possibly because of Carmen's impeccable English and ability to understand and to read between the lines. It only took her two minutes which ended with her question, "Was he really killed by an exploding gas cannister?"

She could hear Carmen shuffling papers in the background and after nearly a minute heard her pick up the receiver again. "I think we need a more private conversation. Can we Zoom later this afternoon?"

Details were swapped. Patricia decided she needed some fresh air anyway.

***

Sir Neville was only too keen to accede to Justin's request to see him at short notice; even at seven-thirty in the morning. As he was ushered into his office, he could see Sir Neville standing at a hinged bookshelf.

Chapter 11 - Collaboration

"Whisky?" He held a tumbler in each hand and offered one as Justin approached. "Before you ask, I sometimes start the day with a large scotch. No excuses other than I like it." He indicated for Justin to sit. "Especially if there's to be a surprise. I know, I know, how do I know there's going to be a surprise if it's a surprise?" He took a deep swig and savoured the peatiness. "Because my nose says so, so tell me, what surprise have you got for me today? Oh, and before you start, you ought to know that one of my inside men heard a rumour that you're not the person you claim to be, but someone from a far more sinister background." He was his usual pert self and it seemed to Justin that he thoroughly enjoyed encounters such as this and he asked himself if it was the scotch that helped put the slightest of smiles on his face.

It took him less than three minutes to relate the relevant parts of what he and Patricia had been doing in Sofia and only once did Sir Neville interrupt him with a query. He kept their meeting with Bayev until last and raised an eyebrow at Sir Neville's reaction.

"You actually met him and managed to walk away. Both of you." It was neither a question nor a rhetorical statement and he held up his half-empty glass in salutation. "Only the bloody lucky manage to survive his clutches." He leaned forward. "How much did he demand?"

"You know him then." That was Justin's rhetoric statement and he instantly regretted opening his mouth as the answer was obvious.

"Know him! Nobody forgets him. Him and his... go on... what happened?"

"He recommended a quality restaurant to us for lunch and I must say it rounded off our trip quite nicely." He smiled as he said it. It was very much a tongue-in-cheek response but Justin felt he wanted to get it out of his system and let the man in front of him know that he was his own man and not one of his lackeys. If he could get Sir Neville to disclose what he knew about Bayev and his operation, it was quite likely that it would make his job easier.

Sir Neville narrowed his eyes a little. "I know a little levity goes some way to alleviating a tense situation but I don't believe you and I are at that stage, but I get your point. OK, I'll tell you." He took a small sip from his glass to whet his lips. "Some years ago, when I was earning my stripes in The Ring, myself and a very close friend and colleague of mine decided to delve into the wholesale dealings of the metal market and in particular, gold. Our aim was to try to cut out the middlemen and buy direct from the mines in South Africa; see if we couldn't make a small fortune on the side while still representing the firm that we worked for at the time. Of course we weren't allowed to buy directly from the mines and had to go through official South African channels, but we had our own man on the inside. Krugerrands were all the rage back then and while it was illegal to import them into the UK, they wouldn't have been listed on any manifest, so it was quite simple for us to include them in a shipment of legal gold. It was all going swimmingly until we came

Chapter 11 - Collaboration

across Bayev who was staying in the same hotel. Both Leo and I were acutely aware of the consequences if we were found out and neither of us told a soul, and the only other person involved was our contact at the treasury. He was one of our own from London who'd emigrated a few years earlier so we knew we could trust him. God knows how Bayev found out about what we were up to, but he did. At the time he was a junior attaché to the Bulgarian embassy in Johannesburg and we thought nothing of his comings and goings, along with other 'attachés' from other embassies." He raised his hand to indicate inverted commas. "We wondered if he'd had our room bugged by his pally Russians or perhaps it was because he was up to the same thing as we were, but the upshot was that the Krugerrands were stolen from our consignment just before it was loaded onto the aircraft." He paused for a brief slurp.

"We suspected Bayev and his crew so Leo insisted on confronting him and went to wait in a bar-cum-coffee shop opposite the entrance to the Bulgarian embassy, while I went off to consult our friendly contact to see if he could add anything to the disappearance of our Krugerrands. The bar Leo was waiting in exploded without warning, instantly killing him and badly injuring several others. Of course there was nobody we could complain to, and officially the explosion was put down to a plumber who had left his tool bag, complete with gas cannister, under the table next to where Leo was sitting. The police had better things to do other than clear up what was a relatively minor incident, yet according to one of the locals who I managed to catch up with, it wasn't the sort of place where plumbers spent their lunch hour."

He finished off his glass, got up, refilled it with an ice cube from his 'bookshelf', and sat back down again.

"I still have bitter memories of kicking my heels and having to stay out there to arrange for the return of Leo's body, or what was left of him rather, as the authorities were asking some awkward questions, and it took me nearly two weeks before they released me and his cadaver for return to the UK. Then I had the devil's own job covering the loss of our money." He placed his glass down in front of him and seemed deep in thought. Justin didn't dare interrupt. "Yes it was our own money, not the companies, and it very nearly bankrupted me. His sister had to sell everything she owned as we'd used her money as well."

The background hum of the building accentuated the silence as Sir Neville stared into the cuts of his glass.

"How certain are you that Bayev was responsible?"

It was as if a spell had been broken. Sir Neville looked up with steel in his eyes and his voice sharpened. "Oh it was Bayev alright. His timing was perfect for rubbing my nose in our misfortune. It was the week after I had returned from South Africa and the day after Leo's funeral at which I'd had to repeatedly explain to his family and close friends that he had died in a tragic accident. I'd had to lie to some of those whom I knew intimately, knowing full well that the real story mustn't ever come out. I was appalled at my own guile. That's when I got a call from an anonymous third party offering to sell me some cut-price Krugerrands and I instantly

Chapter 11 - Collaboration

knew that Bayev was behind it, so I told him where he could stuff their Krugerrands." Sir Neville briefly jutted his chin out. "The bastard even offered to meet me in a café to make a cash exchange; as if I would, but it was like the knife was being twisted after being stuck in, and it hurt like hell."

He went to drink from his glass but paused mid-air and put it down on his desk while glaring at Justin. "It still hurts like hell which is why I'm telling you all of this. Oh I've got to the stage now where I don't care if you repeat what I've just told you. I've reached the top and can't go any higher, get paid a whopping great salary and make even more with my dealings, earned a knighthood, and travel the world whenever I want. There's very little I can't do all except for one thing, and that's get back at that bastard Bayev. And not just for my own satisfaction but to even the score for Leo. Believe me, I've tried." He picked up his glass again but before it reached his lips he added, "And I know for a fact that he's shafted others as well. Well and truly shafted, and if necessary I'll prove it to you."

This time whisky managed to find its way into his mouth but Justin didn't take the opportunity to interject as he felt that there was more to come. He wasn't wrong.

"For example, about eighteen months ago there was an opportunity for those Eastern Bloc countries to create their own derivatives market aimed specifically at rare metals, and it was Bayev who scuppered the framework just as it was being set up… he made a packet from that failure. And I'll bet you don't know how he came to be in the ministerial position he enjoys today." Sir Neville paused. "Don't take it from me but look it up when you get the chance."

Justin looked down at his half-drunk scotch and tried to rattle the now non-existent ice cube.

"You see, after our first meeting and my subsequent discovery of who you used to work for and who you work with now, I decided that you could turn out to be my perfect weapon... against Bayev." He watched a frown form on Justin's forehead. "No... no... don't take umbrage at being used, because throughout your entire career that's all that's happened to you, and contrary to what you are probably thinking right now, at least acknowledge that I'm being straight with you. Opening your eyes to what you haven't realised." He watched Justin's frown grow and his body language readying itself to rise. "Before you walk out of here, please listen to what I have to say because I'm sure you'll find it beneficial... to both of you."

Justin's initial reaction had indeed been to leave but once he managed to gain full control over his emotions, realised that Sir Neville was not insulting him; quite the reverse. He was affording him that rare commodity – the truth. Coupled with his own recent experiences in Bulgaria, he realised that he stood a good chance of getting to the bottom of how the market had been manipulated. He hoped that along the way he'd have the chance of using Sir Neville like he was being used right now. "I'm listening," was all he could manage.

"Bayev specialises in manipulating anyone who he thinks can be of use to him and in this instance, you and your fiancée. I asked you how much a few minutes ago."

Chapter 11 - Collaboration

"Half a million euros… in two tranches."

"That'll be the thin edge of the wedge," Sir Neville immediately countered. "I'll tell you what's going to happen when he doesn't receive that half a million and realises that he's been had. He'll send his dogs along to remind you what you owe him."

"We've thought of that one. When he finds out that we weren't from the Department of Trade and Industry and since there'll be no mileage in him pursuing us, he'll have no other option than to close down his operation. He may even have to resign and go into hiding. Emigrate even."

"You're wrong," Sir Neville retorted with conviction. "Remember, I know this bugger and he's as vindictive as they come. From what you've told me you met his strong-arm man Hana and it's he who'll be sent to find you and torture you before killing you. It won't matter to him that there really was no deal on the table. It won't matter who you once were or that your fiancée is a decorated policeman… policewoman. And he won't care how many others get injured if they just happen to be in his way. Bayev's the type of person who takes that sort of affrontery to a whole new level and he won't want any rumours getting out that a couple of English tourists managed to get one over on him. He'd lose too much face, and face is all important in that part of the world. Your only chance is to find some way of scuppering him which means both of you, and I, pulling our resources together, because we'd never manage it independently. I'll supply all the background information I have on him and to a certain extent, the machinations and contacts of the metal exchange while you and your fiancée supply all the latest intel, then together we formulate a plan... a sting if you prefer to call it that... and by the way, you don't have much time."

"You mean we don't have much time." Justin had kept up with the logic of it all and had quickly come to the conclusion that they needed to work with Sir Neville.

"No. Both of you in particular. Was there any timeframe mentioned?"

"Not that I recall."

"Well at least that's one thing on our side, but he won't wait long in any case. A week or ten days at the most if we're lucky. And talking of luck, just before you arrived I had a very useful message from my man out there – Paul Wiltern if you remember me mentioning his name before. He was rather complimentary of you two."

"How's that?"

"Said you acted the part of a pair of disparate government employees perfectly."

"We never suspected the two girls but eventually we worked out they had come from him."

"He told me once he calls them his 'nieces' and that they come in very useful when prying information from those who are unsuspecting. Here, do you want some coffee?" Sir Neville was looking at Justin's empty glass as he pressed a desk-mounted intercom and ordered some. "Now, please tell me more of your suspicions rather than what you were actually doing in Bayev's backyard."

Chapter 11 - Collaboration

Justin described their hypothesis regarding the two mines and at the end, produced the stone-sized piece of rock he'd retrieved from the ground and placed it on the desk. Sir Neville looked at it for a few seconds before picking it up and hefting it, rotating it in the light, sniffing it, rubbing it with his thumb and finally subjecting it to the sharp end of his letter opener. A small peppercorn piece flicked onto the table and was immediately seized upon and popped onto the end of his tongue.

"Salt."

"Not even 'salty'. Just plain old salt?"

"Ummm... To be more accurate, sodium, which indicates a reasonable chance of good quality coal."

"How about something a little more precious like... platinum?" Justin's sceptical tone wasn't lost on Sir Neville.

"Unlikely. Can you remember exactly where you picked this up? I mean, was it right next to one of the cooling pits or out in the open where it could have come from anywhere?"

He unfocused his eyes and pictured the scene of him bending down and picking it up. "About ten feet or so from the cooling pit. There were several similar-looking pieces all around, but I couldn't swear that it came from the platinum pit."

The door to his office opened and in walked a well-dressed gentleman bearing a tray.

"Ah, Greg. Coffee at last," commented Sir Neville and as the tray was put down on his desk, he added, "Here, get this off to the lab and let me have their usual report as soon as they can." He tossed it in Greg's general direction and Justin wasn't surprised to see Greg deftly catch it as though he had done so on a regular basis.

"Yes Sir."

Sir Neville didn't wait until Greg had left the room. "I'll be a monkey's uncle if that sample's got more than a trace element of platinum in it, but it's best to make sure. Might hear back by tonight but I suspect it'll be tomorrow morning. I'll text you."

"You've told me a bit about Bayev but what about Hana? Do you know for a fact that he's the enforcer?" Justin wasn't about to reveal that his other half was looking into Hana's activities as it may jeopardise the response.

"Good question." He tinkled his spoon in his coffee cup. "I've had nothing in the past to directly link them together until now. Only rumours. But when you told me you saw them in the ministry, well... when one adds up two plus two then there's only one answer, isn't there?"

"They weren't just together... Hana was clearly under Bayev's orders. You could tell from their demeanour, so that makes it a certainty. The only question remaining is for how long." Before Sir Neville could comment, Justin added. "They looked to be about the same sort of age, but Hana may have been slightly younger."

"If they've been working hand-in-glove since the year dot, then it might well account for certain sinister happenings back then, such as exploding bars." He

Chapter 11 - Collaboration

sipped his coffee. "I do believe you now have another snippet of information that may help our case. So, if I can ask you to put your investigative skills to good use, between you and your fiancée, perhaps it may lead us to what to expect next and be one step ahead when they do decide to make their move."

"You make it sound so simple, but finding out anything about someone who wants their past to remain anonymous is often fruitless, especially when they are in a position of power. And by the way, her name is Patricia. It sounds so much better than 'my fiancée'."

"It also sounds rather intimate. Apologies. Now, rather than rush into formulating some sort of plan, why don't we wait until this time tomorrow when we know what that stone's made of, and you may have a bit more information on Messrs Bayev and Hana. And don't forget that there are local connections as well in the form of Todor Yordan. You can bet your bottom dollar he's up to his neck in this."

"There'll be others as well and it'll take us a little time to discard or collate what's relevant."

"Naturally, but the clock's ticking so concentrate on our main men. How about I meet up with you sometime tomorrow? I know what, I'll buy you both lunch and I know just the place… been itching to try it out for days now." Sir Neville's grin was as wide as Justin had seen it.

"I'll tell Patricia to skip breakfast then."

"Splendid."

Chapter 12

Worry lines

Justin strolled towards Finsbury Gardens to clear the heady early morning mixture of scotch and coffee. As he wandered round the bandstand on the tarmac path that dissected the neatly trimmed grass he mulled over what Sir Neville had said, and sceptically hypothesised that it was all a load of bullshit and that he was using Justin to satisfy his own ego. He decided to keep that one in the background, but not so far in the background that he wouldn't remember it should certain anomalies arise. Sir Neville had been right when he had pointed out that Justin had been used throughout his career, but it still irked him that it had had to come from someone else rather than him being able to figure that one out for himself. In retrospect, he was rather glad that it had been someone of Sir Neville's calibre and not some grubby overpaid psychoanalyst.

With his mind concentrating, he nearly bumped into another gent and decided it would be better if he sat down on one of the park benches and as he did so, he remembered that he still needed to investigate those numbers and letters from the postcard. He scrutinised the photo he had taken on his phone and decided they

Chapter 12 - Worry lines

were most likely bank related, so entered some of them into a search engine. The response was immediate and he blinked as the answer stared back at him. Of course. The letters IM stood for Isle of Man and when followed by 833, represented the IBAN of an offshore account held there. It was obvious, now that one had a clue, and obvious that Bayev wouldn't have held any serious amount of money in any bank in his own country. He was curious as to why the Isle of Man had been chosen rather than say Monaco, Jersey, Switzerland or any of the other countries that welcomed those who wished to maintain secrecy of their financial affairs. Certainly the IoM was a safe place to deposit monies and as safe as those others, but he recalled that one needed to be introduced by someone who already had an account there, or by a resident. In any case, whatever the banks' quirky rules, there would have needed to be checks on the origin of the money to ensure it wasn't criminally linked. Bayev could have quite easily claimed that it was Bulgarian government money and therefore circumvented the system and then tailored the account to suit his needs. Another thought came to Justin. Why stop at one account? There may be two, three, four, or several other accounts. If he was repeating the scam, quite possibly one account per customer.

One thing was certain. Because those banks jealously guarded the identities of their clients from the prying eyes of governments, it was very unlikely that neither he nor Patricia would be able to discover whose account it was by just enquiring, even if it was through official channels. He scrutinised the postcard again and looked for the name of the account, because after all, every account needed a name, didn't it? He had to break off as Patricia was calling him.

"Finished with Sir Neville?"

"Yes, about half an hour ago and I think our partnership became more complicated but I'll tell you when I see you. How have you got on?"

"It's like swimming against a treacle tide going in the opposite direction but we can swap notes later. I've arranged to see the photofit girl at ten o'clock; that's in just over half an hour's time. Can you make it to New Scotland Yard by then?"

"Westminster's on the Circle line and as Moorgate's just round the corner, I should just about make it providing that there are no sudden tube strikes. See you then."

Justin waited outside with his back to the Thames, looking up at the several storeys of uniform white blocks interspersed with regular blank windows. It reminded him of that game Connect4 but on its side; except the windows were square rather than round; and it was very black and white instead of colourful. He decided it looked more like one of the Led Zeppelin albums but couldn't remember which one; perhaps it was IV. He needed to wait for Patricia as he wouldn't be allowed in without her and he heard her footfall as she approached from the same direction he had come. He noted that she was several minutes late.

"Don't even ask," she commented as she stomped past Justin who followed right behind her.

Chapter 12 - Worry lines

He didn't.

The inside of the building had a rather clinical feel about it, not like the outside yet not so clinical as to be unfriendly. Nothing had changed since they were both last there but even so, and probably because Justin was no longer a government employee, they were escorted to a windowless room on the third floor and told to wait.

"Go on then," asked Justin as they sat down on a red-leather-covered bench that ran the length of the room. He was referring as to what had delayed Patricia.

She fidgeted at first, then, "Do I look like a bloody terrorist?"

"Only when you're angry," he immediately quipped.

She looked at him and after a small pause, began. "My pistol set off a security alarm at the station and it took me a while to convince them I really was Special Branch. While the two of them waited for confirmation, this poxy bitch insisted on body searching me while her colleague toyed with my Browning. But she got a bit too friendly so I decked her."

Justin appreciated the way she put it by asking, "Twice your size was she?"

"As it happens, yes. And before you say anything else, no she wasn't my type."

They heard footsteps approach the other side of the door, but Justin managed to get his comment in before it opened. "I'm glad all that training hasn't gone to waste then."

In walked a pair of wooden clogs with a teenager on top of them, wearing a body-hugging pair of faded jeans and a scruffy cardigan. They could tell she was a teenager because of the spots on her face, and anyway, everything about her cried 'youth'.

They managed to maintain deadpan faces when she spoke, as her voice was straight out of Cheltenham Ladies College. "Good morning. My name is Vivian and I presume you are Inspector Eyethorne and Mr Crawford." She smiled and stepped closer to shake hands and scrutinise their badges and when finished, she turned to Justin. "Since you are a visitor here, please do not take any photographs or touch anything, and if you become lost you must report to the security desk on the ground floor."

Justin couldn't help himself. "Oh I definitely won't get lost as I used to frequent this place up until recently." He smiled back at her.

She held his eyes for a moment before replying, "In that case you will know the consequences if you stray." She turned back to Patricia in empathy at her rank, and no doubt her badge which depicted her as an existing approved person. "I'm sure you will be able to keep an eye on him. Follow me please."

Justin felt that he was back at school again but decided to keep his mouth shut as he trailed the two women. He decided there was more to this teenager than met the eye.

Three doors further down the corridor was an entrance to a small atrium with an armed guard seated on a tall stool behind a lectern; he scanned their passes as they went through an electronically locked door.

Chapter 12 - Worry lines

"This is one of our secure rooms and you can talk freely as there are no cameras or microphones. I suggest you sit down there." Vivian pointed to two of the several plush cinema-type chairs in the front row as she sat herself down at a console off to their right. The room resembled a cinema which had a deathly hush about it, intimating that it was probably soundproof, but they didn't get much of a chance to look over the rest of it as the lights dimmed and a large silver screen lit up directly in front of them.

After a minute or so, Vivian looked up at them. "I understand you will both be describing an individual with the aim of identifying him, so, I will ask you questions and I would like you to answer with Inspector Eyethorne going first on each occasion. You Mr Crawford can qualify her remarks only after she has finished. You are now wondering why I am being specific with who goes first." It was a statement, not a question. "It is because with this method we are more likely to end up with a very close depiction of the individual concerned and not someone resembling a Martian. Clear?" She hardly waited for their response. "Right, a person will appear on the screen in front of you and we start with the basics." The screen showed a human outline. "Height?"

The human form began to take shape but it didn't take long before Vivian's questions became more difficult. "Skin pallor?" Once this was agreed upon and adjusted on the screen she asked, "Depth?"

"Depth of what?" asked Patricia.

"Depth of skin. For example, was it smooth like alabaster plaster or were the pores more open?"

Try as they did to follow her instructions, after a short while, Vivian butted in. "Please try not to confer, but give me your answers one at a time." It was like being lectured by the headmaster.

A few questions and answers later she zoomed in so that the human frame was reduced to a headshot and Patricia gleefully described the earring.

"I will leave it as octagonal for the moment. Left ear you say, but how was it attached?"

Detailed questions continued. Eyebrows, eyelashes, nasal hair, uniformity colour and shape of teeth, if his lips were showing signs of cracking. Vivian's expertise led them on so that at the end he looked nothing like the aforesaid Martian and she zoomed out so that his full frame was visible. "Now for his dress."

Neither of them had much of a clue there other than he had been wearing a white shirt, a suit and tie, and they hadn't the faintest idea as to what he wore on his feet, so Vivian put a pair of black lace-ups on him.

The pair of them commented that although he looked realistic, it wasn't quite him, but then they got a shock. Vivian rotated the man slowly through 360 degrees and adjusted his frame so that he stood a little more upright.

They got even more of a shock when he started walking; first towards them, and then left to right and back again. He was so lifelike. After a few comments, more adjustments were made, particularly to the way his arms hung and moved in relation to his body. Then he ran.

Chapter 12 - Worry lines

"You may be asking yourselves why we go to this much detail and the answer is simple. We cannot do much about a criminal's facial disguise if it is good. They can extend their cheeks, alter their eye surroundings, lips, nostrils, etcetera etcetera, but they cannot alter the distances between their joints, nor can they disguise the way they move; unless they are extremely good." As she was speaking, she got the man on the screen to bend down, kneel, jump, stretch. Then look directly at them and smile.

"You probably already know that we have facial recognition technology at our major ports and airports, but only recently have we begun to expand this extension to the program to cover certain arears of London. So, if your man somehow evades the UK entry points and ends up in London, sooner or later he will be flagged up."

"That's pretty impressive," commented Justin.

"Isn't it just. This definition program is something I learned how to do with a little help from our computer here, and because of these details, I might be able to give you a name, his ethnic origin, and other such useless information. Just give me a second." She attended to her console.

"Why do you say useless?" asked Patricia.

"Why?" Vivian paused what she was doing momentarily. "You can work that one out for yourself surely."

They looked at each other in the half-light and it didn't take them more than a few seconds to realise that names and faces were now historic in view of the modern detection methods that were now being displayed in front of them. Names and faces could be altered, but bone lengths, radii and skull shapes were far more difficult to forge.

"Can we go over his ears again?" Vivian had enlarged the one with the earring, but panned out a little to encompass both. "Do you think they were level? With each other I mean."

When nothing concrete came from them, she added the background of a plain room and made the man walk back and forth.

"I reckon that's about him," suggested Justin as he glanced at Patricia who nodded.

"OK then. The mainframe analysis time can vary but we ought to have an answer later today. I'll let you know." Vivian had obviously decided that that was the end of the session as she turned on the overhead lights.

As they walked towards the lift, Patricia complimented her on her efficiency.

"Us numpties like to think of ourselves as the backbone of the intelligence section. Of course, we are surrounded by brilliant minds but they all come to us in the end." She pressed the call button. "And then we tell them where they went wrong." Vivian smiled briefly.

"We look forward to being told then."

They shook hands before the pair of them got into the lift and once the doors had shut Justin commented. "She's nearly young enough to be my daughter."

"Don't kid yourself. You being a man wouldn't have noticed the feint creases at the side of her eyes. I reckon she's pushing thirty."

"With acne."

Chapter 13

Over and under

"Other than Vivian, I'll tell you where we go from here," commented Patricia as she finished slurping unladylike through the top of a cardboard beaker in the coffee shop just off Westminster Bridge. She peeled the lid away and flipped it on the table. "Bloody things."

"I had to break off Zooming with Carmen de Rosa to make it here in time. She's one of the Pubblico Ufficiales in Italy where there'd been a possible suspicious death a while back. She's the equivalent to one of our coroners over here in the UK and fortunately she was most cooperative. I've a Zoom with her in…" She glanced at her watch. "Bloody hell. Doesn't time fly when you're enjoying yourself. Forty-five minutes. I'm sure she wouldn't mind if you wanted to join in." She primed him further about the chap being a witness and the gas cannister theory.

Justin listened trying to maintain an open mind. "That's only one case out of many but I suppose it's a start."

Patricia wasn't to be put off. "I sometimes treat each clue as a small bubble and see where it floats and when three or more bubbles meet, then I encompass them into their own bubble. The bigger the bubble, the more the chances of coincidence disappear. Like a Venn diagram if you like." She saw Justin frown. "You remember Venn diagrams from school, don't you? You know, those circles that overlapped each other and where they did, you shaded in the area, and ergo, that was your common denominator. That's exactly what we have here." She didn't give him a chance to comment. "I've started digging into other cases as well and when you get below the surface you find that there are just too many coincidences. Granted they're minor but they all add up."

She looked earnestly at Justin. "That grey area is turning out to be a bit black when you include more circles that intersect, and those bubbles are now far too big to ignore. I reckon I'll need another three or four days to come up with some proof, but this Italian gent is the most concrete so far."

Justin was looking at the photo of the postcard on his phone. "That reminds me, I've yet to somehow trace this bank account number and find out if it has a name."

Patricia looked at his phone from her upside-down perspective and cocked her head to one side. "What's that there then?"

"What's that?" he said, enlarging the screen a little. The word 'nothmail' centred the screen. "I presume it is the name of their man at the bank."

She leaned over for a closer look. "I may not be the world's expert on anagrams, but 'nothmail' rearranged spells 'hamilton'.

They looked at each other, almost in horror.

Chapter 13 - Over and under

"It can't be." Said Justin ticking off the letters. "What else does it spell?"

Both sat there playing with the tips of their fingers.

"I can't think of anything."

"Neither can I but I'll put it through my spellchecker." After a minute or so she conceded. "It doesn't spell anything else. If we've interpreted this correctly, you know what this means, don't you?"

"Maurice 'Bloody' Hamilton's got his fingers in a big fat juicy pie. It's just the sort of thing he'd get up to."

"And what's more, Bayev and Co. are just the sort of people to embrace Hamilton. Shit. Now what do we do?"

"This opens up a whole new ball game." Justin reverted to one of his favourite analogies.

"Let's not get overwhelmed but take one aspect at a time and it'll all unravel itself." In thought, Patricia nibbled her bottom lip lightly. "We have to start somewhere, so let's say that somewhere in the past Hamilton met Bayev and introduced him to one of his banking buddies on the Isle of Man. For his introductory services Hamilton receives a fee; doesn't matter how much, but then Hamilton wants a bigger piece of the action so puts in some of his own money into the operation. Bayev's happy, Hamilton's happy and the bank are happy."

"OK. I'll go along with that as far as it goes."

"I'm making this next bit up… Bayev reckons that Hamilton isn't going to want to be involved with any, shall we say, disappearances or kidnappings etc., either current ones or previous ones. So now that he's got

Hamilton's money, he's got him by the balls and reduces Hamilton's cut. I can't remember if I told you but there was a fire in Streatham, south London last year. Nothing out of the ordinary there except this fire spread from the adjacent fish and chip shop and destroyed the printing works at the end of the terrace. I've yet to interview the senior fire officer and I haven't had time to delve much deeper, but I'm going to make that a priority once this Zoom call is over, because I'll bet you there's going to be yet another unexplained detail somewhere. Something tells me that Hamilton's name is going to crop up."

"It might just be a coincidence that nothmail spells Hamilton."

"Oh come on!" Patricia exclaimed indignantly. "Since when have you started believing in coincidences?"

Justin conceded that point with a shrug, so she continued. "Once upon a time we may have considered the odd coincidence here and there when it came to Hamilton's affairs, but not any longer. Quite the reverse in fact. In my eyes, he's guilty until proved innocent."

Hamilton's acrimonious efforts to rape and imprison Patricia as well as his despicable method of having got Justin fired from his job was all too recent for either of them to forget. If it hadn't been for their own dogged diligence, it was probable that they would no longer be a couple, engaged to be married. In the end it was only because they had saved his life that Hamilton had been forced to back down and leave them alone. His reputation as a proper cad and a bounder, a liar, a cheat and philanderer was rife, but somehow he still managed to retain his position as Minister of State for Northern

Ireland and a very senior member of the Cabinet. The few friends he still had were well positioned, and besides which, he was a dab hand at blackmail. While she had been speaking, Justin had been looking past Patricia and out of the window across the Thames, watching the London Eye rotate. "There are you circles and bubbles," he nodded.

She looked round at the tourist-laden bubbles attached to the giant ferris wheel the other side of the river. "Do you know, I've never been on it."

"Well, that's definitely something to put on the list then. What are you doing tonight?"

She turned back to face him. "You know what we're doing tonight... Oh I see. You've caught me again. Watch it mate or I'll tie your slipper laces together."

"Lucky me." He grinned back and moved his legs out of the way in case she decided to kick him under the table, but they caught the shoes of a gent on the adjacent table. "Sorry." He looked at the nondescript man who was attending to his mobile. "This place is becoming crowded. Let's take a walk."

The tourists on Victoria Embankment were milling around in the spring-like atmosphere in their usual fashion so he led them past the newspaper vendor and away from the bridge towards the small green space of Whitehall Gardens overlooking the Thames.

"OK for your Zoom here?" asked Justin as he steered them towards one of the park benches.

"Provided I've got a signal and it doesn't rain. Look, unless Carmen comes up with a negative, I'm going to be working on the principle of 'if it walks like a duck and quacks like a duck, then it must be a duck'. It'll tie Hana to his murder and possibly an arson attack; although I doubt either can be proved."

"OK then. For the moment let's assume you are correct on that one, how does it help our situation? Don't answer that straight away, because let's now assume you are wrong. We're still facing the same question either way."

"Certainly, but remember my current remit is to prevent any kind of attempt on the life of Kiril Hirov and if I can find out that Hana just so happens to be in London at the same time..." The inference was plain. "I know what I'd do. I'd move heaven and earth to locate Hana before he strikes. And even if he doesn't, we still have grounds for holding him if I get a positive from Carmen." Her phone rattled and she attended to it.

Justin admitted to himself that she had very valid points and it would probably be in their own interests to have him detained and put away somewhere secure. He looked around while Patricia set up her laptop for the Zoom and although not looking, noticed the nondescript man from the coffee shop sitting more or less opposite on another park bench across from a plinth-mounted bronze statue. He'd been concentrating on their conversation and ignoring all other factors, but now his surveillance mode kicked in. He nonchalantly angled his head away from the man but kept his eyes on him, all the while noting the man's features and mannerisms as he thumbed his phone which rested on a folded newspaper. He was itching to point his phone camera in the right direction and take a photo, but that

Chapter 13 - Over and under

would surely be noticed and give away the age old 'we know that you know' scenario. Best to feign ignorance.

Justin estimated that the distance between them was getting on for two hundred feet and therefore too far away for eavesdropping, unless the man's phone had an extended listening device hidden in his newspaper. He half-heard Patricia in the background say something like 'Zoom's starting'. He toyed with the idea of walking over and confronting the man and was about to do so when the chap got up and walked out of the far end of the gardens. He rebuked himself for being overly suspicious as the man was clearly innocent, but then he reminded himself that this was exactly what he had been trained to do – spot potential terrorists. He was about to discard the incident but instead decided that there was definitely something out of kilter with him. He couldn't put his finger on it and was less than half-listening to Patricia and Carmen's conversation as he visually went over their brief encounter in the coffee shop. How long had he been on the adjacent table and had he heard what their discussion had been about? Had he followed them to the gardens or was that another coincidence? Why had the man left the coffee shop when he did and why had he left the park bench just now? They had only been sitting down for less than five minutes, so what makes a man get up from his relatively comfortable seat after only four minutes?

He heard Patricia laugh and was glad, but it interrupted his thought process as he tried to focus. Instead he wondered what there could be to laugh about.

Feigning boredom while the laptop mediated for the two Zoomers, he looked round the rest of the elongated garden to see if there might be anyone else taking an interest in them. Of the half a dozen benches, three others were occupied. One by a pair of businessmen deep in discussion, one by a couple of female secretarial types, and the third by a couple of young fit men, one of whom was dressed as if for a marathon who trotted on the spot as he talked to the one sitting down. He assessed that there was nothing out of the ordinary until a middle-aged man dressed in jeans wandered in from the far end and stopped to talk to the pair of fit-looking types for a few seconds. It may have been just to politely say hello or comment on the weather but he asked himself what else would those three men have in common. Without facing their direction, he saw the one sitting down crane his neck a little round the torso of the trotter for half a second and stare in their direction before hiding himself again.

There was no question about it. Someone was definitely keeping an eye on them. Of all the things going through his mind, his first concern was for Patricia's safety and his instinct shouted at him to get her out of harm's way, but once again he tried to look bored by looking in the other direction. The man in jeans had now left the gardens from one of the far exits and the fit-looking pair departed from another in the opposite direction. To the untrained, there was nothing to become excited about, but Justin knew that something was going on. Whatever it was would have to wait until the two women had finished their Zoom.

To Justin, it seemed to take far too long but within five minutes Patricia had said farewell, closed and put

Chapter 13 - Over and under

away her laptop. She smiled as she looked directly at him. "Now that was worth it."

"I sincerely hope it was. Let's take a walk." He led them back towards Westminster Bridge and took the steps down to the pier. "Let's catch the ferry." He didn't wait for an answer and holding onto her hand hurried along to catch the westbound service that was clearly about to leave. As they got on the boat he half-turned to see if anyone was hurrying to follow them and was gratified to see that one of the fitter looking types from the gardens had failed to make the barrier before it closed.

Rather than sit beside a window as most tourists would do, he chose one of the centre cushioned benches, sat a fidgety Patricia down and described what had been going on in the gardens while she had been Zooming. He was pretty certain that nobody would be able to listen in to their conversation as the thrumming from the boat's engines, mixed with the background chatter, would drown out any attempt, even with the use of a sophisticated electronic device.

"There's no point in asking if you're sure because you wouldn't have gone to all this trouble if you thought otherwise, would you?" He didn't need to answer so she continued after a moment's thought. "The chances are that they are Bayev's boys, aren't they?"

"Well if they were MI5 they were piss-poor at it."

"In that case I see little option than to update Commander Gibbons and get some counter surveillance going."

"Errr, before you do that do you want to tell me what... what... Carmen revealed? Sorry I couldn't remember her name straight off."

"I was right," she beamed. "She told me it was her second case in her new job and she was told in no uncertain terms that all she had to do was rubber stamp the report that had been drawn up before she joined. It was only a few weeks afterwards that she decided to look at the details before it was filed and lost in the dusty corridors of wherever, that she realised that it had falsely been put down as an accident. Boats of that size never carry butane or propane cannisters and certainly not of a size that would explode in such a way so as to obliterate a body. His body was destroyed and strewn over a wide area as attested to by the dive team." She added as an aside, "Then there's the matter of the man with concussion and first-degree burns to his hands who was taken to Sofia's main hospital, and that man had been named by a reporter as Otrino Tuvo." She paused for effect. "That reporter's name was Signor Antello Fraschini and it was he who was blown to hell in the boat."

She had a smug look on her face, so Justin decided to agitate her. "Still not proof."

"There's no arguing that there was an arson attempt on a print works just off a minor square at the back of the railway station because the police report found the failed valve of the gas cannister. The cylinder had ignited prematurely and that's where they found Otrino Tuvo – next to it. They theorised that when it had exploded he had hit his head on the cobbles and knocked himself

Chapter 13 - Over and under

out." Another pause. "I concede that there's no proof but if we follow the duck principle, how many more eggs do you want before admitting that the probability is too high not to come to the same conclusion?"

Passengers swapped seats at Battersea so they ceased talking until they had settled down; both of them looking closely at the few new arrivals.

Justin re-started. "OK I'll accept that Hana is most likely responsible but as you say, it'll never be proved."

"Right, now that you accept that, it follows that he might well be responsible for other mysterious events. All I have to do is keep digging and I'm bound to come up with something… the only problem is that we haven't the time, so can you please agree in the meantime that Hana is definitely a serious threat?"

"It's not me you need to convince but Gibbons."

"Yes Gibbons as well, but I'm also thinking of our own security."

"So am I, but I really needed to hear your arguments."

"Thanks for putting me through the wringer." A sarcastic tone went with her comment. "So now we hand this over to the authorities, right?"

"You are the authorities."

That got her thinking but only momentarily. "Shit!" She nibbled her bottom lip a little. "Once we get off this tub I'll let Gibbons know." She patted her laptop case.

"Talking of which, from the speed this tub's going we've only got about five minutes before we reach Chelsea Harbour and if Bayev's boys are smart enough, they may well be waiting for us when we get there."

"Oh. I'll text him then."

Before she could reach her phone, Justin put a hand on her arm. "I don't think you understand."

She frowned a question as she looked him directly in the eyes and didn't need to ask him to carry on.

"If I'm reading this right, there were too many of them just to observe. You only need two people to follow someone efficiently, and there were four of them. First there was the man in the café, then the three others who appeared in the gardens. And those are just the ones that I could see; all of them healthy males."

He left her to reason out what he was coming to next and it took some time. Perhaps it was reluctance on her part but eventually she came out with it. "They're after us, aren't they?"

"As I said, that's if I'm reading this correctly, and that leads us onto the next question. How come Bayev figured out that we weren't who we said we were so quickly?"

"Our credentials were perfect otherwise he wouldn't have granted us that meeting. We must have given something away."

Justin thought about this for a few seconds. "No, we gave nothing away otherwise we wouldn't have been allowed to leave the country, so that means he's found out something while we've been in England… and it also means that he's probably had a team in place in the UK ready to do his bidding."

"Like assassinate Kiril Hirov." She jumped on the conclusion.

"Like assassinate Kiril Hirov. And while they're already over here, why not use them to bump us off

Chapter 13 - Over and under

beforehand, because we obviously know what he's up to."

"Oh shit."

They sat in silence trying to think things through, knowing that they didn't have long before they would need to disembark.

Patricia was the first to raise a query. "Hang on a minute. You said it was only in the gardens that you suspected we were being followed. Do you reckon it was you or me being followed and was it by that chap in the café?"

"When you've been in the counter surveillance game as long as I have, one tends to build up a sixth sense. I'm not being boastful when I say I believe I've developed that sixth sense, but it obviously wasn't sharp enough earlier. Nevertheless, I don't think it was me who was being followed."

She took a bit of a sharp intake of breath. "In that case, if it was me, they must have cottoned onto me when I left home."

"And that means they know where you live, and ergo, me also."

"So how the hell did they find out our address?"

"Oh that's easy. Phone signals, miniature trackers, local enquiries, the list is almost endless. Remember, you have been in the press quite a lot and your stunning looks are a bit of a giveaway. Look, we're nearly here."

The engine note dipped as they approached Chelsea Harbour pier and as it did, Justin scrutinised the queue of people waiting to alight. "I think we might be alright, but I can't see above the quay," he said craning his neck a little.

Once up the sloping jetty and with much looking around trying to spot anyone out of place, Patricia followed him to a Costa coffee shop. "This used to be a handy out-of-the-way meeting place years ago, but I see it's gone a bit upmarket since." He pointed at the sign that said 'Hilton'.

"Tell me more about it later." She made a beeline for a secluded corner where she could use her laptop without being overlooked. "Get us a glass of water, can you?" There was nobody within twenty feet of her.

Justin returned and left her to compose her report to Commander Gibbons while he sat down with a glass of water next to her and called up the photograph of the postcard on his phone again. This time he minutely examined every millimetre of it but the only item of any worth was the alphanumeric bank account details. He hypothesised as to what would happen if he were to pay just ten pounds into that account and then contact them to say that it was transferred by accident and could they please ask the owners of that account to return the money. Unlikely as it was, it might be worth a punt to see if it would at least reveal who the signatories were but the only problem with that was that it might also reveal from whence the ten pounds came; that would be the last thing either of them would want. Considering what Patricia's boss could do, he looked over at her as she furiously tapped the keys of her laptop. He coughed, hoping that she might pick up on his distraction, but had to cough a little louder a few seconds later before she paused and looked up at him.

Chapter 13 - Over and under

"You might want to listen to my idea before you send that off."

She briefly glanced down to ascertain that she'd got to a finishing point. "OK then." It only took her a moment to assess his suggestion. "Good idea. I'll mention it. Give me a couple of minutes. I'm nearly there."

Rather than sit there lemon-like, Justin got up and wandered round the spacious reception room, all-the-while keeping an open mind as to the legitimacy of the other occupants. He ended up standing next to a decorative seven-foot plastic plant by a staff doorway as it offered the best view, but it was pure luck that he happened to glance outside through the panoramic window when the driver of a cab blew his horn at an errant fellow motorist. He froze as he recognised one of the 'fit' men from the gardens standing in the shadow of a doorway across the road. The usual questions ran through his mind before he reacted and looked over at Patricia. From the 'fit' man's perspective, he wouldn't have been able to see her, but he had to presume that he knew she was there. Rather than go over to her, despite it being some fifty feet away, and thus reveal her position, he went to text her. He stopped as his finger hovered over the send button with the dreadful thought that their phones must have been compromised. How else could their whereabouts have been traced, and so quickly? Where there was one, the other wouldn't be far away. From behind the plant's branches he watched 'fit' man start to talk into his phone, surmised that he had only just located them and was reporting such to his associates. This was beginning to feel decidedly uncomfortable so he went over to Patricia. "We have to leave. Now."

It was his emphatic 'now' that made her pause and look up and he silently mouthed the word 'now' as she looked at him. "Send what you've got and let's go. I'll explain later."

It must have been the look of concern on his face that galvanised her into following his instructions and she was ready within ten seconds. He led her through the staff door which he had already surmised led towards the back of the building and an alternative exit onto a street out of sight of 'fit' man, but his worry was that they had a means of tracking them. The Underground might provide them with some respite until they could pick up some pay-as-you-go replacement phones so he led them past Chelsea football stadium and stopped in its shadow.

His explanation to Patricia took very little time. "Here's what we do because we really need to get rid of our phones." He was looking at passers-by as he spoke. "We'll pick someone at random and drop them into their bags or whatever, but we've only got a minute or so before they catch up with us. Let them follow our phones and as they do so, I'll point them out to you so that you too will be able to recognise them. Here, give me yours. Is it locked? Slow her down a bit." He moved off to one side to let a woman wheeling a pushchair along the pavement pass and was pleased to see Patricia let her purse slip from her grasp just in the right place.

Chapter 13 - Over and under

As the woman came to a virtual stop, Justin dropped both phones into a half-open baby's bag that dangled over the woman's shoulder, then strolled off and waited for Patricia to catch him up.

"Get your badge ready." He led them to one of the stadium's railed access gates which was half-open and had a bored-looking security guard standing on the inside. They didn't have to try very hard to get the guard to let them pass into the grounds, but most importantly, virtually out of sight of the road. They watched the woman continue towards Fulham Road and just as she was about to go out of sight, Justin pointed out the 'fit' man who was dutifully tailing her. "Well at least we now know how they knew where we were, but I haven't had time to work out how, where or when they did it."

"Nor do we know if it was yours or mine," she smiled cynically.

"No we don't but more importantly, it won't be long before they realise we've dumped our phones because we knew they were on to us. They won't be quite so easy to spot next time. Time to move I think. West Brom's just round the corner."

They disappeared down the brass-capped steps of West Brompton tube station and into the maze of the London Underground system.

"Where to then?"

Justin stopped them in front of the world-renowned schematic map, then pointed to an empty bench set back out of the way in a semi-niche of the forum, commenting that there was no point in standing out in the middle.

"Right, we've done our running bit, now let's stop and think this through because a nasty thought has just occurred." He paused as he mentally composed what he was going to say and then checked to see if it made sense. "OK but stop me if this is all gobbledygook." It still took him a moment before he continued. "Fact. Bayev must have found out about us after we landed back at Heathrow, otherwise we'd have been detained in Sofia. Fact. He must have access to personnel here already in London because there's no way he could have had them flown in and on to us at such short notice. Fact. They have been directed to locate us, but the way they've been acting it's as though they're getting ready for an abduction. You don't congregate your soldiers in one place just to maintain contact. You gather them for action. Fact. They've managed to get close enough to hack into our phones which means they discovered what you do for a living and decided to tag you and it probably means that they know where we live."

He put the palms of his hands together and offered them up to his mouth, almost as if in prayer, but with closed eyes he was furiously thinking. Patricia didn't disturb his train of thought.

"I reckon that once we had been disposed of, they might well be moving on to Kiril Hirov; he's due here in London shortly. Follow my logic. If it was one or two of them I'd say we were just being followed, but with four, five, six or more, then they're about to strike. And we're their target. Whatever else they may have planned, it is obvious now that we are their priority, so we need to react to that or find ourselves blown to bits with the

Chapter 13 - Over and under

help of a gas cannister or whatever. Going home is not an option, so we're going to have to seek help from Commander Gibbons. By the way, how much of your report did you manage to get off to him?"

"Just about all of it."

"Then he'll probably be expecting you… maybe both of us. OK then, first we need a mobile each so we pick up a pair of pay-as-you gos. There's a shop near Victoria station that sells them and it'll be en route."

"En route to where?"

"Scotland Yard of course. Unless Gibbons wants us elsewhere. Meanwhile I'll get in touch with my contact at the Treasury, a man called Thomas, and pick his brains about the possibility of Bulgarian involvement. By the way, I must give you his contact number; mine are all stored on a cloud. When you do speak to Gibbons, apart from asking him for a safe house, see if he can coordinate the photofit with airports etc., which brings me to my last idea, but my car's parked at Maidenhead station." He paused in thought again.

"Don't stop, because listening to you is like watching a runaway roller coaster."

"Eh?"

"Verbal diarrhoea."

"Diarrhoea it may be but as long as we're on the same wavelength, we'll get through this."

"Come on then. What's your idea?"

He looked at her pensively. "I'd better not tell you in case it compromises you with Gibbons and anyway, by splitting up we can get twice as much done."

"OK. Here's our first problem and I'll bet you haven't even considered it." Smug was written all over her face.

"And what's that?"

"My Oyster card was with my phone, so without my mobile how am I going to get to the tube through the cashless barriers?"

They ended up getting a taxi.

Chapter 14

White lines

With new mobiles and various numbers saved in each other's, Patricia went in search of Vivian and Gibbons while Justin phoned an ex-colleague. He stayed at the back of the shop to reduce the off chance of being spotted. He'd built-up excellent relationships with his fellow officers from his lengthy time in the Diplomatic Protection Squad; even going on cricket tour with two of them, but it was going to boil down to the element of trust. None of them had any sort of respect for Hamilton and had it not been their job, would have quite happily left him bleeding out in the gutter if he happened to fall over into one. The disdain Hamilton had managed to build up among those who were protecting him was staggering.

He had what he wanted to know five minutes later and set off across Westminster Bridge. It didn't matter that he usually crossed it each way driving a car but with the London Eye on the far bank and the Houses of Parliament behind him, it still evoked a national sense of pride in him. His previous posting had been as one of several bodyguards-cum-chauffeurs to Maurice 'Bloody' Hamilton. Then and now, he was the Secretary of State for Northern Ireland and had attained that very senior position by such underhand methods that even his fellow Cabinet members could hardly believe how he had got there. Justin had extreme negative regard for this corrupt man who had had him fired from his posting and very nearly succeeded in having Patricia imprisoned; and that was after his attempted rape of her. He was under no illusions that Hamilton would twist any story Justin was about to confront him with to suit his own purposes. In fact, what he was about to do could very well lead to his own arrest, but he thought it would be worth the risk.

As he walked across the bridge in the pleasant sunshine, he attended to his new mobile to make sure he could voice record easily while wending his way between the myriad of tourists. Reaching The Marriott on the South Bank, he walked through the archway and saw Hamilton's black chauffeured limousine waiting off to one side with his ex-colleague Ben standing next to it. On a cold winter's day, Ben, like Justin had done in the past, would wait on guard just inside the warmth of the building, but having spoken to Justin a few minutes earlier, agreed to meet on the edge of the quadrangle which was also out of camera shot. Despite it being springtime, in the shadows the light north wind had a nip to it.

Out of habit and training, Justin looked around to see if there was anyone posing a threat as he waited for Ben to walk the short distance over to where he now waited.

Chapter 14 - White lines

The 'hello stranger' and hand shaking greeting between them re-affirmed their friendship in the blink of an eye.

"What this all about?" Ben asked after a couple of pleasantries.

"I promise I'll tell you once I can, but for now, I need to ask Hamilton a few questions."

"You know I can't allow that... It's more than my job's worth."

"I know that, which is why you'll be blameless."

Ben cocked an eye at Justin. "Oh yes... and how are you going to manage that?"

"Quite simple really. Who else is on duty with you?"

"Dick. He's up on the top floor outside Hamilton's apartment."

"I know Dick well, but it doesn't make any difference who it is really. It just helps."

"I know you know Dick and I hope this won't compromise him either. Remember we've got to work together."

"No problem. When Hamilton goes to leave, I presume Dick will come down with him in the lift and accompany him to his car here, and I also presume he'll contact you on your radio to tell you they're on their way. Correct?"

"That's right. Nothing's changed since you were here."

"That's what I'm banking on. Protocol states that if there's the possibility of an attack or if the car is compromised, then any mode of transport is acceptable, but in this case, it'll be a taxi."

Wondering what Justin had in mind, Ben eyed him a little suspiciously, then across the inner quad at the limousine that he was chauffeuring in. "I suppose you'd prefer it if Hamilton's ride was a little further away from the entrance than it is now."

"Ideally yes, and it would also help if you just happened to be inspecting something under the bonnet at the time. I don't want any eyebrows raised in your direction. Just don't have his usual door open for him. Say it got stuck or that the auto-lock prevented you from opening it and you were checking the fuses."

"Now that I'll be happy to do... errr... I take it this is all going to happen in the foreseeable future because he's due down anytime now?" He glanced down at his watch.

"So soon you won't believe it." Justin grinned. "I take it he's entertaining somebody else's whore right now?"

"Oh yes, and this one even looks like one. Not up to his usual standard. She's even got the cheap clothing to match."

Justin grinned and patted him on the arm before retracting himself back through the archway while Ben went in the opposite direction to accede to Justin's requests.

Justin walked a couple of hundred yards away from The Marriott towards Lambeth Palace Road, waited at a suitable stopping place where the road widened and hailed a black cab. He knew he didn't have time on his side but he peered into the oncoming stream of empty cabs looking for the right sort of driver. He

Chapter 14 - White lines

wasn't sure exactly what sort of driver he wanted but knew he didn't want one that could become awkward. In the end the one he had chosen turned out to be quite compliant. He briefly flashed his 'out-of-date' badge at the cabbie, lied about the sudden need for the use of his cab, stated that non-compliance was an imprisonable offence, frightened him with the Official Secrets Act and told him he could collect his taxi in an hour's time from under the bridge outside Vauxhall tube station; he knew there were no cameras there. As Justin got behind the wheel and made to move off, the taxi driver shouted at him "Oi... how do I get to Vauxhall?"

Justin leaned out the same way that all cabbies do. "Get a taxi."

It had all happened so fast that the cabbie just stood mouth open at the side of the road. Much to the annoyance of a bus driver, Justin performed a U-turn in front of it, went back up the road and out of sight of the cabbie. Without blocking anyone, he stopped at the entrance of The Marriott and sent a simple text to Hamilton. At least, he hoped it was Hamilton's and that he hadn't changed his number because all it said was 'husband en route'. He reckoned that that would get him moving and that it ought to take about three or four minutes before he appeared; five if he still had his trousers round his ankles.

He had parked the cab in the shadows of the archway entrance and now closely watched Ben fiddling with some unknown part under the limousine bonnet. As he suspected, Ben stopped what he was doing and put his finger to his earpiece which indicated to Justin that Hamilton was on his way down, so he pulled the cab forward, stopped directly opposite where Hamilton would emerge, opened the back door of the cab to make it an easy decision for Dick, who would, no doubt, see that the bonnet of the limousine was up and usher Hamilton into the waiting cab.

This was the nervous part for Justin as his timing would need to be perfect; he wanted Hamilton in the cab without Dick. Not only that, but without either endangering Dick or leaving him in the invidious position of having to explain why he let his charge be whisked off from under his nose. It had to look realistic.

Sure enough Hamilton appeared slightly behind Dick, who looked around making an assessment. As he was trained to do, he almost pushed Hamilton into the back of the taxi, but as he attempted to follow him in, Justin let the clutch out with the accompanying engine speed, resulting in the cab jumping forward so that the back door slammed shut leaving Dick standing on the pavement and holding on to an imaginary door. Hamilton hadn't had time to sit squarely in the back seat and, with Justin turning the wheel to exit the courtyard at quite a speed, ended up lying across it. It took him a couple of shoves against the swerving movement of the taxi to right himself and once he did, his composure returned to something approaching normal; that was until Justin spoke to him.

All he had to say was "Minister." Because he knew Hamilton would recognise his voice.

Hamilton froze, hardly daring to believe that Justin Crawford had kidnapped him and it was only when

Chapter 14 - White lines

he positioned himself onto one of the nearer rear seats and had a good look, did his suspicions come together. "What the bloody hell are you doing here and where are we going?"

"So nice to get acquainted again Minister, and not even a hello. I see you're up to your usual tricks."

"Mind you own fucking business and tell me what's going on. I suppose you're now going to spirit me away somewhere and blackmail me into confessing to something that's going to cost me a lot of money."

"Wrong on all counts… we've decided that because you're such a shit, we're not going to take your money, just kill you outright." As they stopped at a set of red lights, Justin turned round so that he could see Hamilton's reaction. "OK?"

"No it's not OK you supercilious cunt, now let me out of here." He tried the door opener but knew that it wouldn't work until Justin pressed the unlock button in the front of the cab.

"Sit back and enjoy the ride but while we're waiting to get to where we're going, would you mind phoning your security detail and advise them that you have not in fact been kidnapped, but meeting somebody at short notice."

"And why should I do that?"

"Because if you don't, we're going to have all sorts of security types descending upon us in short order and I won't have time enough to help you out of a predicament you seem to have got yourself into."

"No."

"Have it you own way then, but you ought to know that you might well be Bayev's next target."

Slips Catch

Hamilton was dumbfounded. It took him a couple of breaths before he reached for his phone. "You know they've got a fix on this phone anyway don't you, but then you would wouldn't you?" He broke off commenting to Justin to speak into his phone.

He rung off and closed his phone. "Right then, let's be having you because they won't wait long." He looked out over the Thames as Justin drove them along Albert Embankment.

"You let me worry about that and in any case we'll be there in a minute or so, but you can start by telling me about your involvement in the Bulgarian mining operation."

"The last time we crossed swords it nearly cost me my Cabinet position and political career, so what guarantee have I got that if I tell you anything, you won't go using it against me?"

"That's the beauty of it from my point of view... there's absolutely no guarantee. Ha!" He was starting to enjoy himself having Hamilton as a captive. "But depending upon your answers, it may mean I could save you a shed load of money as well as saving your miserable life. Here we are."

Justin drove the taxi under the very long railway arch behind Vauxhall station and onto the narrow pavement where he stopped. He turned to face Hamilton. "No one to worry us down here and the tracker in your phone won't work under this bridge... it's Victorian iron all around us... no signal and no cameras. That's just another snippet of security info one picks up on when working with The Squad."

Chapter 14 - White lines

Hamilton looked at his phone to see the communication bars disappear. "OK then, what do you want to know?"

"We know..."

"When you say we, do you mean that bitch of a policewoman?" interrupted Hamilton. "Because if so, you can go to hell... both of you."

Justin let him calm down before continuing.

"I know you have an account based in the Isle of Man and I also know you have put some of you own resources into that account, but what I don't know is how much. I also don't know who your fellow signatories are but I could hazard a guess."

"And the Manx bank won't tell you what you want to know which is why we're here."

"Something like that, but I also need to know what your arrangements are with Bayev and Todor Yordan, because I think they're about to shaft you; possibly in every sense of the word."

"You seem to know an awful lot considering this is supposed to be a secret deal." Hamilton was no longer quite as sceptic.

"Oh I know an awful lot more but not everything, which is why you're going to tell me the rest if I'm going to be able to help you. I need you to fill in the gaps if you like."

"And I suppose you'll want a fee for your services."

Justin was aware that anything he said would be on his mobile recorder, so responded guardedly. "Some out-of-pocket expenses would be nice." He was also aware that with each frequent passing train, the clatter and boom as it passed over sets of points would probably drown out much of the recording, so he had timed his response accordingly.

"So now that you're no longer employed as my bodyguard by the Civil Service, doing it for king and country is no longer an option. Is that about it?"

"Never mind about my reasons. It's your reasons why we're here having any kind of conversation at all. Stalling for time so that you find yourself not needing to answer my questions is quite inadvisable so let's get right to it shall we?"

Hamilton went to comment but Justin cut him short. "How you met Bayev on some government mission or other is irrelevant, but what is relevant is what sort of deal did he offer you, and before you decide to twist the truth in your usual manner, you need to know I've been down the mine."

Again, Hamilton was totally surprised by Justin's last comment and the crestfallen look on his face was not missed. "I have your word that you'll not go public with this?"

Justin thought about this for a moment. "Not unless it directly jeopardises me."

"Fair enough and I suppose that's about as good a guarantee as I'm going to get."

"Let me make this simple for you and save us both valuable time that neither of us have right now. Those two mines are actually one but why the deception?"

"Oh that's simple. To justify the selling of platinum." Hamilton left it there to see how quickly Justin was going to put two and two together, but it was clear

Chapter 14 - White lines

that further explanation was required. "OK, I see I'm going to have to go back a bit further. Just before I was promoted to the Cabinet as the Minister for Northern Ireland, I was part of a UK trade mission to Bulgaria which is where Bayev put a lucrative option in front of me. Not anybody else, just me because we had met previously on a UN military exercise in Germany. It was there one late night in the officers' mess after everybody else had gone to bed when the alcohol loosened tongues to a certain extent that Bayev mentioned his scheme, so it was only natural that he should approach me again. We were both high enough up in our respective governments and had adequate influence over those that mattered in order to be able to set the scheme up. Sooner or later I would have suspected that his entire plan was a sham even all the way from Westminster, so to ensure my silence he offered me a piece of the action, so they say. At first it was simple enough as he and Todor claimed that they needed some capital to finish setting it all up, particularly at the UK end, and I have to admit that I fell for it hook, line and sinker." He began to gently wring his hands in embarrassment. "It was almost impossible for me to carry out any checks, so I ended up putting in a million euros, but to safeguard my funds to a certain extent, I proposed that we should set up a bank account in a neutral territory; hence the Isle of Man account."

"What was your return supposed to be?"

"That was the beauty of it all. The returns would come from additional investment in the metal markets and depending upon how much or little we released on to the market meant that we could virtually control the price of platinum. Oh I know what you're thinking... how much can the price vary and the answer is not by a great deal; it doesn't have to... except on one or two occasions." He smiled. "I'll give you an example. If you've got a million and you know the price is going to rise by say five per cent, then that's fifty thousand you've made. Not bad for a morning's work. Then repeat that two or three times a month and add in those occasional extra-large jumps which was once nearly fifteen per cent, then you're onto a winner. It was too good to resist. Now times that by a hundred if you're a government like Bulgaria and you get some idea as to the sums involved."

"But what about when the price dropped?"

"Oh we could control that as well and it was just as rewarding financially but even more satisfying. We timed our release of extra platinum months in advance, which naturally forced the price down when we did so, and having already correctly predicted the market price, cleaned up then as well. It was better than having a crystal ball." He watched Justin wrestling with the scenario and added, "It's a classic schoolboy case study of supply and demand, except we control the supply."

Hamilton watched Justin as he grappled with the outline of the operation and was prepared when the next question came.

"I suppose the deception of the second mine was necessary to fool the outside world that that was the origin of the platinum, but if it's not producing platinum, where is it coming from?"

Chapter 14 - White lines

"Right question so go to the top of the class." Nevertheless, Hamilton still hesitated as his reply really would let the cat out of the bag. "It's Russian."

"Russian!"

"Oh yes, Russian platinum and at the right price because if the Western world knew its origin, it would most likely be one of the targets for economic sanctions, should the sanction issue raise its ugly head again. Outwardly Russia retains a certain amount for its own internal industry and sells a small amount of its own stock in metal markets around the world just to keep up appearances. Most of that platinum comes from the Kola peninsula in Siberia and is a well-known commodity in the worldwide markets, but in the past decade they discovered a closer source in the Urals and that platinum gets sold on the open market ostensibly as Bulgarian."

Justin followed the logic through. "And I suppose those in the Russian government decided to line their own pockets in the process."

Hamilton leaned forwards a little. "It's called capitalism." Then leaned back again.

"It's called daylight robbery because capitalism in Russia is not supposed to exist."

"Whatever you call it, the long and the short of it is that it enriches those who take the risk, and I just so happen to be one of them. And anyway, as far as I can see there's nothing illegal about it."

Justin was stunned at Hamilton's last comment. He shut his eyes, clenched his teeth and shook his head in disbelief. What Hamilton was saying was throwing him off what he came to quiz him about and he made the conscious decision to put Hamilton's ethos of right and wrong to one side for the time being. "Well in that case you've nothing to worry about then, have you?" he goaded.

"It's you I'm worried about because so far all you've done is kidnap me, so say what you've got to say and get me out of here."

Justin realised that time was slipping away too quickly so came straight to the point. "I'm not going to go into the morals of what's right or wrong because you and I could never remotely agree on anything. The upshot of what you're doing is that Bayev's got an assassination team over here now who are trying to murder myself and my colleague before moving on to Kiril Hirov and that's most likely planned to happen in the next few days. Once he's dead it'll play into Russian hands and mean that the Bulgarian government will retain its own currency of levs rather than consider the euro. There's more at stake here than you lining your own pocket while a friendly country fails, and to boot, you might have one, two or three deaths on your hands. Now while I appreciate your desire to see my fiancée and I dead, even your miserable conscience probably doesn't stretch as far as being an accessory to a third party's murder. And consider this. If we do manage to thwart Hirov's assassination, you may even come out of this smelling of roses and in the public's eyes you'd be a hero."

He let Hamilton mull on that last thought for a moment before adding on the spur of the moment,

Chapter 14 - White lines

"Were you considering a leadership challenge?" The ploy was a bit of a thin appeal to Hamilton's vanity but he hoped it might just tip the balance.

He reckoned it did, because he watched a thoughtful Hamilton rub his chin in wonder.

"I'm being blackmailed."

"How so?"

"They've threatened to reveal my involvement in money laundering and demanded I release all the funds in the Isle of Man bank account to them. All I'd manage to keep is the profits from our dealings which would just about cover my initial investment. Business is business," he added in defence of his actions.

"Who exactly is they?"

"Bayev and Todor are top of the chain, but there's a strong-arm man called Hana, who, so I gather, goes around topping people who cross them."

"Would that be Hana Otrino Tuvo?"

"You know him then?"

"We met in Sofia."

"That's not all. Hana has direct links to one of the Russian mafia groups who call themselves 'Vogli' and it's they who control the flow of platinum from the Urals mine. You're quite right when you mentioned that I might be one of their next targets but from what you just told me, I suspect I might be fairly high up on their list unless I comply."

"And naturally you haven't alerted any of the diplomatic security services."

"Not bloody likely. My ministerial position would be compromised and I'd have to resign immediately."

"Then I'll do you a deal. Leave this to me and my fiancée and we'll do our best to keep your name under wraps."

"For your out-of-pocket expenses of course."

"Naturally."

"Then I suppose I'll just have to play along with whatever you've got planned."

Justin grinned at him. "You can start by giving me the other names on the bank account and considering the imminent actions of Bayev's assassins, I suggest you tell them that you'll be acceding to their demands, but that you need to delay transferring the money for a few days."

"What delaying excuse do you suggest I give them?"

"I leave that up to you. You're the government minister." Justin frowned. "By the way, have you any pending platinum transactions in the pipeline?"

"Funny you should ask that because that woman I was with not more than an hour ago works for Bayev and she passed me a note. She's just a go-between and knows nothing of its contents, so don't bother wasting your time chasing her. The point is that their next move will be this coming Friday afternoon shortly before the markets close for the weekend."

"And what's going to happen?"

"There's a bogus report being leaked by the Bulgarian ministry stating that their platinum estimates for the rest of the year are grossly exaggerated which will have the effect of upping the price considerably. Twelve to fifteen per cent increase and I was going to transfer half a million euros later today in readiness," he said gleefully.

Chapter 14 - White lines

Justin looked at his watch and considered that they were almost out of time before Hamilton's security details descended on the railway arch. He really didn't want to be put in the embarrassing position of having to try to talk his way out of being in the same cab as Hamilton. He flicked the door release switch and exited. "I'll be in touch, but carry on as normal for the time being and make sure you answer your phone when I ring you." Just before he slammed the door shut he added, "It won't cost you an arm or a leg."

As he walked smartly away he heard Hamilton's response of, "Buggeroff."

***

Patricia fumed through her phone at the functionary on the other end who took up valuable time by doggedly asking questions, but eventually she had access to cash and plenty of credit on her new mobile. She wanted to check a couple of facts before meeting with either Vivian or Gibbons so dived into one of the pubs and sat quietly at a table in the far corner away from the windows. While she waited for her laptop to come to life, the looked up and saw she was in The Cadogan Arms and that explained why it felt so familiar. She'd been taken there by her superintendent on one of her training missions several years ago and she smiled as the memory of arresting one of the barmen came to mind.

She delved into the report on the strange fire that had destroyed a fish and chip shop and the adjacent print works in Streatham, found the name of the senior fire officer and rang him. Once she explained who she was to Frank Bartley, he was the model of cooperation.

"I know I stated that it was to an overflow of hot fat on electric elements, but that's because I couldn't prove otherwise, yet if you look at my penultimate paragraph you'll see that although that was the primary cause of the fire, it could also have been due to a gas leak from the print works next door. It certainly added to the inferno that ensued. Have you ever been near one of those propane cannisters when they go up? Bloody hell. Believe me when I say you don't want to be within a hundred yards of one when it goes off because not only will it blow you off your feet, you don't know what direction the cannister is going to take. In this instance it was rather fateful as when this cannister released its propane, it propelled it across the room and split the internal gas pipe. That only added to the inferno. Oh and by the way, when they go off they're likely to burst your eardrums from the sudden increase in pressure, which in this case blew all the windows out and allowed fresh air, oxygen, in to fuel the furnace. Yes, very nasty. Why do you ask?"

"I'm going over old cases and trying to ascertain which ones were genuine accidents and which ones were possible arson."

"Oh, this one was probably arson but like I say, I couldn't prove it one way or the other. You see, the external valve to the water supply to the fire suppression system in the fish and chip shop had been damaged and was turned off. We come across damaged valves on the odd occasion usually because of neglect, but this one

Chapter 14 - White lines

looked like a van or lorry had reversed into it and bent the spindle."

"Would hitting the spindle with a hammer or other such instrument render it useless?"

"Certainly, but why turn it off first because you surely couldn't turn it after it was bent."

"Well, I think that answers that question then."

"You ought to be asking about the hole in the wall between the two properties."

Patricia sat upright and thought about this for a moment; her interest was now really piqued. "Go on."

"Well, with most of these Victorian-cum-Edwardian properties there were air bricks to allow for ventilation… to help stop condensation and the like. Some at the back and some at the front to encourage a through-flow of air. This one also had air bricks at the side as one part of the building was obviously built before the other, and it seemed that nobody thought anything of leaving the side vents where they were. Somewhere along the line, somebody had blocked off the abutting vents with small sheets of slate and probably wedged them in place to stop the smells either coming into the chip shop or vice versa into the print works. Imagine what you'd feel like if you worked next to a fish shop and could smell food all day long and then imaging walking into the fish shop and smelling printing solvent. The point is that neither of those slate sheets would have stopped the spread of the fire but what did interest me was that I couldn't find any evidence of the nearest vent being blocked off." He could imagine a frown appearing on her face so added. "Slate doesn't burn and there was none in the debris."

Patricia had been starting to lose interest as Frank's voice was rather monotonous, but managed to grasp the salient point he was making. "In other words, it had been removed before the fire."

"We found the one on the print side but not on the fish shop side, but there must have been one. Health and safety wouldn't have allowed it otherwise."

"Frank. You've been a great help. Thanks."

During the taxi ride to New Scotland Yard, she didn't need to dwell long on the coincidence side of things to conclude that the Streatham fire had been started on purpose. She wanted to talk to the owner of the printing press, ideally before meeting Gibbons, but there simply wasn't enough time. She tried ringing Justin and frowned at the unusual tone indicating that his was turned off. She was met by Vivian as she exited the lift.

"Seems like you've set a fire under something."

"Eh?" The mention of fire so soon after considering one caught her off guard.

"Fire. You know. That flame that was discovered by our Neanderthal ancestors a few years ago." Vivian's light-hearted comment reminded Patricia that she was in the presence of a genius. "We're to go straight in," she added as they neared the outer door to the Commander's office. Patricia recognised it from her previous visits but as they were about to go in her phone rang; she was relieved to see that it was Justin so indicated that she was going to answer it. The delay Vivian experienced manifested itself in the form of her mouthing that they shouldn't keep Gibbons waiting, but Patricia held her finger up. It took less than a minute.

Chapter 14 - White lines

The Head of Special Branch sat calmly behind his neat desk and both women felt the enquiring mind emanating through his eyes. Despite there being a set of matching chairs off to one side, they waited directly in front of him before he indicated with a brief look-cum-nod that they should sit themselves down.

He focused on Patricia. "A few days ago I charged you with the low-to-medium risk assignment of keeping Kiril Hirov alive while he's on UK soil, but what I've learned since is that the threat is now as high as it can be. Bring me up to date." As usual, Gibbons rarely minced words and frowned upon those who waffled around the point.

Both women knew they needed to deliver direct answers but since he was looking at Patricia, it was she who spoke first by briefly outlining her recent findings and experiences. She finished up by adding some of what Justin had told her a few minutes ago with regard to possible Russian mafia involvement. What she was unable to relay to Gibbons was that Hamilton was involved, quite simply because Justin hadn't told her.

"You." Gibbons swivelled a few degrees on his chair that now faced Vivian.

Despite being based in New Scotland Yard for nearly two years and having submitted several reports to him, it was the first time Vivian had been in front of Gibbons. She'd heard rumours of his reputation for putting the fear of God into those under him, but nevertheless she managed to take a deep breath and steady her nerves before speaking. "Hana Otrino Tuvo, whom we refer to as HOT for short, turns out to probably be the nasty piece of work we've been trying to pin down for a long time." She went on to explain much that Patricia had discovered and confirmed that he was the one and same person they had met in Sofia. "HOT's parentage is shrouded in mystery but it is probable that his grandfather became one of the few survivors to escape from the ghettos when the Germans evacuated the city towards the end of world war two." She paused. "I'm not certain of this next part because there's no way of corroborating it but if I'm right, then it was his grandfather who was appointed by Stalin himself to hunt down Nazi sympathisers in the city and surrounding area. You can imagine what power he wielded and we all know what happens when power is abused... especially when it comes to women. There's no telling how many offspring he fathered, but HOT's father was one of them and a like-father-like-son scenario began, only this was more like grandfather when it came to Hana."

She had no need to look at any notes as she had memorised the salient points. Nevertheless, she stopped momentarily to collect her thoughts. Gibbons and Patricia waited patiently.

"Communist doctrine pervaded throughout the Soviet Union when Hana was receiving his basic schooling, and we think that it was when his mother disappeared that he was sent to a specialist reform school, probably under the instructions of his father. I say reform school but it is really another name for Russian state espionage training school. There he

Chapter 14 - White lines

would have been taught the rudiments of terrorism and maybe even practised them on the local dissidents, no doubt with encouragement from his father or even grandfather. The photograph Inspector Eyethorne came across was taken at a military camp and included several undesirable types, some of whom are now deceased, but from his central position in it, it clearly demonstrates that he was growing up to be a prominent member of a martial group. Move on two or three years and there are indications that Hana was experimenting with chemicals because reports emerged from various prisons around Minsk about inmates being spirited away and poisoned. He then disappears off everyone's radar around the time of the break up of the Soviet Union, soon after the fall of the Berlin Wall." She briefly glanced at Patricia and added for her benefit, "That was nineteen ninety-one stroke two. He then reappears after a few years in various mainly European cities acting very much as a mercenary, but avoids the political terrorist groups, preferring to be employed directly by governmental officials. He didn't stay a lone wolf for long as it seems that he honed his sniping skills within the Vogli group based in Moscow, one of the mafia gangs, and it is probable that while he was under their wing he disposed of several of their rivals. As far as we know his rifle of choice is a 308 Anschutz with a thumbhole stock."

"That's very precise information," commented Gibbons. There was no scepticism in his voice, but then again, there didn't need to be with an observation like that.

"I'll be pleased to tell you more about how we came by that, but it may not be appropriate right now." She was effectively asking for permission, due to Patricia's presence, to divulge how that information had been obtained.

"Another time. Please continue," agreed Gibbons.

"There's not much more…" She looked down at her mobile for a prompt. "Somehow or other he ended up with our Bulgarian friends and is most likely still secretly working for the Vogli group. We have classified him as a key player rather than a master spy as his affiliations are rather dubious, but he most definitely has the capabilities of mounting significant operations on foreign soils." Now that she had delivered her piece, her slightly drooping shoulders betrayed her relaxing, but a second later she added, "Oh and by the way, it's recently come to light that he may, just may, also be involved with one of the poisonings."

They knew that she referred to recent poisonings of foreign nationals by unknowns on British soil.

The look of concentration on Gibbons' face said it all as he considered their reports. "Wait outside," was his only instruction.

***

As Justin walked smartly to cross over Vauxhall Bridge, he felt it was about the right sort of time for the boot to be on the other foot. Twice they had nearly been caught and he didn't want to give them a third chance. He tried to put himself in Hana's frame of mind and

Chapter 14 - White lines

wonder what he would do if they'd lost contact with their target. Reacquisition was the answer, but how? More importantly, where? He sought inspiration from the flanking skyscrapers being built ahead of him on the north bank of the Thames and a wry smile crossed his face as he recognised Britain's security headquarters off to his left and wondered if, one day, he'd ever get to go inside. Waiting at a set of pedestrian lights to turn green, he instinctively looked about to see if he was being followed. He decided he wasn't but he did spot a suspicious man of Asian extract wearing a local borough hi-viz vest who seemed not to be concentrating enough on his task in hand. The broom was being wielded just a bit too lazily along the pavement not too far from his rubbish barrow. He relaxed as he linked the man to the security headquarters and surmised that he was actually doing what he was supposed to do – keeping an eye out. It gave him an idea and as he got halfway across the road, he did a U-turn and walked back to the pavement where he had been a few seconds earlier. Hi-viz man was very good because Justin noted how he altered his stance just enough so that he could keep half an eye on him. After all, how many pedestrians decided to perform a U-turn in the middle of a heavily trafficked dual carriageway? He had his inspiration and hailed a taxi.

    He considered his logic as he sat back in the black taxi having directed the cabbie to take him to Charing Cross station but via Victoria Embankment, and as they neared Whitehall Gardens, he told the driver to slow right down.

"Can't slow down much guv 'cos there's too much traffic," he said, spending as much time looking in his mirrors as he did ahead of him. "Do you want me to stop?"

"No, just keep going but as slow as you can."

"Blimey, I usually get asked to do that in front of big memorials, not by a set of gardens. Mind you, you get a good view of the London Eye from here. Anything in particular you're looking for?"

"Only someone but I don't want them to see me… if you know what I mean." Justin hoped he was giving an amorous impression.

"Right you are. Here's a break in the traffic."

The black cab rolled along Victoria Embankment at a very sedate speed giving Justin enough time to look through the verdure to see who was hanging around in the same gardens where they had first seen their pursuers. He worked out that they'd been followed there from New Scotland Yard after meeting with Vivian as it was only a stone's throw away, and if he was correct, then it also meant that Hana knew that they were attached to the police.

He made sure he was on the far side of the cab in case he might be recognised and as the cab drew level with the top of the gardens, he melancholically resigned himself that it was too much to hope for, but at the last second he saw someone who looked out of place.

"Turn left here and drop me," he said as he passed a £20 note through the dividing glass.

With the cabbie wishing him good luck behind him, he passed a row of battery bikes, entered the

Chapter 14 - White lines

gardens and hid behind a broad sign so as to observe the out-of-place man. It took him all of two seconds to relocate the man as he sauntered further away from him and watched him as he turned his head this way and that, clearly being far too observant for a tourist. The man briefly stopped on the far side of one of the three memorials, put a phone to his ear for a few moments, then continued towards the far end of the gardens then kept going. Justin followed, kept out of sight and remembered to look behind him in case the man was just a lure, but he didn't see anybody else showing any interest in him. They crossed over Horse Guards Avenue, past some elegant government buildings, to see the man taking up station by leaning against the shady side of a tree. He had a direct view of the entrance to New Scotland Yard.

One or two items were beginning to fall into place as it confirmed to him that they must have been seen going into New Scotland Yard, which meant that someone was expecting them to go there. If so, it meant that Bayev knew who they worked for and had set Hana on their trail to prevent them revealing what they had so recently learned in Bulgaria. But then a nasty thought crossed his mind. Suppose they were to be taken and forced to reveal what they were up to? Even if they didn't resist, they would be tortured anyway before being dumped dead in the nearest canal.

He looked round again before crossing the road and sat on one of the Victorian wrought iron bench seats overlooking the Thames and because it was partially behind a temporary red and white workman's canvas hut with British Telecom printed down the side, it gave him excellent cover. As the man leaned against the leafy tree, he noted how well he blended in, but the woollen half-round hat that he was wearing was what had drawn Justin's attention to him in the first place. And the man kept looking around him to study passers-by, but not obviously. Justin half-laughed to himself because from his own point of view, the audacity of these terrorists was way beyond anything else he had come across before, and it was all happening not far from Downing Street. He found the zoom function on the phone's camera and took a few shots of him and then he looked at the location of the building-mounted surveillance cameras. The man had positioned himself so that he was not in direct view of any of them. All-in-all, Justin decided he was competent and not someone who had been drafted in off the street, but if this was an indication of the calibre of Hana's associates, then they were certainly up against professionals. It wouldn't surprise him to find that there was another at the other end of the block that housed New Scotland Yard but he dared not move and risk being spotted, and possibly lose contact.

He sent the photo of the man to Patricia's phone, waited a few moments and then phoned her but she was not answering. He presumed she was with Gibbons so he texted her. While he waited for a response, he phoned Mr Thomas, his contact at the Treasury, but it took him three goes to get the number right as he had to remember it.

Chapter 14 - White lines

"Aaah, there you are. I was beginning to wonder if you'd decided to stay on holiday in that part of the world. It really is very pretty isn't it, especially the Varna Valley, and did you try the local grape? But the question is, did she enjoy it?"

Tommy Thomas's Civil Service accent and demeanour did him credit as it was that typical sort of attitude that pervaded in the Whitehall offices of government. Justin cynically wondered if he was going to be asked the cricket score before getting down to business and was almost disappointed when he wasn't. He got straight to the point as he hoped Patricia would return his call shortly.

"I have a little bit of interesting news for you and I believe you can give me some in return."

Mr Thomas' attitude changed to one of officialdom, clearly resonating in the timbre of his voice. "Go on," he said sternly, although he didn't mean to be.

Justin told him about the mine's likelihood of it ever being capable of producing any significant quantity of platinum and went on to tell him the probable origin of it. He gave him the bones of his discussion with Sir Neville but hesitated when it came to what Hamilton had told him. He hadn't had a chance to think the next bit through thoroughly, but even as he spoke, he saw light at the end of the tunnel. He knew what he was going to tell Mr Thomas.

By mentioning the forthcoming bogus Bulgarian report, Justin knew he would be passing on a small, but valuable, snippet of information to his superiors who would presumably react to take advantage of the impending price rise. Initially on behalf of HM Government but it wouldn't surprise Justin to learn that several others had taken advantage to line their own pockets; much as Hamilton intended to do. He didn't know how senior Mr Thomas was but knew that sensitive financial information such as this spread like wildfire. Friday was the day after tomorrow and an eternity as far as these sort of people were concerned.

"I've one last item to check before I submit my report to you hopefully tomorrow, but I think you will find that the platinum market is going to be manipulated this Friday."

"Up or down?" Mr Thomas asked, just a little too anxiously for Justin's liking and he had his answer.

"That's what I've got to corroborate and I'm not going to point you in any particular direction at the moment because that depends upon what I'll be learning a bit later today," he half-lied.

He may have been a little unfair with his assessment of Mr Thomas as he pictured him with compressed lips waiting for a definitive answer, but on the other hand a snippet of information such as this was too good not to pass along the old boy network and curry favour.

He continued, "And in order to complete my report I need you to tell me which clearing bank handles the most financial transactions between buyer and seller when it come to the metal market, and if it's the same when it comes to hedge funds."

"Oh that's quite an easy one." His voice was back to its usual self. "Basically, the major banks created

Chapter 14 - White lines

their own consortium for these transactions which is labelled LPMCL and it's all sanctioned by the Loco London Precious Metals Market. Sorry there's no snappy acronym but we usually refer to it as Loco for short. I suppose if I had to name one bank in particular it would be JP Morgan."

"Could a buyer or seller utilise the Isle of Man Bank?"

"Oh yes, but they'd still need to clear it through Loco."

"And does HM Government have, shall we say, influence within Loco and LP… blah blah blah… because there may be an opportunity here to turn the tables?

"I think you may have used the ideal phrase when you say 'influence within Loco'. Not only are they independent in the eyes of the media and the outside world, but the chairman of their governing body is a real terrier when it comes to defending their corner. Quite recently he publicly lambasted a junior minister for even suggesting that there was any sort of link between HMG or any other government, and Loco. They're fiercely protective of their non-political status and to my mind, quite right too. Can't have governments around the world trying to manipulate global metal prices, especially gold, but they try on the odd occasion. Brussels had a cack-handed go the other week and were laughed out of the room." He sounded quite gleeful.

"That doesn't really answer my question."

"Ummm. That rather depends upon what you're after. If it's a triviality then there's not much of a problem but if it comes to anything more serious, then I'm afraid you're stuck." He let Justin muse on that one.

"Thanks. I'll get back to you."

"Tomorrow?" came the hurried question as Justin hovered his thumb over the red button to end the call.

"If possible." He hung up and tried Patricia again; it rang and she answered.

"How are you getting on? See the photo I sent you? I'm on a park bench outside."

"We've just come out from seeing the Commander." And she described what Vivian had revealed while showing the photo to her and she asked for it to be forwarded to her. She got to work on it straight away from her mobile.

Justin was eager to butt in and eventually did so. "Look. It's clear we're up against a professional outfit with an agenda, so let's hope Gibbons appreciates it and acts accordingly. What we need right now is more personnel because I'll bet my last pound on there being another looking out for us further down the street. When Gibbons calls you back in, tell him so will you. Hang on a minute…"

She could hear talking in the background but it really was nearly a minute before she heard Justin's voice again. "Sorry about that. The telephone engineer wanted to know what I was doing, and at the same time our sneaky friend was briefly joined by another but he's gone now. I've sent you a photo of him as well, but the light's beginning to fade so it might not be as clear as the last. Ring you shortly."

Chapter 14 - White lines

As she showed the latest photograph to Vivian, both girls looked up as Tates walked into the waiting room and went straight into Gibbons' office without giving them a glance.

"Can you access your photofit programme from your mobile?" asked Patricia.

"Oh yes, but not in the same detail as you and Justin saw the other day, so I've given it the simple task of trying to work out who these fellows are while we're waiting. It also cross-references with other crime agencies so with any luck we'll have an answer soon."

Patricia thought about this for a moment. "Would that include the OSCE?"

Vivian looked up from her mobile. "Oh, you mean the Organisation for Security and Co-operation in Europe? Normally yes. Why do you ask?"

"I discovered it a few days ago but never had the chance to find out more and when I tried digging deeper, it locked me out."

"Yes, it would do. Only accredited personnel can access it."

She nibbled her bottom lip lightly as she thought her way through. "Are you allowed to access it?"

"Yes. I have to logon each time but our computer is given automatic access; otherwise it's quite secure."

"Can you tell me more about it without incriminating yourself?"

"Of course I can because it's no secret," she said with a hint of astonishment in her voice. "OSCE is about fifty years old now, well before I was born, and I gather was created to help prevent another Cold War between east and west. It's like the oil that greases the machine when it comes to negotiation between governments. A marginally smaller version of the UN but for Europe."

"Smaller?" commented Patricia sceptically. "When I looked at its website it said it employed nearly four thousand people. That's hardly small."

"Ummm. I know. And it's grown even more since I've been here and it seems to me that the mandarins in Brussels are trying to commandeer it bit by bit. Rather like the Americans have easy access to the UN mainly because its headquarters is based in New York, those expansionists in the EEC would love to be in certain positions of power within OSCE. It's like there's a little cold war going on underground and one of those frontiers looks like being Bulgaria, Moldova, Hungary and Slovakia. It can be quite frightening when one finds out what's really going on, especially as there seems to be a lot of new activity when it comes to arms controls, shipments and troop movements. All sanctioned by the contributing governments, but you don't need to worry because its security section is extremely well-guarded."

"And that's exactly my point because if Bayev's bribed enough officials then he's bound to have his own man inside it, and ergo, able to find out whatever he wants. I know Bulgaria's part of that organisation but consider what amount of pressure Russia or say Belarus can bring to bear if they want their way. Hana was born in Belarus, or was it Minsk, and because of his Russian links, it follows that he's running operations on behalf of various criminal groups. If I'm right then

Chapter 14 - White lines

he's the rotten apple in the barrel and his infectious activities are spreading like a cancer across Europe. Right now, his focus is on England, a) because of Kiril Hirov's imminent visit and b) because we rumbled his platinum operation. And here's another thought that's just crossed my mind. If your computer is looking to identify certain individuals that Bayev has indirectly employed, then he's going to find out about it because OSCE's computer will alert his chap inside." She paused to catch up with her thought process. "And also, once Bayev tells Hana that his chaps in London are blown, then all Hana has to do is swap them for others… but on the other hand, time is rather short for him." She added the last part as an afterthought.

Vivian followed her assessment for a few moments, then attended to her mobile. "You're right. I've paused our computer's continental search and kept it to the UK, but I'll continue it once I've had a chance to access it directly; not with this though." She waved her mobile. "I can set it to exclude OSCE's mainframe so once Commander Gibbons has finished with us, I'll get right on it. Oh, but hang on a mo." Her fingers scampered across the face of her mobile. "Here's what the computer's come up with so far. Looks like the first chap could be one of three. Here, have a look." She showed the photographs at an angle. "Any look familiar?"

Patricia wasn't as adept as Vivian with a mobile but after enlarging and looking again, replied that none did.

Vivian took full control of her mobile and after a brief finger recital announced what she had found so far. "The first's name is Alexi Petrov, Russian naturally with a name like that... the second's George Hiranu, possibly Albanian... and the third's Ceasar Tiernmann, unknown country of origin. Heard of them before?"

"No. Remember up to a few months ago I was plain Inspector Eyethorne based in Maidenhead who dealt with local crimes, so I've not come across international criminals before." Patricia's bottom lip was receiving more than its fair share of attention that day. "But what if Hana already has a second team in place?"

Both women looked at each other but it was Patricia who continued. "If Hana's first team is set up for Hirov and he diverted them on to us because of the urgent need to keep us quiet, then he'd probably have a second team standing by to deal with Hirov..."

"I don't follow you."

Patricia suddenly realised that Vivian wouldn't know quite a lot of what she and Justin had been through over the past few days and couldn't possibly arrive at the same conclusion.

"Ah... here we are. Your chap outside is Alexi Petrov." She showed Patricia a full-size clear photograph. "And yes... he's believed to be a member of the Vogli group based in Moscow." She paused to scroll. "Usual story... born in Moscow's suburbs, parents sidelined, etc. They specialise in smuggling medical, chemical, biological, etc. and of course drugs which come under the category of either medicines or chemicals."

Patricia needed to talk to Justin but as she reached for her mobile, Tates opened the door to the Commander's office and beckoned them in.

Chapter 14 - White lines

The two girls sat to one side in the same chairs but Tates was seated alongside Gibbons who didn't look up until he had stopped writing. "Seems like we have a priority situation on our hands, not made easier by Hirov and his deputy arriving at Heathrow airport tomorrow, a day ahead of schedule. I've designated two four-man teams to look after their arrival, transport, stay at The Lancaster Hotel and general well-being while they're here in London. You," he said looking directly at Patricia, "I want as a floater based there and to act as a secondary liaison in the hotel so get there asap, check-in and familiarise yourself with the building. Fire escapes, kitchen exits, staff shortcuts, deliveries and so on. Before you ask why you're needed as my liaison it's because Special Branch will have its usual official communication channels which the press will naturally be aware of but they won't be aware of you, so make sure you keep your head down and report directly back to me only. Understood?"

"That might not be possible, Sir," she stated before Gibbons could continue.

He didn't show any surprise but the mere fact that he paused before asking why not, betrayed that he was. It was also something that Patricia picked up on.

There was no other way of putting it, so she just blurted it out. "Events have developed since we've been sitting in your outer office and it looks like Justin Crawford and myself are the target before Hirov arrives because of our knowledge of the bogus platinum operation. We know who some of them are and are pretty certain who's bankrolling the operation." She pointedly looked at Vivian who took her cue and repeated what she had said a few minutes earlier. The two of them didn't quite cross-talk over each other, but by the time they had finished, it was clear to Gibbons that there was a lot more going on than he had been aware of only a few minutes ago.

The room fell silent while Gibbons considered their options, but that silence only lasted less than half a minute. "Under normal circumstances either I, or in my absence Tates here, would decide what to do and issue the necessary instructions down the line, but events are unfolding at such a pace and one that I've not seen for quite a while, that I think it best if we include you in the decision-making this instance. Are you in direct communication with Crawford?"

"Yes Sir. He's outside keeping an eye on them."

"Assuming you're correct in your assessment that you and he are their target, then I think we ought to respond immediately because you're no good to me if you're dead."

"I think that goes for both of us Sir," Patricia added with a deadpan face and the touch of cynicism in her voice was noticed by the other three. It took them a moment to realise that she was referring to Justin rather than Vivian.

Gibbons looked down as he lightly tapped his pen on his desk a couple of times, then without turning, directed his next comment at Tates. "Tower Bridge exercise."

Tates perceptively nodded his head. "Perfect." He smiled.

Chapter 14 - White lines

"I assume you can get a team in place in say one hour?" He looked at his watch. "Commence at 20.00?"

"Leave it to me Sir." Tates had the look of a person with a mission as he left the room and indeed he did have a mission to complete on time. Rounding up that number of personnel at the drop of a hat was going to be a stretch.

Gibbons addressed Vivian. "Thank you for your contribution but I don't think we need detain you any longer."

The chagrin on her face was clear. Just when she thought she would be included in an active operation, she was being dismissed. What she didn't know was that it was for her own safety and once she had left the room, Gibbons commanded Patricia's full attention. "We'll deal with one problem at a time so let's get you and Crawford sorted so that you're both free to operate effectively." It was a cold-blooded comment but not unexpected from Patricia's perspective. After all, she was just another of his minions.

He continued. "We've practised exactly this scenario at various locations, but Tower Bridge, apart from being just about the closest, is the perfect setting for capturing the enemy, and it works like this. You and Crawford are the target but you'll be referred to as 'The Cheese' because the enemy will be classified as 'Mouse 1', 'Mouse 2' and so forth depending upon how many there are of them. You'll lure them into following you onto Tower Bridge from the north end, enter the north tower and make your way up to the overhead walkway which joins the two towers at a hundred and fifty feet above the Thames. The Mice will naturally follow you and when you get to the far end you just walk down the stairs in the south tower and exit back onto the bridge."

Gibbons was about to continue when a nondescript man entered after the briefest of knocks, walked up to Patricia, told her to stand with her arms out wide and proceeded to attach radio equipment about her body. He shamelessly tucked a small box into the cup of her right bra and carefully inserted an earpiece into her right ear and indicated that she should make it comfortable herself. He added a watch/cum/microphone to her right wrist and finished by asking her to respond through his own equipment, which she did. Once he left, she sat back down and turned her attention to Gibbons. "One question Sir. I expect there'll come a point when the Mice smell a rat, so should the need arise you'll expect us to turn and confront them. When do you envisage that to be?"

His eyes narrowed just a touch; he recognised her ability for foresight which he had rarely come across before. "There'll be two teams of two following behind you making sure the Mice are following you and one team at the base of the south tower to act as a blocker. I leave it up to your discretion as to when you turn and stand but probably as you exit the south tower." He let her consider the scenario for a moment. "Once they enter the north tower behind you they'll be trapped."

As she looked at her real watch, stood, adjusted her right bosom, shifted her left armpit to ease her Browning holster which evened up her figure, he added, "Treat this as you would a training exercise and you'll be fine."

Chapter 15

Walkway

Even before she closed the door on the way out of Gibbons' office, her mind was conjuring up all sorts of scenarios which in turn raised even more questions, and without realising how she had arrived there, stopped just two paces out of the lift as it arrived at the ground floor. Trancelike, she didn't notice either of the two male receptionists' reactions from behind their tall desk opposite the main entrance several yards away, nor the woman who had to steer herself around Patricia as she half-blocked the access. She concentrated only on what lay ahead; she wasn't even nibbling her bottom lip it was that intense. It took a while to dismiss her daydreams and focus on what was the other side of the one-way glass and she spotted Justin briefly peering round the side of the stripped temporary hut no more than fifty yards away. Then she saw his target innocuously standing besides a London plane tree. He could end up being Mouse 1. She knew the second she walked out into the open that she would be taking her life in her own hands, but not only was this what she was paid to do, but it seemed the right and natural thing to do. She readied herself to go outside and hail a London taxi to take her to Tower Bridge when two things dawned on her. Justin didn't know the plan and she'd have to stay on this side of the carriageway to ensure the driver took her along the north embankment rather than shortcut across the U-bend in the Thames.

She phoned Justin and outlined the Tower Bridge operation but before she finished speaking had a further idea. "Why don't you hang back and follow the crew who'll be following me? That way we may be able to bag more of them in case they also have a long stop."

Justin's delayed response was to be expected. "Will do, but watch yourself because these people know what they're doing."

"See you on the other side then." Hoping that Justin would interpret the bit of levity correctly. She then spoke into her wrist mic to advise control and went through the large glass door.

She didn't have to stand kerbside of Victoria Embankment for long before pulling up a taxi and as casually as possible, looked round to see Mouse 1 trotting through the gardens in her direction with a phone glued to his ear. Once she had instructed the cabbie, she surreptitiously looked over her shoulder and saw Mouse 1 getting into the passenger side of a silver Audi that had appeared from nowhere, presumably driven by Mouse 2. She couldn't see Justin but guessed he was somewhere in the distance and hypothesised that as he knew where she was going that he might take the shortcut via Elephant and Castle and conceal himself somewhere at the base of the south tower.

Chapter 15 - Walkway

On any other occasion she would have looked out of the window and admired the numerous landmarks that abutted the Thames, but not this evening. Instead she took the opportunity to phone Justin for a longer conversation; he was indeed cutting across the U-bend in the river.

"You're new to this sort of thing and there isn't time to give you a crash course in counter surveillance so I'm going to wait out of sight by the north tower. You won't see me but I'll be there to see how many of them there's going to be. I'll also be able to watch you back. One thing for certain is that they won't be in front of you at that point as they can't know where you're going, but the only danger is that once you disappear up the tower, they may send someone to cover the south exit, so watch out for him. Once they're inside, I'll make my way to the bottom of the south tower."

"I'd better tell control what you're doing."

"No don't so that as it'll only distract them. They'll find out soon enough if they're any good."

There was silence over the phone but it was Patricia who broke it. "Justin… I've never had someone try to murder me before… not like this anyway… it's not a nice feeling, is it?"

"What, not even that chap the other day?"

"That was on the spur of the moment. This is different… it's premeditated."

Justin could almost sense her nervousness. "Just remember your training and it won't let you down. In any case, I'll be there. Where are you now?"

She looked up out of the window then behind her. "Approaching Monument and they're a few hundred yards behind me."

"I'll be in position in a couple of minutes... see you on the south side."

She hung up, looked at the time on her phone and decided she had the timing about right. When she looked behind her again, she noted what cars were following the silver Audi and tried to remember if they were the same as when she had looked previously, but nothing stood out. On her wrist mic she reported her whereabouts and confirmed that Mouse 1 and 2 were still following in their silver Audi and was relieved when a dispassionate voice told her that they were waiting for her. "Head for the door on the western side which will be unlocked. Try to look as though you are meeting someone before you go in, pause and look around, then take the lift to the top."

Being typically British, she'd never been on the sightseeing tour of Tower Bridge, only driven over it, but she recalled the basic facts from her schooldays. Built during Queen Victoria's reign at a time when the sun never set on the British Empire, the ornate bridge adjacent to the Tower of London where the Crown Jewels were securely kept, was just one representation of the wealth of the country. When it was originally built, it was the gateway to London from the seven seas around the globe and its twin towers housed the mechanism that raised and lowered the drawbridges to allow high-masted ships to sail further up the Thames to dock at the many wharfs. As a testament

Chapter 15 - Walkway

to the engineers of the day, as far as she knew it was still working as well today as it did over a hundred years ago. She wasn't to know that chaperones strictly controlled the guided tours of the overhead walkways, nor that its floor and sides were now made of several layers of glass to enable better viewing from that lofty viewpoint. These daily guided tours had finished a few hours ago, the tour guides having gone home for the night long ago, and she wasn't to know that she'd be all alone once she ascended the lift. No doubt the access doors had been opened by one of Gibbons' other operatives.

She acknowledged control as they passed the Tower of London on their right. The cabbie was asking exactly where she wanted to be dropped and she told him on the right as they approached the northern-most tower. He started to comment on how the tourists usually milled around just where they had stopped and added that the sightseeing tours finished several hours ago. She ignored him as she got out making sure that for a moment she was facing backwards. The Audi was negotiating the light traffic but was clearly intent on pulling up to where her taxi was. It was followed by a blue Range Rover; the same one as she had noted a short while ago. She didn't think she'd have enough time to follow control's instructions to the letter but headed for the heavy oak door at the base of the western tower, pulled it open and slammed it closed knowing that her pursuers weren't far behind. She ignored her instinct to look for the lock but after a brief moment of anxiety trying to locate the lift, half a dozen paces bought her to the control panel where she jabbed the call button which mercifully opened the door immediately. Once again she jabbed at the obvious ascent button but her nerves jangled as she waited for the sedentary door to close, and when it eventually did, she consciously exhaled.

She didn't count how long the lift took but it was long enough in that clinical stainless-steel box to assess what was actually happening, and it was anger that came to the forefront. She was angry that she was being pursued by foreigners on British soil intent on either killing or kidnapping her, angry that she had been manipulated into this position and angry that Justin wasn't beside her. Her anger intensified as she thought back to the conversation she had had with Gibbons regarding Mice, Rats and Cheese and resolved never to volunteer to be The Cheese again. She decided that being the bait and irrationality went hand in glove. She was angry at just about everything but it stiffened her resolve that they weren't going to get their own way. Bastards. She knew Justin would have witnessed her flight from the taxi into the tower and she didn't waste any time wondering where he had secreted himself but instead concentrated on what was about to happen when the lift door opened. She readied her Browning as she worked out that it was conceivable that they had climbed the staircase quicker than the lift had taken to arrive at the walkway as it seemed to be taking far too long. Her body tensed as she felt and heard it come to a stop.

As the door opened, she flicked the safety catch and levelled the gun downwards to point at gut-level

Chapter 15 - Walkway

knowing that it would kick up slightly, but there was nobody to aim it at. Nevertheless, she cautiously peered out into an empty space and almost pulled the trigger when the door rattled as it automatically tried to close itself. All was briefly silent but in the background she heard footsteps pounding up the staircase. She returned her Browning to its holster and didn't waste any time wondering how far up they were, but turned and trotted across what seemed to be some sort of vestibule and then smartly down the nearest of the two unlit glazed walkways, but what she did have time for was to glance sideways through the layers of glass towards the setting sun and only then did she realise that she was treading on glass. The fading sun cast eerie shadows through the criss-cross patterns of the lofty walkway and despite her predicament, she experienced a sense of smallness within the great structure.

Absentmindedly she slowed down a little as she passed the halfway point but when she heard her pursuers behind, decided it was time to sprint. Never had halfway seemed more like quarter-the-way but she could see the corresponding vestibule entrance ahead. She supposed that the lift would be off to the left with the doorway to the stairs of the south tower and knew she would be out of their sight within a few paces.

Bang. Bang.

She felt the wind of one of the bullets as it passed close to her right ear and she instinctively jinked left and right; and now she was round the corner going towards the stairs instead of waiting for the lift that was directly in front of her where she would have made a perfect stationary target. It was a testament to her abilities that she had discarded the idea of waiting for the lift and with her mind now being at its most sensitive, she briefly looked at the elegant staircase. Rushing footsteps were coming up from below, but whose footsteps were they?

Not knowing, in an instant she opted for another door which she knew wouldn't be locked as it was underneath a green 'emergency' sign and going through it was confronted by a narrow spiral staircase that led both up and down. Closing it as quietly as possible she chose to go up, hoping that her pursuers would assume she had gone down. In any case, something told her that it probably met the main staircase just below her and would therefore turn out to be useless.

Very little light penetrated this staircase which was steep and narrow with a polished handrail on the outside of the solid metal central support, but it suddenly terminated next to an ornate window at a wooden door with a pair of linked iron levers keeping it shut. She yanked them sideways and they released with a loud clang. Now everybody knew where she was.

The first thing that struck her was the wind as its pressure helped push the small door open violently against her and she realised that once she went through it, there was no way she would ever be able to close it again from the outside. It wasn't gusting and it was pleasantly warm, but nonetheless it was something she hadn't considered. Bracing her hands against both jambs, she eased her head and shoulders through the narrow doorway and discovered that it opened onto a narrow castellated parapet from one of the round

Chapter 15 - Walkway

turrets. She depicted Tower Bridge in her mind and deduced that it must be one of the high-up four gothic towers that accentuated each corner, and leaning out a little further saw that there was enough of a gap between the extremely steep slated roof and the upright of the castellation that formed a gutter below her, and that it was wide enough for her to step onto. She did exactly that as she thought she heard noise behind her.

Even under these stressful circumstances, she was aware of the magnificent uninhibited view and though it was only for a split second, it was the sort of view that makes an indelible imprint in one's memory. She bought up the mic to her mouth, shielded it from the wind and reported her predicament to control, who were no doubt expecting her at the base of the south tower, not near its pinnacle. What she didn't report to them was what she proposed to do next.

There was no doubt in her mind that unless she acted quickly, all they had to do was stand in the doorway and shoot her until dead, so with little regard for the alternative consequences, she eased herself out of the door, slid the few feet down the slates until her feet touched the narrow gutter, then swung herself between two of the castellations and dropped a couple of feet onto the top of the slippery metal-domed roof of the walkway. And now she was faced with only two choices and discarding the running-along-the-top option where she would make a perfect running target, instead chose to flatten herself with her back against the stone wall of the tower. She had seen that the castellations jutted out quite a bit and for somebody to see where she was, they would have to lean out quite a way and therefore present themselves as a target to her. Hopefully they would waste time looking for her round the parapet and by the time they worked out where she might actually be, Gibbons' crews would come to the rescue. She hoped.

She reckoned she had little more than a minute before they showed themselves and it didn't help when control's remote voice asked her to repeat what her exact location was. Drawing her Browning and holding it pointing up, despite the twilight she scanned the parapet's edge for the outline of heads in case they should look over.

On more than one occasion, she had wondered what she would do if she ever found herself in the conundrum of having to shoot first or not and had put off making that decision because it was unlikely to arise. Now it was crunch time and she recognised that it was a kill or be killed situation. She thumbed the safety catch and readied herself to fire but she was really caught out by what happened next.

The external floodlights came on. Not instantly blindingly white, but warmed up gradually from a dull yellow, yet after only a few seconds it became clear that she was going to be in the shadows rather than highlighted like a fly on a white wall. Anyone looking down on her from above would be staring into one particular light that pointed towards the top of her tower and was no more than six feet in front of her, yet she was standing just outside of its angled beam.

Chapter 15 - Walkway

She flicked the safety catch to safe and holstered her Browning, reached for her phone and rang Justin.

When he answered she could tell he was running from the heavy breathing. "On my way up. Where are you?"

"I'm outside above the walkway."

"Say again."

"On top of the bloody walkway," she shouted down the phone and listened to his laboured breathing and deduced that he was running up the stairs.

It must have been her shout that attracted attention because she heard a bullet whine off the corrugated roof, followed by another couple of shots which also missed. They knew roughly where she was but couldn't see her in the shadows, otherwise it would have been an easy kill for them. Angry at herself for being so foolhardy, she took a couple of paces forwards so that she was right next to and slightly behind the floodlight, knowing that she would be invisible to them. Withdrawing her Browning for the third time and flicking off the safety catch, she took her time because her two assailants were perfectly lit up from the waist upwards and about four feet apart between adjacent castellations, no more than thirty feet away. First one then the other disappeared as she loosed off two shots at each of them in turn, then she knelt down on one knee to lessen herself as a target in case she had missed or if there were more of them.

She heard shots coming from inside the tower and saw movement at the doorway. Stay put she told herself, stay put. I'm safe enough here for the moment. But she kept her gun at the ready.

Two minutes... three minutes and still nothing, but she became aware of a buzzing noise at the same time that Justin called out from the doorway. "Don't get trigger happy... it's me."

He appeared and, like Patricia a few minutes earlier, slid down the steep tiles so that he was standing above her on the parapet. He shielded his eyes. "I know you're there but I can't see you. It's safe to come out now."

She made him wait while she stood, holstered, and ran her hands down her clothing. "Nothing like being on time, is it?" she jested but had to shout a little.

"I didn't want to steal your limelight. Here, let me help you up." He leaned over offering his hand but he could tell that the gap was still a bit too great for direct contact. "You'll have to jump," he shouted over the buzzing and they both looked up to see a helicopter nearing.

Her first attempt was a bit half-hearted but with her second he managed to half-grab her wrist and she let out a gasp of pain as she felt part of her hand dislocated; her thumb maybe. Her slender wrist slipped through his hand and she fell to one side of the top of the domed roof and he stared in horror as she began to slide off to one side.

The pain in her wrist masked her sliding sensation but only for a moment as she suddenly realised she was nearing the edge of the walkway roof. She knew the curved roof was made of metal but what she hadn't noticed was the thin layer of verdure that covered it and made it extremely slippery, and it didn't appear to have anything to grab hold of to slow her descent. The roof

Chapter 15 - Walkway

wasn't semi-circular, only arched slightly, but she knew the further she slid down it, the more difficult it would be to stop. She somehow managed to straighten out her body and pummelling her legs on the lead in the hope of making a toehold didn't really help. Just when she thought she was going to hurtle over the edge and drop into the Thames an awful long way down, her right foot found the gutter, and it really hurt as she whacked her toes on the iron. Being designed and built by the Victorians, the gutter was typical of their desire to make things last, and it was just as well, because it didn't budge as she felt for it with her other foot. But age and decay go hand-in-glove and she felt more than heard a splintering noise from just below her, then felt the slight movement as the gutter brackets started to give way. They had only been designed to catch rainwater, not retain the weight of a woman.

She cursed as she was blinded by the helicopter's search light which at last pinpointed her and she briefly wondered if they had some sort of rope ladder they could throw out. Above the engine clatter, she felt the gutter bracket move significantly, and much as she tried to take the weight off, there was no denying that she only had a few seconds before it gave way completely. She started to decide how she was going to enter the water as she acknowledged that she was inevitably slipping off the roof, when she felt a hand clasp her wrist; the painful one, but that didn't seem to matter now. She looked up to see that Justin was trying to tell her something over the mechanical din and she cried out in pain as he heaved her off the gutter.

It seemed to take an age but finally he pulled her up to the flat apex of the roof, hefted her onto her knees, and held her tight. He also waved the helicopter away as its downdraught was being very unhelpful and as the noise abated he managed a quip. "Gotcha just where I want ya."

It took her a while to react and she tried to think of something smart to say but all she could manage was, "You can let go of me now."

"What... after all the trouble I went to?"

He saw that she managed a weak smile which told him that she was going to be alright. He still clung on to her with a reassuring cuddle; she reciprocated as she felt she had earned it. "Can I get off my knees now please?" he asked in a plaintiff voice into her ear.

She closed her eyes and imagined that they were back on that rocky tor on the south Welsh coast. "The last time you asked me that on your knees, you proposed. What are you suggesting this time?"

They pulled apart and looked at each other. "How about a curry?"

She had less difficulty standing than he did. "Only if you're paying and have figured out how we get off this bloody roof."

He looked up at the castellations in time to see someone emerge from the doorway behind. "Why don't you use your radio to whistle up a ladder?

Even though there had been chatter in her ear, with her own imminent demise and the racket from the helicopter, she had forgotten all about it.

Chapter 15 - Walkway

***

Seated in a contemporary-styled armchair, Justin looked at his lightly grazed knees, rubbed them in unison, and turned his attention back to the TV on the countertop. "You're on telly again," he called over his shoulder at the open door that led to the ensuite bathroom but there was no reply; Patricia was submerged at that moment.

The dubious quality video had been taken on someone's mobile as they had been dining al fresco in one of the many riverside restaurants, and for a few seconds showed Patricia's legs kicking in the air as they neared the gutter. Not an hour had passed and it was already being circulated to the news agencies, and the usual speculation went with it but mercifully there was no mention of the security forces being involved. A City of London police inspector decried the reckless foolhardiness of inconsiderate tourists, while on another channel there was a suggestion that dogging had been the motive.

"I'm on telly again." Justin looked over his shoulder to see his fiancée looking at the TV as she dripped on the carpet, despite the short towel that provocatively dangled from around her chest. "Seen the hairdryer?"

He went and looked out of the window at a splendidly illuminated Tower Bridge for the next few minutes as the noisy dryer did what it was supposed to do, and ran over what had happened since he had taken up station near the base of the north tower. He had seen Patricia slam the ground-level doorway and he remembered hoping that there had been enough time for the lift doors to have closed before the pair chasing her managed to get a foot in the door. He had had to wait quite some time before two Special Branch chaps followed them in and wondered if they hadn't left it a bit too late, and had been about to go after them all when he saw the Range Rover surge forward, stop by the south tower and disgorge another couple of chaps before driving off. He'd decided to get up to the walkway using the south tower as the north was already taken care of by the pair from SB, and he now knew that the reason why they had held back for so long was because there would be another pair of them already waiting up the top.

As he had been about to enter the base of the south tower through a similar door to that in the north, he had heard the pair from the Range Rover clattering up the stairs, despite the near darkness. He had looked at the lift indicator that had shown it wasn't moving from the top, presumably disabled by someone from SB, and had thought he had heard the return of the Range Rover pulling up outside. He had been torn between chasing after the ascending pair or seeing what the Range Rover was up to, and chose the latter as it was only going to take a moment. Gingerly opening the heavy door and creeping round the tower so that he could see into the car on the roadway, he squinted, trying to see who was at the wheel. He looked harder as he thought he recognised Hana, but his head was in the shadows and he couldn't be one hundred per cent certain. Not wanting to be seen, he had headed for the staircase.

Chapter 15 - Walkway

The hairdryer stopped with a sudden silence and he turned to admire the graceful lines of Patricia's nearly naked body sitting on the bed. "How's your wrist feeling now?"

She flexed her fingers and winced. "Fair enough but I expect it'll take a bloody age to get better, so I reckon I'll need a compression bandage of some sort."

He moved towards the room phone. "Good idea. I'll see if reception can find one."

"And some ice."

While he spoke to room service she combed her hair and daydreamed about her latest brush with death and it briefly sent shivers down her spine; or it could have been the whiff of breeze from the window that was ajar that gave her brief shivers. She held out one hand to see if it was shaking and decided it wasn't. She had no headache and her vision was as it should be, so apart from her bruised wrist and slightly painful toe where it had come into contact with the gutter, she concluded that she was in pretty good shape and that she really oughtn't to worry about herself. She smiled to herself as she recalled the old-fashioned rope ladder that the pair of SB guys had found and had dangled over the parapet, because she had nearly fallen off that as well. They had helped them both over the castellations and had told them that they had been booked into a room in The Tower Hotel just opposite on the north bank and that they were to stay there until contacted. She stuck a finger where her earpiece had been and wiggled it for a second to clear an itch, because they had taken that back from her along with the remote.

Justin hung up. "He reckons they have one somewhere and will send someone up with it."

"That's if he can get past the two guys outside the door." She referred to the two SB officers who had been detailed to stay outside the door to their room on the third floor. "Rather thoughtful of the Commander to put us in such a plush hotel for the night but I wish I had a change of clothes."

Justin wandered back to the window and gazed at the superb view. "Oh look. I can see Tower Bridge from here," he teased.

He ducked as she threw her towel at him but she hurriedly retrieved it at the knock on the door and disappeared into the bathroom where all her clothes were. Tates entered the room followed closely by a woman with some carrier bags in each hand and she proceeded to disgorge their contents onto one of the beds before leaving. He opened his mouth to speak but was interrupted by the crash of something metallic from the bathroom. Both men furrowed their brows for a moment, and a few seconds later Patricia stuck her head round the door with an apologetic look on her face, then spotted the array of clothes on the bed in front of her. Immodestly, only her towel keeping her half-decent with one hand, with the other she scooped up several packages and disappeared back into the bathroom.

"That's about the first reaction I would have expected from any woman," commented Justin.

"Restores one's faith in them doesn't it," replied Tates with a brief beam. "But I'm here to update Miss Eyethorne in particular, but the Commander has told

Chapter 15 - Walkway

me to include you as you seem to have elbowed your way into this operation with good effect."

"All I can offer you is some bottled water while we're waiting... unless you prefer room service?"

Tates had sauntered over to the window, gazed at an illuminated Tower Bridge, then sat down in the armchair. "No thank you, but while I'm waiting have you and your fiancée decided on a wedding date yet?"

Justin recognised the apparent nonchalant but purposeful query that went with the question knowing that nothing was ever 'off the record' when it came from someone of Tates' seniority.

"No, not yet and the way things are going at the moment, it's looking like next year, so you've got Patricia for a while yet." He referred to her employed status that was likely to demand that she be available almost at the drop of a hat anywhere in the world. A thought occurred to him and he took his chance to put the record straight. "But don't go thinking just because we make a good team that by ordering Miss Eyethorne on a job that I come with her. That's not part of any deal. I know you're considering that because of my previous posting with the Diplomatic Protection Squad, but you also have to take into account why I decided to leave it."

Tates half-smiled. "Of course we wouldn't take you for granted, but there may be the odd occasion when we might be able to come to a mutual understanding. In fact we have a job that's right up your street for tomorrow."

"Now why am I not surprised?" He let Tates chew on that while he tried to work out what was coming

Slips Catch

his way, and when he did, he knew he would have to accede because of Patricia. "You want me in on Hirov's protection operation don't you... now let me guess..."

"Don't waste time guessing because we haven't enough of it, so let me tell you. On top of our visible teams orbiting around Hirov and his aide while they go hither and thither, Miss Eyethorne will be invisible in the background, blending in with the scenery and to complete that picture, you ought to accompany her as a doting fiancée. We think Hana is likely to strike when Hirov is in or at least near his hotel, but in reality it could be anywhere. You'll be her second pair of eyes."

"And for this you'll pay me handsomely I hope."

"Don't be absurd. Why should you be paid to look after your fiancée?"

"You're not. You're going to pay me to keep my mince pies peeled."

"Pardon?"

"Mince pies... cockney rhyming for eyes, and by the way, I charge a bag-of-sand a day."

"Eh?"

"Bag-of-sand... grand... that's a thousand to you."

"Do speak the Queen's English."

"I am. We're in England's capital city and in case you didn't know, a cockney is one who was born within the sound of the Bow Bells, so I expect that makes me more of a Londoner than you. How much more English do you want me to be?"

"We're getting off the point..."

"No. That's exactly my point. Cockneys always look after themselves and I choose to look after my

Chapter 15 - Walkway

fiancée by staying in the same hotel as her. Reporting back to you will cost."

"I can see now why the Diplomatic Squad let you go, but I have to admit, your services would be of some use to this department."

"Possibly. Even though Hamilton wanted my head on a platter, I left because of the political interference. Being freelance means I get to cut through all the bullshit and achieve the correct result instead of one that is 'desirable' by the client."

"Hmmm…. that's still baffling us just a little and I don't suppose you want to tell me why Hamilton didn't persecute you?"

Justin smiled at first and retorted, "I don't think he had the balls for it in the end."

Tates was raising an eyebrow when the bathroom door opened to reveal a freshened-up Patricia in slightly unusual clothing. "Whoever chose this had my size right but I really don't like cerise." She picked at the woollen top with her forefinger and thumb. Justin ignored the colour as he was admiring the way it accentuated her very womanly figure.

"I'll get straight to business as there's pressing matters." Tates tone of voice was rather business-like, but he waited until they were both sat on the edge of the bed before continuing. "The reason why you're here, in this room, is because when we sent someone round to your Maidenhead flat we found that it was being watched and we're finding out right now how connected they are with this bunch." He tipped his head in the direction of Tower Bridge then looked at Patricia.

"The Commander concurred with your appraisal and quite rightly concluded that they would naturally stake out where you live in the hope of catching you when you eventually returned. For the moment I believe they're being held at your previous station in Maidenhead."

He paused and adjusted his pose in the chair as he got round to the main business of the day. "Turning to this evening's escapades, they're a few outstanding issues, one of them being the honing of our well-planned exercise, because you were never meant to have had to go out onto the roof."

"You don't have to tell me that."

Tates waited a moment for effect before he continued. "When you got out of the lift and crossed the hallway, you ran down the eastern walkway when you should have gone down the west one. The team that was up there were in the right place but couldn't have known that you would take the alternative walkway, hence the delay in them coming to your assistance. And by the way, because of your choice of walkways, they were under threat themselves from the pair of terrorists coming up from the south tower. These are issues that will be reviewed at a later date."

"You can tell the Commander that next time he can choose which bloody walkway to go down himself. They might only be fifty feet apart but when you're under genuine pressure and it's half-dark, then one looks very much like the other." She didn't go into more detail as she suspected there'd be a proper debriefing at some point soon.

Chapter 15 - Walkway

Her comments didn't seem to have any impression on Tates whose visage hadn't changed. "Because of the activities of these particular terrorists, the Commander felt it was better to put you in a 'safe house' but errr... suffice to say... this is a better option." He waved his hand.

"Are you leaving a team outside?" Patricia's eyes briefly darted towards the door.

"No. That's just for the moment and they'll leave with me. After all, there can't be many of them left because we caught them all. Even those at Maidenhead."

The inference was that the pair outside were there really to accompany Tates, but Justin wasn't being hoodwinked. "So if you managed to detain Hana, why the need for safe houses etcetera?"

Tates looked at Justin and a small furrow appeared on his brow. "Hana? Nobody's suggesting that Hana was actually in on this operation. Only organising it."

"I am."

"Why?"

"You do know that Hana was driving the Range Rover, don't you?"

"Nobody mentioned it."

Justin thought of retorting 'well I'm mentioning it now', but instead said, "He's still out there and bloody dangerous, and I'll bet you that right now he's putting his second team together from wherever he's holed-up. I wouldn't put it past him to even have a third team somewhere." His facetious remarks weren't lost on Tates.

"The question now is will he overlook us in favour of going after Hirov?" Patricia added.

"And that'll depend upon what his boss Bayev says." If Tates had had a transparent skull, one could have seen the cogs going round, but they were moving quite quickly. "As far as I am aware, tomorrow's operations are going ahead as planned, but you're quite right. Hana's going to be more dangerous now because he knows we're onto him."

"What little we know of Hana, he'll consider tonight's failure as a temporary setback, but if Hirov is the prize, then he's likely to concentrate on him tomorrow. He can come back to us at any time, which means we have to resolve this one way or another before Hirov leaves the UK. I don't want to be walking down the street in a month's time and be shot in the back of the head out of the blue."

Tates suddenly stood up. "Make the most of your luxurious lodgings."

Chapter 16

Twist

Kiril Hirov had been to London only once before as an exchange student, but that had been for nearly an entire year and he had been looking forward to returning to what he considered to be the most appealing capital city in the world. Twenty years ago, while attending an intensive course at the London School of Economics and flat sharing in Bayswater, he'd found time to enjoy the cosmopolitan social scene, but he'd never over done it. His father's governmental influence meant that his 'year out' was sponsored and would be spent advancing himself and making contacts at a level which would hopefully bear fruit in the years to come. Now in his late-thirties, unmarried, and as finance minister for Bulgaria, he was about to put his expensive education and links to good use. His command of the English language was rather good for an Eastern European and anyone held in conversation with him would have had difficulty pinning down his origins, but for his 'clipped' words that is typical of that part of the world. He wasn't a linguist but had naturally managed to pick up on a few idiosyncratic phrases and had joined in laughing at himself with his new friends when the explanation of whatever had been said became apparent. One favourite expression still was 'you're joking, aren't you' as it could be taken both ways and he had used it to good effect only yesterday when he had been engaged in discussion with one of the EEC commissioners in Brussels.

The Lancaster was one of the favoured hotels chosen for visiting dignitaries by the mandarins in HM Government as it was just the right distance from their offices off Pall Mall; not overly luxurious yet palatial enough to impress. The Diplomatic Protection Squad also favoured it as it was relatively easy to monitor and indeed they had installed permanent security cameras in selected positions.

Hirov was ensconced in one of the suites on the fifteenth floor with an impressive view over Kensington Gardens and the curved dome of the Albert Hall in the distance. He smiled recalling the memory of seeing Eric Clapton play there many years ago and rather than attend to the almost menial tasks on his laptop, instead he sat down in one of the chairs next to the large table and continued to gaze over the remarkable vista. After lighting one of his favourite cigars, naturally. Two minutes… just two whole minutes peace and quiet before his thoughts were interrupted by a knock on the connecting door and after a respectful lag, in walked his aide, Martin.

"Wonderful isn't it?" He pointed out of the window. "But there are too many trees in the way."

"Shall I ask to have them cut down for you?" asked Martin facetiously.

Chapter 16 - Twist

"Only the green ones. I remember that Buckingham Palace is on the other side somewhere and that Queen Elizabeth really does live there sometimes. Not like our own palaces, eh?"

"They're about the only decent things the communists did build for us."

"Those and the railways, but let's not talk of home when we're here in London. We've got two days and nights and I don't want to spend them in endless meetings. Before you confirm timings and what other arrangements you've crammed in, please tell me there's some time off for indulging ourselves."

Martin produced his tablet and rattled off where and whens. "…and after your official engagement with our own ambassador at the Bulgarian embassy tomorrow night, which is also just the other side of this park, you have the rest of the night off." He waited only a moment before adding, "Flight back to Sofia at midday the following morning."

But Hirov was already back in business mode. "What did you think of the reception we received at Heathrow airport this morning? A little over the top security-wise don't you think?"

"The western nations are becoming more and more paranoid about security, but now that you mention it, they did seem a little overzealous; especially when compared to Brussels… or our own."

"I wonder why it is that they offered to put us up here entirely at their own expense when we could have quite easily stayed at our embassy?"

Martin briefly weighed the question and looked at his watch. "I expect we'll find out shortly. A man from their diplomatic security service is supposed to be calling on us in a few minutes. Why don't you ask him?"

Hirov raised an eyebrow as he looked at Martin. "You expect a straight answer?"

"Perhaps."

It was just as well that they didn't have to wait long as Hirov's first appointment was to be held at the Bank of England in Threadneedle Street within the hour. A pinstripe-suited middle-aged gentleman introduced himself as 'Mr Johnson' and was clearly a diplomat from his manner; after the expected pleasantries he asked if he could seat himself down as he had learned that it created a more relaxed atmosphere. The three of them went over the timetable with Mr Johnson tactfully answering the raised queries and it was only towards the end of the discussion that Hirov bought up the question of their accommodation.

"Now that's a very topical point and I'm glad you asked me because I was about to come on to that. Your meeting with our chancellor Mr Jerry Rodgers could be viewed by some as an opportunity to protest at whatever they want to protest about, and we would rather not put yourselves in the invidious position of having to explain yourself to the hostile press that will have been alerted. These protesters will likely have been tipped off if your visit were official… which it would have had to have been if you were staying at your embassy." What he didn't add was that it would also save Jerry Rodgers some face. "Some hardcore protesters have a

Chapter 16 - Twist

knack of turning a genuine protest into a street brawl which obviously won't do either yourselves or our government any good."

"That's very astute of you." Hirov was referring to the entire arrangements rather than crediting Mr Johnson personally; he was only the messenger. "Is this level of security normal?"

"Oh yes, but only because we recently received intelligence that there may be an attempt on your life while you're here in the UK, and we certainly wouldn't want that happening." Johnson tried to make his voice sound as mundane as possible. "But let me assure you that this is rather typical and there's rarely a visiting government official that doesn't come with a death threat." He leaned forward in an avuncular manner and added jokingly, "It's just another world-class service that we provide."

Hirov marvelled at the British sense of humour. "Even though I have my own two bodyguards in the next room."

"Yes, we're very used to this sort of thing which is why we do our best not to let anything happen." Glancing at his watch, he continued, "We are very pleased to chaperone you around to all your appointments over the next couple of days and I think you will find that there's a car with a driver, an additional car for your own bodyguards together with another one for our own security details. I expect they're waiting downstairs for you now." He produced a business card. "Here are my contact details should you need me; day or night."

***

Justin was familiar with The Lancaster from his previous visits and knew all that Patricia had to learn. She followed him through various back doors and corridors as he pointed out useful shortcuts, service elevators, laundry chutes, fuse boxes, hydrants, and by the time they had finished, she felt like she had just emerged from a rabbit warren. He even introduced her to a couple of the staff whom he had got to know by name over the years, so handing over a master pass key was no problem. Back in their basic room on the second floor, she flopped down in the chair to rest her feet; in particular her toes, some of which had turned blue.

"Double aspect windows so if we want, we can keep an eye out on two fronts. The problem with this hotel is that the two main entrances are diametrically opposite each other which makes it impossible for one person to see who's coming and going unless they're sitting in the lobby."

"Which presumably we'll be doing a lot of."

"No. You haven't quite got the gist of professional surveillance yet, have you?" Justin stopped drawing on a pad of paper on the desk and looked at her. "You stay in one place for more than a few minutes and you'll be spotted by whoever is on the lookout. It's all too easy to pick a comfy chair, order up a coffee, pick up a newspaper and stagnate, so we tend to move about a bit, swap places, talk to strangers, change clothing... use our imagination etcetera. Hana knows what we look like but he can only have given our description to his lackeys, so I reckon if there's an attempt in the hotel, we'll have the advantage."

"Unless it's going to be Hana himself."

"Like you say, unless it's Hana himself, but if I were him I'd send in a couple of chaps to sound out the level of security first, so they'll probably saunter in and take a circuitous route to reception. They'll ask something inane like how to get to Tower Bridge for example, which'll take time giving them the opportunity to look round." He held up the pad of paper he'd been drawing on which showed the basic outline of the reception area and pointed out various vantage points and sightlines. "But here's an easy one. We could borrow a white board on an A-frame from the hotel and set it up in the reception area, draw something irrelevant on it as quite often somebody asks, and this makes us look as though we're supposed to be there and gives us a legitimate excuse for hanging about."

"Sounds perfect, but how about adding a name tag to stick on one's lapel? We'd look even more official then." Patricia was pleased with herself that she had come up with an idea.

Justin gave a half-laugh. "Yes, that's been done before but so long as one doesn't do what a colleague of mine did a few years back. As a bit of a joke and to see how observant his boss was, he printed his lapel name as Fred Flintstone."

"And..."

"His boss, and mine later, was observant and demoted him out of the squad."

"I suppose they had a bit of a 'barney' then."

Justin nearly groaned at the reference to Flintstone's neighbour Barney Rubble. "Come on then, let's go and have coffee in the lobby and remember, we're stuck in this hotel for two days so there's no need to rush anything."

They had hardly taken the first sip from the cups when Justin recognised someone from his old detail walking towards them, and he motioned that he was welcome to join them on one of the spare chairs.

"Ed, meet my fiancée, Patricia and before you ask, yes she's cleared. Coffee?"

Ed briefly glanced at Patricia; professionally. "No thanks. This can't be a coincidence... you sitting here when we've a hot target to look after."

"No coincidence, but even though I've left The Squad I've other strings to my bow and happen to be working for another department of HMG at the moment. I'm not surprised you haven't been told as we're just keeping an eye on things."

"Reporting back to the boss more likely."

"How's our target this morning?"

"I haven't seen him but apparently he's off to the Bank of England any time now." He looked up at the lobby clock. "He'll be taking the lift straight to the underground car park, so whatever you're up to here looks like being wasted."

"Just enjoying the coffee and keeping Patricia happy."

Ed cocked his ear in automation just a little. "Must dash." He went to move away.

"Ed. Don't tell the others we're here."

Chapter 16 - Twist

When he was out of earshot, Patricia asked Justin, "Good guy or bad?"

"Oh, Ed's alright. Just don't ask him to put his hand in his pocket when it comes to buying the next round though. Talking of which, did you notice that chap wandering through to the bar area? Don't look round," he hurriedly added.

"Should I have done?"

"Not particularly, but he didn't quite fit the profile of someone who's staying at the hotel. Stay here… I'll go and look at the menu."

She knew he meant that he was going to use that as an excuse for looking into the bar-cum-restaurant and decided she really ought to start paying more attention to who was around. By the time Justin got back, she was paranoid.

"The chap at reception's been there far too long and there's a strong-looking woman standing by the lifts who's been playing with her phone, and I'm not too sure about the man sitting behind you."

Justin sat back in his chair, adjusted his pose and sipped his coffee. "Reception desk man is North American and asking where he and his wife can get a decent hamburger, the woman by the lifts is waiting for her daughter to come out of the toilet further down and the man behind me looks too innocent; too large round the middle."

The look on her face said it all. "Well how about giving me some on-the-spot training as we're sitting here not doing too much. Explain to me how to spot a terrorist."

Slips Catch

"Oh they're easy to spot... they're the ones with bulges in their pockets."

"What the bloody hell are you talking about?"

"Instead of balls between their legs they carry handgrenades in their pockets."

"And what about the female terrorist; what does she look like?"

Justin started to describe Patricia before his foot got stamped on. Nevertheless, an hour or so later she felt a little more confident and an hour after that and knowing that Hirov was going to be busy until well into the afternoon, they took up positions in their room overlooking the entrance. It took a while before boredom set in and a short while later they found themselves in a long-overdue amorous embrace on the bed, followed by a shared shower.

The sharp rain shower had moved on depositing pollen and other verdant debris collecting kerbside, leaving a crisp sunny afternoon. Patricia grabbed a book and sat right at the back of the lobby. Contrary to what she had been told about not staying in one place, they had agreed that in this hotel it would be worth the risk and to any onlooker she was totally engrossed. Justin took in the fresh air by walking the outside perimeter and spending a while sitting on a park bench next to the Italian Gardens across the road in Kensington Gardens. He remembered that one of his duties soon after he had joined The Squad had been to do just this at another hotel, and to pass the time he started to note down on his phone the taxis who were dropping off or collecting guests and decided to include delivery drivers as the

Chapter 16 - Twist

cabs weren't really that frequent. There was no pattern to all the comings and goings and to his mind, all was as it should be. So engrossed had he been that when Hirov's entourage returned it took him a few seconds to realise he had been noting the time of their arrival so he shut-up-shop and went to join Patricia in the lobby.

He decided to test her powers of observation and was a little disappointed when, as he crept up behind her chair, all he got was a "hello stranger" before he even got close.

"Fancy a drink as it's well gone six o'clock? G&T?"

She looked over the rim of her book at him. "I suppose this ought to count as expenses as we're keeping up a pretence."

"Huh. Some pretence and fat chance."

"They haven't come across my womanly charms yet, so keep the receipt. Do I look like I'm pretending? Guinness for me please."

Justin had to admit she blended in well. "What's the book? You seem well into it."

She flicked the cover briefly so that he could see its title. "It's a fascinating story of a Lieutenant Colonel in the Royal Engineers during the second world war. I didn't think I'd like it but it's engrossing and so far he's spent most of his time blowing up things rather than building them. Right up your street."

Justin turned to fill her request and drummed his fingers on the countertop while waiting to be served at the bar. Typically of bars around the world, the etched mirrors behind the bottles made it seem like there were an awful lot more spirits to choose from and he looked up at the angled-bevelled mirrors just above him. His mind started to wander and he wasn't really thinking about the job in hand, but there was something not quite right about what was going on behind him. He nonchalantly turned to look directly outside in favour of looking at the reflection but couldn't see anything or anyone out of the ordinary. He couldn't put his finger on it, but there was a niggle in his own mind that he ought to have paid attention to. The barman interrupted his thoughts and when he turned back to look outside, the tenuous thread was gone.

He persuaded Patricia to put her book down. "Something's not right... not sure if it's inside or out but I've a feeling I've missed something."

They fruitlessly batted ideas and possibilities about. "Why don't you go to the bar and see if you can spot anything? Ask for some nuts or whatever."

It took her five minutes. "You're nuts." She let the small glass bowl drop onto the table and hurriedly went to stop it tipping over the side.

"Nothing?"

"It all looks normal to me, but then again, I haven't your trained eye."

"That's the problem... it isn't trained enough."

"Just enough to know when something's amiss eh?"

"More or less. More of a feeling and less of anything tangible."

They sat in silence for several moments occasionally looking at people toing and froing, trying to guess.

"I'll tell you what." Patricia rose from her chair. "I'll take a walk round outside while you ogle the leggy brunette that's just walked in."

Justin glanced over at reception. "Can I frisk her?"

Chapter 16 - Twist

"Shouldn't take long with what she's not wearing."

Patricia took her time and saw that Justin had made a mess of the peanuts over the table. "Stopped dribbling yet?"

"Naah. Not worth it... but her sister was," he teased.

"All quiet outside." She had slurped most of her Guinness. "Here, let's have a look at that list of taxis on your phone, I might spot something." She handed it back after scrolling through. "You're probably not very hungry as you've scoffed most of the peanuts, but I fancy a bite. Restaurant?"

"I thought you'd never ask."

Towards the end of their main course, Patricia received a text on her phone. "I've got an update on Hirov's schedule tomorrow, but I can't access it without my laptop. Do you reckon we're getting the same information as the Diplomatic Squad boys?"

He finished chewing before answering. "Now that's a very good question, and the only way to find out is by comparing one with the other."

"Well, we can do that can't we? Would your friend Ed cooperate?"

"Probably... if he's still here."

"If he's not here now, then presumably he will be in the morning."

"Probably."

"So why don't we finish up here and do what we've got to do?"

It was gone midnight by the time they returned to their room, having had another walkabout and a comparison with Ed.

"There's as much security in this hotel as what Hamilton usually requires, and we know there are several people who want to see him dead," remarked Justin as he fingered the TV remote.

Patricia emerged from the en suite. "OK then, let's break it down as we did when we figured out how that attempt on Hamilton was going to happen." She sat down in the other chair facing Justin. "If Hana's going to try to assassinate Hirov, then how would he do it? We know he's a sniper, we know he blows people up using propane cannisters, we know he likes to set fire to places. We know he's in London and we know his target, so it can't be beyond our reasoning as to how he's likely to go about it."

"He also knows you and I are involved and we're probably his next target."

"But he doesn't know our whereabouts does he? So let's use that to our advantage if we get the chance."

"Okaaay." Justin drew-out the affirmation.

Patricia held her index finger upright. "Sniping. He's not going to get much of a shot while Hirov's in his room as he's on the top floor and this is the tallest building for several hundred yards around, so that leaves while he's in the car or arriving at whatever location he's going to. Suppose he waits directly across where the underground car park joins the road? He could even get one of his chaps to stall a car in the right place so that Hirov's car is stationary."

"I suspect the car will have bullet-proof glass."

"What if he's using a high-powered rifle at short range? Would that penetrate?"

Chapter 16 - Twist

"It might?"

She could sense his negativity from his sceptical tone, so she discarded that line of thought. "How about an RPG? That…"

"No good. Remember he likes to keep an invisible profile so anything that's remotely attributable is not an option. He'll set up something that when investigated could be put down to shoddy workmanship, metal fatigue, act of god, or anything other than the actions of a terrorist."

"Unless Bayev's ordered him to send a message to the outside world and make it public."

"You don't half make life difficult sometimes," Justin growled.

"It's a possibility."

He was about to reply 'and so is landing a man on the moon', but as that had actually happened on more than one occasion, decided that her argument couldn't be totally discarded. "OK, OK, but we can come back to that if nothing else fits. What was the second thing you said?"

"Errr, blowing people up with gas cannisters and setting fires, but I've left out plain old thuggery and I'll bet you he's used a knife before."

She watched his frown grow at the mention of gas cannisters; he was clearly trying to put two and two together but nothing added up. "Look… there's no way he can smuggle a gas cannister even outside Hirov's room let alone in it, and if there's a fire, the hotel alarm and sprinkler system will activate."

"Unless it's been disabled."

He focused on her. "You might have something there, but what guarantee does he have that Hirov will be the victim?"

"He'd have to deactivate the lifts and block the staircase."

"No, no, no, no. There are too many variables."

"Why don't we go and check?"

Justin looked at his watch. "We're not going to be popular if we accidentally set off the fire alarm at this time of night."

"Then we'll just have to be careful then, because whatever Hana's planning might just be happening right now." Patricia slipped on her shoes, then paused. "And here's another thought. He's only got a little over twenty-four hours to do it."

"If he's going to do it in the UK."

"Now who's making life difficult?"

Chapter 17

The face of the enemy

After their preliminary session on fixed cycle machines in the underground gym followed by a brisk trot around the perimeter including in and out of Hyde Park via the Serpentine Bridge, they tucked into a relatively unhealthy breakfast.

"Hirov's got a busy schedule today culminating this evening in a soiree at the Bulgarian embassy which is a stone's throw across the park here, then flying out of Heathrow at noon tomorrow." Patricia sipped at her second cup with elbows on table and waited for a response. "Coffee's not too bad for you is it and pink marshmallows taste like they've been thrown up by Bugs Bunny."

Justin wasn't paying attention but was looking at the mirrored wall behind her. "Uuuhuhhh."

"Hoi. What you thinking about?" She gently kicked his leg under the table.

He refocused his eyes to Patricia's proximity. "Not pink marshmallows that's for sure."

"Well give me a clue then."

"You know yesterday when I came back with your pint of Guinness and said I wasn't one hundred per cent happy... well looking in that mirror behind you reminded me, but I still can't see what was bothering me."

She turned round to look at the wall behind her that was almost entirely mirrored. "Just as well you hadn't cut yourself shaving otherwise you might have recognised yourself," she jibed.

She recognised he was in deep thought and let silence prevail for the next few minutes but eventually bought it to an end. "Right. Time to move on. If you can't put your finger on whatever's bothering you now, go and stand in the same position at the bar and see if anything comes to mind."

He did exactly that after breakfast while she waited just in his sightline in the lobby, but after five minutes, he wandered over to her. "I don't know... I just don't know what I saw and it didn't come back to me."

"Might it have been the barman? He's obviously not there now as it's closed, but somebody else perhaps?"

"No, not the barman, I've dismissed him. He was real alright. Saw him making cocktails later and it takes skill to do that. Not something you casually pick up on your way to work if you know what I mean."

"Well then. What are we going to do for the rest of the day?"

They spent it inspecting laundry rooms, cellars, fire escapes, the showers in the gym, and every possible cupboard off the behind-the-scenes corridors. They visited the hushed, heavily carpeted corridors of the top floors and checked every room that had a 'keep locked' sign on it. They stopped and chatted to some of

Chapter 17 - The face of the enemy

the staff but none of them had seen anything out of the ordinary. They unlocked and locked access cupboards in the underground car park and ensured the electrically operated gate was working correctly. Patricia cursed at the lack of phone signal as her mobile beeped just once indicating that she had a missed call. There wasn't enough space to sit down in the room that housed the security video recorders, and they strolled outside and in the park on two occasions.

From their vantage point in their room and with six o'clock on the horizon, they saw Hirov's cars approaching down Bayswater Road.

"We could nip down to the underground car park and have a word with his security detail," suggested Patricia.

"Let's not. Remember we're not officially here as far as they're concerned."

"I'll bet you they do know we're here."

"You're probably right, but unless they actually see us then they can't report mere hearsay. What I'd like to do is wander across the park and see what the Bulgarian embassy looks like; when Hirov happens to be there of course, but I suppose we need to follow instructions and stay in the hotel." He looked at his watch. "He's probably only come back to change as he's due there in a few minutes. I don't envy his schedule."

"I'm not sure I envy ours. This is starting to get boring."

"Well it'll only be boring for another eighteen hours or so, and a little of that will be spent sleeping."

It took her a second or so to cotton on to what he said. "What do you mean by a little?"

"It's logical isn't it? If Hana hasn't succeeded by now, then his window of opportunity will be tonight only, so we're going to have to take it in turns to see him coming. Before you point out that it's The Squad's job, just think back as to why the commander put us here." He watched Patricia blink and lightly nibble her bottom lip and continued when he saw that she had come to the same conclusion as he had. "It's not going to do our reputation much good if we allow Hana to succeed on our watch, is it?"

They watched Hirov and his party return not long after midnight, Patricia from the room and Justin through the window in the bar area. He had just enough time to take the stairs down to the underground garage and hide in a relatively unlit corner to watch the party disgorge. There was nobody lurking in the shadows and no unexpected movement, so he returned to their room.

With only borrowed light from London's street lamps, from the corner of the room next to the window that gave him a good view, he watched his fiancée as she snuggled down to sleep. So beautiful. So serene. So... his attention waivered, but not so much that he didn't miss the lone hooded figure, head down, as they shuffled along the pavement in the direction of the hotel. At first he thought it was someone turning up for their shift when they disappeared towards the staff entrance, but it was getting on for a minute later when his somnolent mind decided to wake up a little. Despite his drowsy state, his mind casually started to question why someone would turn up for work at two something in the morning. He shifted his seated position, then stood

Chapter 17 - The face of the enemy

up and stretched; yawning was virtually mandatory. People don't usually go to work at two or three in the morning even in a busy London hotel. Do they? What job would require a shift change at that particular hour and where would a lone worker be? Bit early for a chef. Perhaps one of the laundry staff, but he discarded that idea as he knew that the hotel's laundry was picked up and returned in a large van. He started to tick off other occupations and came to the conclusion that one wouldn't normally come into work in the small hours unless one worked in an airport, post office, or the like.

Now he was fully awake and that little niggle was starting to ping around his head. Without waking Patricia, he silently went to the ensuite, splashed some water on his face over the basin and looked at himself in the mirror trying to decipher what the headstrong pin ball was trying to tell him as it bounced off the sides. Something was out of kilter; or at the very least, required investigation. He put his shoes back on with the aim of questioning the night manager in reception, and on his way out, he spent a valuable few seconds looking down at his serene fiancée's face.

The night manager's name was Paul from Senegal; easy to remember thought Justin. Paul stood to one side as he reviewed the security footage in the small room and watched the hooded man enter the staff entrance, then go along the corridor and enter the utility lift in the far corner. Nothing anywhere after that.

"Where's that lift go?" The instant he asked he wished he hadn't. "No don't bother, but does it go down as well as up?"

"No. Only up."

"All the way to the top?"

"All the way."

Even though Justin had been in the lift before, he hadn't checked to see how far it went. "Just through there and turn left, isn't it?"

He didn't wait for a reply as he rushed out the door and reached for his mobile at the same time. He was about to press the lift call button then stopped his finger a mere inch away. If he did press the button and the wall-mounted number-counter started counting either up or down, and if the hooded man was looking, then he would know that somebody was after him. There was also the matter of noise as the sound of an elevator travelling in either direction tends to make a specific sound. Justin swiftly ran along the corridor, round a corner and along another short corridor, through a set of swing doors and he entered the lobby foyer where the guest lifts were.

"Wake up damn you…" as he pressed a button.

A drowsy Patricia answered as the doors closed behind him. "I think Hana's in the building… hello… hello. Shit… poxy phone signals."

All Patricia heard was a crackled '…shit…'. She hadn't undressed when she had lain down on the bed and it now took her less than thirty seconds to pass the webbing of her holster through her arms, holster her Browning and be out of the room. She had already thought about what she would do before nodding off, and headed for the vestibule that housed both the lift and the staircase. A glance at the lift told her that it was

Chapter 17 - The face of the enemy

going up and she did likewise via the stairs, not even slowing down to call the lift to her floor. Her aim was simple. If Hirov's life was in danger, then she needed to be near him, on the fifteenth floor.

As the lift doors opened, Justin walked slowly out showing his hands well in front of him for the simple reason that he didn't want to get shot.

"Three paces forwards and keep your hands where I can see them."

Justin complied and saw half a head and a pair of arms holding a revolver from behind the corner of a wall. The gun was, of course, pointing at him.

"My name's Justin Crawford and I used to be with you lot. My presence here is sanctioned and I've come to warn you that there's someone here to try to assassinate Kiril Hirov."

Silence for a moment.

"How do we know it's not you?"

"Are you kidding…? I haven't even got a knife let alone a gun. Look."

The half head turned into a full head and a tall man warily took a pace into the open. "What do you think Tab?"

Justin kept his hands high but looked down the corridor towards Hirov's room and saw Tab's outline in the shadows of the darkened corridor; darkened no doubt to give himself the advantage. On top of that, Justin though the man was dark-skinned making it even more difficult to see him.

"I remember seeing the name Justin Crawford, but I never met him. How do we know who you are?"

Justin wasn't prepared for this line of questioning but started rattling off names of his former colleagues and after about the tenth one, the man nearest him lowered his revolver. Justin decided to call him number one. "OK... OK... that's enough. Ed mentioned he'd come across an old friend yesterday and that you weren't officially here, but why are you here?"

Justin told them and noted that Tab professionally stayed in the shadows.

"No one's come up here since we got back," said number one.

"Well, that hoodie came into the building and hasn't left, so he must be here somewhere."

Their ears picked up as they heard running footsteps. Tab stayed where he was, number one resumed his half-hidden position and Justin backed into a niche next to the lift and half-hid behind a tall pedestal-mounted aspidistra.

Patricia burst through the swing door from the stairway and Justin shouted that she was with him. He didn't want her getting shot at either.

She bent double and rested her forearms on her thighs. The others looked on while she got her breath back, and once she more or less had, the discussion about the hooded man continued. Even Tab came closer. One thing they had to agree on was that there was no way anyone could get to Hirov, his aide or his guards along that corridor.

"That leaves one option only. Outside." Patricia stated what the others were just beginning to think.

They all looked at each other. "Roof," three of them said in unison.

Chapter 17 - The face of the enemy

"You two stay here and keep an eye on the windows. We'll go and check it out. Get your passkey ready," Patricia said as she and Justin headed for the stairway. Before he pressed his electronic key to the pad, Patricia readied her Browning. There was no barging the door open noisily and no shouting; they went quietly through the doorway and onto the roof, separated a few feet from each other, and hid in the shadow of a large air conditioning unit.

"We never thought to check the roof, did we?"

"Why not?"

"I'd have thought you'd have had enough of roofs lately."

She didn't need to say anything.

Their half-whispers couldn't have been heard more than ten feet away over the noise of the big fan motors as they looked around the rooftop which was flat, other than other aircon units, aerials and several vent pipes. But then Justin spotted the window-cleaning gantry at the far end. "You go left, I'll go right and watch behind you. Meet you at that gantry, but quietly."

They skitted from shadow to shadow occasionally looking to see what the other was doing en route to the twin hangers of the window-cleaning platform located near one of the corners.

"Nothing here," said Patricia raising her voice a little as she holstered her pistol.

"Well where did bloody hoodie go?"

"Maybe he was a guest who didn't want to be seen creeping back in the small hours."

"Via the tradesman's entrance?"

"It's possible."

"I don't believe it because he didn't show up on any of the CCTVs on each floor. There isn't a camera on this door because nobody comes up here except maintenance men and they don't start working at two o'clock in the morning, so he's got to be up here somewhere."

Had there been enough light, Patricia would have seen the desperate look on his face as he looked about forlornly. "Hang on a mo… what's that there?"

A few feet away was a pile of discarded cables, pipes, ropes and boxes. In the gloom it looked like a couple of tarpaulins draped over some crates which were part sticking out underneath.

"Ready?" Justin asked. Patricia readied herself with her Browning as Justin yanked back one tarpaulin, then flicked it further to reveal exactly what they had both thought it was – left-over materials.

"Wow." She took a sharp step backwards as did Justin. The unmistakable sweet smell of gas overwhelmed both of them for a moment to such an extent that it made them both gasp.

Walking a few paces away to breathe in fresh air, Justin spoke first. "Now we know what hoodie was doing." Before he could say anything further, hoodie detached himself from the shadow of one of the aircon units and clobbered Justin over the head with something. Patricia watched him collapse and with frightening speed the attacker was on to her with a midriff headbutt, knocking the Browning out of her hand. He was lifting her towards the edge of the roof and with horror she realised that he intended to push her over the side.

Chapter 17 - The face of the enemy

She hadn't recovered fully from sucking in a substantial quantity of gas, seeing her fiancée assaulted, and now about to be murdered; and all within the space of a few seconds. A few weeks ago she probably would have cried out or screamed and was on the verge of doing so, but as she sensed the fast-approaching lip of the roof, somehow her training kicked in. She shifted her right leg so that it tripped her attacker up, and at the same time grabbed his other leg. He went sprawling and she heard him grunt as he landed, but the momentum was just enough to carry Patricia over the edge. Falling, she couldn't reach the disappearing concrete lip and before she knew it, she had landed on the suspended window-cleaning platform several feet below. Despite being dazed and unable to focus her eyes, she thought she saw the outline of what looked like hoodie peering down at her; and then he disappeared from sight. She closed her eyes, explored the sharp pain on her left side and felt for the bump on her head. She tried to get up but found it extremely difficult to move a muscle, so she opened her eyes again in the hope of being able to see how far she had fallen and thought it was about ten or fifteen feet. It was difficult to tell in the darkness.

Her eyes opened wide when she felt the platform abruptly jerk and if it were possible, widened them further because only one side of the platform was moving. Down. Within a few seconds, the angle steepened to such an extent that she needed to grab hold of something to stop herself sliding off the side and this time she had no trouble in moving. She scrabbled for anything remotely solid as she felt her feet slip off the edge and for the second time in only a few days, was momentarily in the precarious position of dangling over a very unhealthy long drop to certain death. She looked around in desperation to see if there was any sort of rope to cling on to but all she could find was one of the abrasive steel hawsers that suspended the platform; and that was far too thin to hang on to for long. Nearing the vertical, the platform suddenly stopped moving but then the entire stage started to ascend. Straight away she knew hoodie was bringing her up so that he could finish her off. She had perhaps twenty or thirty seconds before she would be within his reach, but then she saw him heft some sort of metal bar in his hands and guessed he aimed to clobber her on the head as it levelled with the lip of the building. Her stark choice would be to either let go and end up on the concrete below or hang on and be beaten until she let go. It was all she could do to hang on, let alone defend herself, and a wave of desperate anger flooded over her. She was determined that she would not die at the hands of this scum and braced herself to swing her legs up and kick him while she still could.

She almost cried out when she realised she would never be able to reach him and watched helplessly as he raised what looked like a big crowbar. As he was about to strike, he brushed back his hood with his free hand so that she would know who it was that was going to kill her. She could just about make out his smile.

Wallop.

On the very point of bringing the iron bar down on her head, what looked like a weighty plank of

Chapter 17 - The face of the enemy

wood thudded into hoodie's head and she watched him go down. She had no option but to hold on while the platform continued its ascent. The unthinkable happened. The top edge of the platform had reached its 'stop' point and it did exactly that, transferring the entire weight of the platform onto the lower pair of hawsers as they struggled to continue lifting. The system had clearly been designed so that a hawser on each corner would comfortably raise and lower the platform with two people on; even three cables would have managed it, but with only two… and both of those were on the same end. She could hear a creaking noise as they stretched under the extra weight but they continued to wind the platform towards the concrete lip. Her only hope was to hang on until it raised up enough for her to swing herself onto the concrete lip of the roof, but she wasn't certain she could reach it.

Another creak and the definite sound of cables snapping… just another few feet… please she thought… just another few feet. The quiver of the cable parting above her made her look up. This time she did scream. Her fingers were inches from the pulley wheel which would undoubtedly take them clean off and leave her to plummet. She needed more room where her fingers were, less room from the building, and more time to work out how to go about getting those things. None were available. She swung towards the building just as the cable parted with a loud crack and she managed to curl the ends of her fingers onto the lip but almost immediately knew she couldn't hold that position for more than a few seconds. She felt rather than saw the whoosh of the platform as it disappeared from under her, and cruelly, part of the hawser whipped at her legs as it was pulled down. With no strength left in her fingers, she let go at the same that Justin's hand appeared and grabbed her wrist. She cried out in pain once again as her wrist dislocated and she bought her other hand over to grasp whatever she could to ease the agony and found the lip again. It felt like her hand was being separated from her arm, but Justin's other hand came to the rescue and with grunting and gasping, pulled Patricia over the lip and onto the safety of the flat roof.

Neither of them counted or were even aware of time as they both lay there panting and gasping. Justin had blood covering half his face and limiting vision in his right eye, while Patricia struggled to work out which part of her body hurt the most. Feeling like an eternity but in fact in very little time at all, Justin raised himself, stood over Patricia and bent down to tap her gently on one shoulder.

Her immediate response was "Aaagh" as she shifted herself from the foetal position.

"You're still alive then."

After a racking heave of her lungs, she replied by turning the air blue, but she managed to slowly roll over onto her back and gaze up at the starry night.

"Which hand do you want a hand up with?" Justin's shadow asked.

"Neither... I'll do it myself," she coughed.

Once he had vanished from view, she gingerly rolled back over, manoeuvred herself onto all fours and stood nearly upright. Looking around, she couldn't see him.

Chapter 17 - The face of the enemy

"Over here," came the response from the blackness of the shadow of an aircon unit.

"What are you doing?" she asked as he dragged the unconscious body into the open.

"I've trussed him up with that rope we saw earlier. There's no way he's getting out of that but I still don't trust the bugger. Keep an eye on him, will you?"

"Where are you going now?"

"To find out where that stench of gas is coming from, and don't even think of using your mobile."

Her nose told her that Hana's penchant for utilising propane was still very much with them, despite him being out of action and for the first time in several minutes she turned her mind to the main reason they had come onto the roof. When she looked down to look at the entwined body, all she could see was the vague outline of someone bound with rope. Just the mere thought of what he had tried to do to her sent her into a rage but as she brought her leg back to kick him where it would hurt, she stopped, for two reasons. It hurt her to move her leg and she couldn't see where to aim. She swore at him instead.

Justin returned. "Get back downstairs and tell them to move Hirov to another room, preferably at the other end of the building without turning on any lights, and then get number one up here; not Tab though. Then ring Tates and get more help."

"Why move Hirov now?"

"Because that bugger has drilled a hole in the roof and piped a couple of cannisters of propane into the roof space directly above his room. With gas being heavier than air, it'll be sinking and if the fumes don't kill anyone in the rooms below, then the first time they turn a light on the spark will set off an explosion that'll probably take the corner of the building out. Make no mistake, until that gas has dissipated, we're all in danger, so watch it. In fact, we know Hirov likes his cigars so let's just pray that he's asleep right now and not awake. That's probably what Hana was counting on. Cigars."

She didn't need any repetition, and as she turned to follow Justin's instructions, she caught her already painful foot on her Browning. She put it back where it belonged. Rather than run across the roof and sprint down the stairs, she took it a little easier as her body complained with almost every movement, but the pain was generally easing. Or it could have been that her mind was concentrating on what she was about to do.

It took her a while to persuade 'number one' with Tab listening in the background but the convincer was when Tab thought he smelled gas. The three of them sniffed and after a brief look at each other, they sprang into action. Number one and Tab in Hirov's direction while Patricia backtracked to the ventilated stairwell, got on her mobile and reported to Tates.

She found out later that Hirov's bodyguards had gone round opening every window they could find before allowing their charge to leave his room. It was that kind of Eastern European logic that Patricia couldn't fathom, but nevertheless, all of them managed to relocate to the other end of the hotel in an unused suite. While this was going on, more officers from the

Chapter 17 - The face of the enemy

Diplomatic Squad arrived and Patricia squared things with their senior in charge before returning to the roof with two of them to watch over Hana. When they arrived, she got a shock.

"It's not Hana," announced Justin as they neared. He turned the torch on his mobile on and shone it in the face of the bound man who was now conscious.

Patricia's mind raced as she pictured herself as she rose on the platform no more than fifteen minutes ago. So intent had she been on staying alive and grabbing the concrete lip that she hadn't taken in that her assailant hadn't been Hana. The man at her feet looked a little like him, but a younger version. She crouched down for a closer look at the bloodied face, then smashed her fist into his face twice before Justin caught her arm. He pulled her upright and held her tight. "I've already done that for you," he whispered into her ear.

She backed away a little. "Bastard shithead tried to kill me… and you come to that. Let's throw him off the edge like he tried to do to me." There was real venom in her voice.

"I'll get his feet, you get his head… but only after we've questioned him." If Justin could have seen the look in her eyes, he would have quailed, despite being her fiancé.

"Why fucking bother?"

"Because we don't know where Hana is yet." Justin had to raise his voice to get through to her.

"Fuck." She stamped her foot and spun round simultaneously, instantly regretting it as it sent painful shockwaves through her leg and torso. "Well let's get on with it then and perhaps he'll tell us where the bugger's hiding." She turned to the pair of Squad officers. "Either of you got a knife? I'll gouge his fucking eyes out first."

They tried to look at each other in the greyness without answering.

"Not a good idea here," Justin quietly interjected then looked at the pair. "Take him away, chaps, while he's still alive."

Patricia turned and huffed her way to a point not far from the pile of building materials and was instantly reminded of gas from the hanging odour. Justin joined her after watching the body being carried towards the roof exit.

"Much as I would have liked to twist the bloke's bollocks until he told us where Hana is, I don't think it's quite compatible with our status as human beings… or that of Special Branch."

She was about to retort that he wasn't there on the platform, but checked herself as it was Justin who had knocked him out with a bulk of timber.

"Well he can rot in fucking hell then," he said resignedly knowing that he'd be taken to a secure cell somewhere secret and therefore beyond her reach.

"Come and have a look at this so you can see what kind of a man thinks up these nefarious schemes."

Dawn wasn't too far off, and from the reflection of the lightening sky she saw that Justin had pulled back the tarpaulin all the way revealing six orange propane cylinders. Two of them were twinned together with orange tubing that disappeared down a hole a few feet away, while the rest were patently empty from the way

Chapter 17 - The face of the enemy

Justin rocked one. "There's another couple of holes here as well, hence the need for the tarpaulin to stop the gas being wafted away."

"That would have been some explosion." She recalled being at a warehouse some years ago when the fire brigade had tried to make an adjacent caravan safe by towing it away. No sooner had they decided upon that course of action than the cylinder inside had caught and the entire caravan instantly disintegrated dozens of feet in all directions. She had been told that that had been a five-kilogramme cylinder. These on the roof were forty-eights, nearly ten times the size. Six of them with their deadly gas having seeped into the confines of the hotel's structure.

Her mind ignored the aches and pains that pervaded her body as it absorbed what Justin was telling her. "Is this all of them?"

"Eh?"

"All of them... did he leave any more?"

A worried looking Justin started looking around; then they both started to re-examine the rest of the roof. It was so much easier to walk across in the growing daylight and they converged on the opposite corner. It only took one minute to see that there were no other piles of discarded materials or tarpaulins.

"Well how about elsewhere in the building and how did he get all this up here without being noticed?" probed Patricia.

Justin was about to shrug his shoulders but instead his jaw dropped. "Oh shit. Now I know what's been niggling me the past couple of days." He clenched his teeth and raised his fists to the heavens. "Oh the sneaky bastard... and it was in my face the whole time. Aaarrghhh."

She waited for him to calm down instead of rushing him.

"You know I said I thought there was something unusual when I came back from the bar with your pint of Guinness? Well, I know what it was now. The angled mirror between the wall and the ceiling reflected outside, and it was an open-sided gas delivery van that I must have seen." He closed his eyes trying to reconfirm the image.

"Oh I don't think anyone could blame you for not querying that."

"Oh yes they can because immediately before that I was sitting outside and noting who was coming and going and I saw that same van come and go." He reached into his pocket for his phone, tapped it a few times and retrieved his notes. "Look here... it says arrived 17.01 and left 17.32 Vauxhall van. I was at the bar buying Guinness about an hour after that and when I saw the same van return via the mirror, it didn't click."

"If you're right, then that's how he got all this stuff up here."

"What, all of it including the crates and tarpaulin?" He swept his arm round.

"You said you saw him arrive so he could have spent half the night shifting this up here. The crate was probably here in the first place."

"I'll bet you he had someone to help him 'cos those cylinders ain't light and that someone was probably that chap who's now under arrest."

Chapter 17 - The face of the enemy

"Hang on a mo... you said you saw the van arrive... did you see it leave?"

He thought about that for a moment. "No, but that doesn't mean it didn't as neither of us could see the exit."

"That's not what I'm getting at. The van could still be here... in the underground car park."

The instant reaction bought forth an expletive. "Oh fuck, If it's still here then..."

They both raced for the roof exit. "Probably not yet safe to take the lift yet," panted Justin. As they passed the top floor and tramped on down the concrete stairs the sickly smell of gas filled their nostrils, but they didn't notice that it disappeared once they reached the next level. Patricia, trying to ignore her complaining body as she leapt two steps at a time, desperately tried to work out Hana's strategy and came up with a frightening scenario. If the van was still in the car park then it would probably have other gas bottles, including exploding ones. She was beginning to wonder if charging into the basement was such a good idea.

"Justin. Wait!" she shouted as he was getting too far ahead.

He stopped, turned and waited a few seconds for Patricia to catch up. He was about to resume his headlong rush, when she shouted again. "Stop!" So he did.

"Wait just a sec." Patricia was in quite a bad way and she leaned against the wall while gasping. "The van might be another bomb."

Justin considered what she had said while she gulped down some more air.

"Think about it... He's not one for leaving things to chance very much and if he wants to ensure Hirov dies, then he'd need some way of detonating the gas." Gasp, gasp. "Hoping that Hirov's going to light his cigar in his room at the right time is asking too much." Gasp. "Don't you think?"

Justin thought. "Double bollocks... you're right. If only we had a radio."

She waved her mobile. "I'll talk to Tates."

"I'd talk to the Commander as well, but do it while we get a move on. Let's get outside rather than head for the car park."

Another flight of stairs brought more expletives from Patricia. "No fucking signal... what is it about bloody phones. Never give you a signal when you want one."

They emerged outside through a side door; off to their right the wreckage of the platform was strewn across the building-side of the wall adjacent to the outside car park but unusually had not set off any car alarms. While Patricia paced further from the hotel trying to get a signal, Justin looked up and saw a few of the rooms had lights on, presumably because guests were wondering what the noise had been all about. Approaching sirens could be heard and in no time at all the familiar dazzling blues and reds of cars lurched to a halt at random places around the hotel. Some were saloon cars while others were the larger Range Rovers all liveried with the familiar blue and orange reflective stripes down their sides. Fire engines could be seen hurtling down Bayswater Road and the arrival of two

Chapter 17 - The face of the enemy

ambulances added their flickering lights to a colourful scene that would have done a disco proud.

Past the platform wreckage and across the other side of the side road, in the lightening pre-dawn Justin saw the outline of the two officers strong-arming their man into the back of a waiting van, and was about to turn away to look for Patricia when he saw someone appear out of nowhere. The stroboscopic effect from several blue and red lights didn't help and he had to shade his eyes and squint to focus on what he was witnessing. The two officers had just closed the back door of the van when the shadowy figure attacked one then the other, knocking them both to the ground. He initially blinked but started to walk towards the van, ignoring a plethora of intermediate police officers who seemed to be aimlessly going about their jobs of finding out what they were supposed to be doing.

The shadow tried opening the van back door but it wouldn't open, and he looked around before getting in the driver's side and half disappeared below the dashboard. Justin could only guess that the shadow was Hana and that he intended to steal the van with their captive still inside. Perhaps it was anger that Hana was about to get away again, or that he had had enough of being outwitted by this foreign terrorist, because he quickened his pace to a run and headed for one of the police Range Rovers not far away. He didn't have time to explain to the copper waiting by the Range Rover, so threw a punch knocking him to the ground. He jumped in, thanked his lucky stars that the keys were in the ignition, started it, shoved the gearstick into reverse, simultaneously floored the accelerator pedal and released the handbrake. It shot backwards T-boning the van and pinning it against a brick wall.

Immediately after the jarring impact, he could clearly see in the door mirror that he had hit his target perfectly. The back of the Range Rover was hard up against the van's driver's door while the passenger door was wedged against the wall on the other side. Hana was trapped; at least he hoped so because he couldn't see him.

Within seconds, the immediate area was swarming with police; some held laser-sighted machine pistols, others had their tasers ready and those without any sort of weaponry other than pepper spray and torches just looked on, all from a safe distance. Several were shouting at Justin who had little option than to raise his hands and try to look innocent as he sat in the driver's seat. He could only follow instructions to get out, but as he did so, into the circle stepped Patricia who shouted back at them. One by one they lowered their weapons away from Justin, but hardly had the threat of being tasered or shot dissipated than they all heard the windscreen of the van being kicked out.

"The bastard who's responsible for all of this is in there. Make sure he doesn't get away." Justin yelled and in an instant the armed police targeted the van, verified by wobbling red dots. "Don't shoot him as we want him alive."

The windscreen crumpled outwards, bounced off the bonnet, landed on the pavement and out of the aperture poked Hana's bleeding head.

Chapter 17 - The face of the enemy

Justin turned and made way for Patricia. "I believe this is your arrest."

She didn't smile but took her time. She took a pair of handcuffs from a nearby policeman, walked towards Hana holding them out in front of her and was within two paces of the van when she stood stock still.

Hana slowly lifted one hand high in the air. It clasped a mobile and his finger hovered over one of the buttons. Only she and Justin immediately knew what they previously suspected, and he groaned at the prospect of a van full of propane being detonated in the confined space of an underground car park.

Hana smiled. "You let me and him go."

When nobody did or said anything he shouted, "NOW. There is bomb in car park."

Still nobody moved except Patricia after several seconds. With great delight she smiled back, lifted the handcuffs higher and took the remaining steps forward so that she was within touching distance of him. "You vile piece of shit. You will rot in hell." As she went to clip on one half of the cuffs on Hana's hand she watched as he pressed the send button with his other.

Nothing happened so he pressed it again. Still nothing happened.

She pouted. "What's the matter you fucking simpleton? Don't you know that mobiles don't work underground in this country?" She lunged and managed to cuff his other hand, sending the mobile clattering into the gutter.

She had to step back smartly as he tried to take a swipe at her while spitting and shouting obscenities in mixed languages.

Chapter 18

Roses

Paddington station is renowned for several things, one of them being that inside there's a bronze statue of that same named bear. The fact that there were several other more colourful versions of him dotted around the lofty atrium really didn't concern either Patricia or Justin as they woke no more than a hundred yards away in a 'safe' house.

"Oh god I ache," she groaned as she tentively stretched her arm out to turn off the alarm clock and missed. "Why do they always put these bloody things just out of reach?" She wiggled nearer the bed's edge and slammed her hand down on the noisy gadget. "Fuck. It's nearly eleven-thirty" She went to get up but mid-bend, flopped back down again. "Owww."

"Oh stop complaining. Just be grateful you've still got a nervous system." Justin wasn't feeling anything like as bad as Patricia who seemed to have taken enough injury for both of them, but he still wasn't feeling on top of the world; it had been a long night. "That gives you half an hour to get yourself ready for the Commander."

"You're bloody lucky I can't turn over very easily." But she did manage to whack a pillow in his general direction without looking.

Chapter 18 - Roses

It had only taken a few minutes at that time of the morning to be driven to the apartment in Westbourne Terrace, just across the road from Paddington station. The resident housekeeper of the safe house told them that Commander Gibbons would be carrying out the debriefing himself at noon.

He was punctual. He didn't have to say much as he left them to do it all, and he only raised the occasional question. After nearly three-quarters of an hour they had run out of things to say and they sat there while he appeared to be contemplating.

Eventually he looked at Patricia. "I believe I charged you with keeping a low profile and never to be seen by the press, but on this occasion I can understand your timely intervention. Fortunately matters occurred so quickly that the media hadn't had time to arrive in force, and only one photograph managed to appear on the internet. We have already provided a plausible explanation to this morning's events but as a result, you will be asked to comment. Tates will be along shortly to provide you with the necessary."

He turned to Justin. "If you have found out what Mr Thomas from the Treasury wanted to know, Tates will take that from you and pass it on, but I do want that resolved one way or another. I'd prefer this morning's matter to dissipate a little first but tempus fugit. Good day to you both and errr... well done." He abruptly left.

Patricia felt like she had emerged from a confessional box. Justin went to the sideboard and poured out two neat scotches and they sat there going over what had been said to Gibbons.

"I suppose that's his way of complimenting us."

"It's more than most get," Tates added as he silently walked in. "And I'll have one of those too, but a small one with water." He was looking at the matching pair of tumblers in front of them. He sat at the central table, withdrew a laptop and some documents from his briefcase which naturally drew the couple to sit either side of him.

He didn't ask after Patricia's bandages nor how she was feeling. "Have you any idea as to the loss of life and damage that would have been caused if that delivery truck had been detonated?"

Justin had a good idea but thought it better to remain silent.

Tates continued, "Not only did the van contain a further fifteen large propane cylinders mixed in with some containers of nitrous methane but also three full-sized acetylene bottles. If you think propane is destructive, then acetylene is a hundred times more powerful." He paused to let that sink in. "It would have been the equivalent of a four-ton bomb going off and would have destroyed the entire building and most likely damaged any others within a hundred-yard radius." He showed them an A4-sized colour photograph of the remains of what was once a multi-storey building. "Beirut 1983, two trucks containing gas cannisters exploded and reduced this building to rubble. It killed over two hundred people." He showed another. "I think you will remember the London 2005 bus bombing that killed fifty-two." He saw the look of horror on Patricia's face in particular. "I don't think I

Chapter 18 - Roses

need go on, but suffice to say that you probably saved the lives of more than two hundred people this morning. One thing is puzzling us at the moment... how did you know that Hana's phone wouldn't work?"

She gulped. "I didn't. I think it was working perfectly, but when he showed it to me as he leaned through the van windscreen, it was obviously his method of sending a signal to the remote detonator. The previous day I noted that one couldn't receive a signal down there so took a chance that nothing had changed."

"Had you considered that he might have been on a different network?"

She withered at the suggestion. "No," she said guiltily.

"Or that he might have been signalling for somebody else to detonate it?"

Her patience snapped. "Look. I took that decision on the spur of the moment because there and then I believed he would have detonated whatever we did. Hirov was still in the building and as he was Hana's number one target, he would have had to set it off. Don't you dare criticise my actions. You weren't there. You weren't the one that was thrown off the top of a building and you weren't the one who put himself in the line of fire when it came to handling those trigger-happy police. Half-blinded by flashing lights with a fucking maniac threatening to blow us all to kingdom come. So you just crawl back behind your ever-so-safe desk and leave people like me to do your dirty work. And don't tell me I can't say that to you because I just have. And I mean it."

Her face was contorted with rage and she turned on Justin. "Get me another scotch," she ordered tersely before returning to look Tates squarely in the eyes, daring him to challenge her.

Justin hadn't seen her anger surface to such an extent before and was glad he wasn't on the receiving end.

Tates met her stare until the spell was broken by the appearance of another whisky. He looked down, shuffled a couple of papers, and without showing nerves continued.

"Now this surprised us and will surprise you. The other man in the back of the van turns out to be related to Hana, but it's too early to tell what their relationship is."

Despite the strange news Patricia's anger was still on the boil. "And just how did you find that out?"

"Through the usual blood tests. We're waiting for DNA confirmation as we speak."

"And when do I get to question them?"

"Oh I don't think that'll ever happen. You're not qualified to…"

"Don't give me that because we're just about the only people in the Western world that have actually met Hana and survived. We've studied his mannerisms with the help of Vivian and I've had in-depth discussions with foreign counterparts, and on top of that, in my previous job I was used to interrogating suspects and have built up a knowledge of how they lie, so stop shovelling me that crap." She leaned forward and closed in on Tates' face. "If you want answers, send me in, otherwise I might as well go back to my own job."

Chapter 18 - Roses

"I… I'll see what the Commander says." It was his turn to gulp. He turned to a subject that he felt fairly safe about by revolving his laptop round so that she could see better. "This is the one and only photograph that has appeared over the internet and we think it'll be the last. As a result of this being seen by hundreds of thousands, we've had to draw up a statement for you to read out at a press conference. That's arranged for three o'clock this afternoon outside New Scotland Yard." He produced an A5 sheet of typed paper and spun it round for her to read; it took her less than twenty seconds. "You'll be introduced by one of the assistant commissioners and because of that photograph I expect he or she'll have nothing but kind words to say about you, so prepare yourself to reciprocate."

The photograph had been taken at the exact moment she had slapped the second handcuff on Hana and showed him grimacing threats in her direction. She tried to remember who was standing where the photographer had been but couldn't remember. A cynical thought crossed her mind that it may have been one of the constables.

Tates allowed her time to digest the implications of the photograph. "I'm sure you won't forget how to smile at the right time." He forced his own smile. "A car will collect you at two-thirty."

Justin leaned over to see the photograph. "Looks like you'll be on the front page again and it even shows your good side." His comment lightened the atmosphere with Patricia visibly calming down.

"Now I come to the subject of your enquiries relating to the Treasury's request." He looked at Justin who sat down again. "We'd all like to know what you discovered."

"And why do you want to know? It's a matter for the Treasury, not Special Branch or the diplomatic section."

"Who do you think inaugurated that enquiry, mmm?" Tates held his head high and looked down his nose at Justin. "We like to at least try to keep level with the game when it comes to national interests and that sometimes means we have to ask questions through a third party. In this case it was Mr Thomas of the Treasury, so I ask you again, what did you find out?"

Justin mulled for a moment. "You remember our brief conversation just after the Tower Bridge incident... when you and I were in the hotel room discussing something about employing Miss Eyethorne and not getting me for free? I believe you owe me for that; five grand so far by my reckoning." Before Tates could respond, Justin continued, "And I'm sure you'll remember saying that you wouldn't take me for granted. And I'm sure I said I'd never go to work for you again, but it seems you have manipulated matters so that I'm included in whatever schemes you have dreamed up for my fiancée here. That's exactly what you have done in this instance and that's exactly why I won't be part of your grubby operations. The only time you recognise the truth is when it suits you."

The umbrage Justin felt manifested itself in his next comment. "I'll present my report to Mr Thomas first thing Monday morning but that'll cost you another five grand. Make sure it's all transferred into my account by then. Remember, I don't work for free... for anyone."

Tates was definitely on the back foot and he recognised that today's meeting with Messrs Eyethorne and Crawford was not going the way he had hoped. But he still had the Commander's orders to carry out.

"One last item... Kiril Hirov added some more meetings to his agenda and now isn't flying out until tomorrow. He learned of your... involvement at The Lancaster and has asked to receive you both at the Bulgarian embassy this evening at 8 pm. I assume you will have the grace to accept his personal thanks?"

Patricia and Justin looked at each other. Patricia nodded and Justin replied, "You'll be making a car available for us for that as well then."

Tates had no option but to agree. He packed up his things and went to leave. "Oh by the way, the Commander felt it would be safer for you both to stay here until Monday." He watched the couple wondering if they could work out why, and when it was clear they they couldn't he added, "It's because Hana's henchmen are still out there... for the moment."

"I must say you do have a knack of coming up smelling of roses," was his leaving comment.

Chapter 19

Sand

"I'm beginning to go off the Sunday papers." Justin threw his comment over the top of *The Sunday Times* into thin air when really it was aimed at Patricia as she emerged from the kitchen.

She ignored his remark and instead put a couple of slices of slightly burnt buttered toast down on his plate before sitting down at the table opposite him.

"It says here that you single-handedly arrested a disgruntled activist." He lowered the paper to look at her. "It also says that you did it with total disregard for your own safety."

"Well that bit's true."

"Yes I know that bit's true and all the papers say more or less the same thing."

"Well they must all be true then."

"No. The single-handed bit. There had to be at least a dozen police officers almost within touching distance. That's why I'm going off the papers."

"What you really mean is that they didn't mention you," she half-mumbled as a worm of marmalade threatened to escape down her chin.

Chapter 19 - Sand

"I'd have liked to have been a fly-on-the-wall when Gibbons got told about your photo, he must have shown some sort of reaction. Maybe even raised one eyebrow a smidgen?" He resumed his reading.

"*The Mirror* still calls me 'our golden girl' and who am I to argue with that?" Patricia looked past the Marmite jar at another paper.

"I'll bet you *The Sun's* just interested in your bust size."

"I wonder how much they'd offer me to go topless on page three?"

Justin thought about this for a second. "Go on then I dare you. Give 'em a ring. You know how to pose."

"That was just for you." She blew him a kiss.

The housekeeper came in carrying a very large bouquet of flowers and placed it on the floor. "Compliments of Mr Hirov, and yes… it is safe." He left nearly as soundlessly as he had arrived.

Justin leaned over, plucked out the stick-mounted card and read it. "May the radiance of the beautiful always be with you… Isn't that nice… I suspect that's aimed at you rather than me."

She glanced at him momentarily. "Then why don't you go and have a shave?"

"Haha."

"I'll tell you what, let's take up his offer for a VIP trip to Bulgaria next year, because right now I fancy a stretch on a hot sunny beach not far from a man who serves pina coladas with fresh pineapple."

Justin mused for next to no time as he rubbed his bristles. "You're on. Let's book it online now and go

295

tomorrow morning. Sod whatever Gibbons has in mind. Where do you fancy?"

"Caribbean... definitely the Caribbean."

"Antigua? Jamaica?"

"Barbados."

"Barbados it is. One week or two?"

"Errrr, one week. I'm not sure I'd know what to do with two."

"Leave it to me."

"Not likely." She sidled up to him as he opened the laptop. "You're more likely to book us up next door to a bloody cricket pitch in a shabby three-star hotel rather than a pool-side four star one."

Chapter 20

Epilogue

For the second time that week, the BBC weatherman gleefully announced that another record had been broken as he palmed his hand over the screen behind him. Apparently it hadn't been this wet in the UK since Glastonbury in 2007, but a record is a record, no matter how one connives it.

Had Hamilton been bothered with looking at any weather forecast, even he would have had to agree as he watched the rain cantering down the road towards an already full gully through his chauffeured car window. They were parked outside Kerridge's bar and grill on Northumberland Avenue; as salubrious a venue as they come in London and a perfect place to have a discreet business luncheon meeting. He was waiting for the 'all clear' signal from one of his bodyguards before dashing the few feet to the awning that would protect him and his newest suit from being ruined by the downpour, even with an umbrella.

He was ushered to one of the semi-circular booths where Commander Gibbons was already sat, and seeing the look on his face wasn't sure if he was to be on the menu. Visions of a crocodile about to snatch its own dinner sprang to mind, but he had no choice in the matter; not the way the invitation to lunch had come across from Gibbons' office. He'd reluctantly agreed and had had to postpone one of his lunchtime sessions with his latest paramour.

They'd only met once before which was why Hamilton was nervous about this one.

"Water?" enquired Gibbons as Hamilton seated himself. There were no greetings and no hellos.

"Water?" Hamilton replied with effrontery.

"That's what I drink when I need a clear head." He didn't need to add that he always had a clear head.

"I manage a clear head perfectly well without water, thank you." He turned to the hovering waiter. "I'd much rather have some of that excellent premier cru Chablis I had the other day. Do you have another bottle?"

Gibbons didn't want to be drawn into a long lunch with Hamilton who he considered to be one of the most odious men he had had the displeasure to encounter. Similarly Hamilton didn't want a protracted lunch in the presence of Gibbons as he had too much to hide from such a person, but at least he'd be able to enjoy his wine of the month while there.

Gibbons got straight to the point. "Platinum."

"Um. Very useful stuff so I understand."

Gibbons didn't say anything but just looked at the deceitful Member of Parliament next to him with disdain. Cabinet minister he may have been but in his eyes, he was a crook. Granted, a powerful crook.

Hamilton used the excuse of waiting for the bread waiter to leave before responding further. Ever

Chapter 20 - Epilogue

since he received the virtual summons from Gibbon's office earlier that day, he knew what was going to be discussed. "OK, OK. We both know that I've been a little indiscrete with the buying and selling of shares, but we do live in a capitalists' market, and one is entitled to make a profit from time to time."

His explanation clearly didn't impress Gibbons.

"We're going to turn the tables on Bayev and his Russian backers and we're going to use you to do it."

"I... I'm not sure that's a good idea..."

"Oh it's perfectly straight forward and we wouldn't want to burden you with anything too complicated. We'll be using the information that Bayev will be telling you for our own ends. We believe they'll be in touch with you later this week or early next week to make another killing on the metal exchange. Once funds have been committed and just before their bogus information comes out, we make our own statement, release our own platinum figures and with American help, this will severely reverse the market direction. Once our statement challenges the validity of their own platinum mine, coupled with tonnage figures, it ought to expose Bayev to such an extent that he'll be forced to resign and quite probably he'll have to go into hiding for the rest of his life. It'll also have the desired effect of Bulgaria retaining its own currency very much along the lines that Kiril Hirov has been advocating."

The appearance of the wine waiter with a bottle distracted Hamilton who just nodded his head in approval of it. "You didn't have to tell me all of this, did you?"

Gibbons let him speak without interruption.

"You've told me this for a reason." Hamilton thought the crocodile next to him smiled a little more.

"I know you fellows. You don't tell anyone anything unless you have an ulterior motive, and this time you've told me. What is it that you want from me? I'm just a Cabinet member in charge of Northern Ireland so anything I do that's officially connected with Bulgaria will raise eyebrows." His brow furrowed. "Unless you want me to link last Friday's explosion with a story about Bulgarian platinum and a disaffected Irish separatist group?"

Gibbons gave the impression of not being surprised at Hamilton's suggestion, but in reality he was a little taken aback with his ingenuity. "No. Not that complex. You will be our go-between man."

"How do you mean?" The crocodile was now showing a tooth or two.

"When you're contacted, you'll give them the information that we'll supply you with. They'll believe anything you tell them because they know they've got you in their pocket and won't dare to cross them."

"But that'll mean they'll hold me responsible for when it goes wrong."

"Exactly… and they won't suspect any involvement from Her Majesty's Government, nor will the rest of the world when the dust settles. Especially the Russians."

Hamilton could see it all now and the crocodile's jaws were starting to open. "They'll kill me… a contract… I'll be ruined… have to resign…"

Chapter 20 - Epilogue

"Think about all of that for a moment." Inwardly Gibbons was really enjoying this moment, but he daren't show it. He watched Hamilton's stress levels rise and decided not to intercede straight away. He noted that Hamilton had not bothered to mention his family when it came to adversity; only himself. "Look at it from a dispassionate point of view. You'll be doing your Queen and country a great service. As a minister of the Crown that ought to be your first and foremost thought, but knowing you as I do, I suppose that's about as far from your mind as it's possible to be… next to consideration for you family of course. I don't think this will do your reputation any harm at all as you can put it about that you were acting selflessly. Whether or not people believe you is an entirely different matter, so it'll be up to you to defend your corner. Oh and by the way, when Bayev and his cronies realise what is happening, they'll have no option but to run for cover; back to Moscow I should think. They probably won't have the wherewithal to carry out their threats to you, but on the other hand they have been known to be vengeful."

This was all going a bit too fast for Hamilton, and Gibbons was relentless.

"Then there's the chance of redeeming your recent transgressions in the form of financial compensation."

"Eh?" That certainly piqued his interest.

"Think about it… you'll be telling your Bulgarian friends one thing when actually the complete opposite is going to happen."

Gibbons sipped his water in a timely fashion to allow Hamilton to work it out for himself. The wine waiter prepared a taster and stood back. It didn't even touch the sides but he nodded for the glass to be filled out of automation.

"You mean... you don't mind me making a profit on the side of all this?"

"Why should we stand in the way of such a capitalist venture and anyway, half of your profit will return to the Treasury in taxes."

Hamilton gave a worried look and was still working it all out when the menus were presented to them; Gibbons didn't look at his. "What I've just told you is strictly off the record and in case you have ideas of trying to cover you own backside, we may just have to drop a hint to the Inland Revenue and suggest they delve into your recent platinum deals a bit deeper. It would be a great shame for such information to potentially embarrass a minister of the Crown. Some have even been bankrupted for less."

The threat was clear. Either do as he was told or pay the consequences.

Gibbons stood up. "I am afraid I won't be joining you for lunch, but my colleague here will provide you with all the details you need to know."

At every turn, Hamilton had been put on the defensive and he hadn't liked it one little bit; but he'd had no choice. Problems followed problems which seemed to compound themselves. He looked up as Gibbons departed and was replaced at the table by a young man who introduced himself as Oliver.

"Commander Gibbons has told me that you've offered to buy me lunch and I must say that this is by

Chapter 20 - Epilogue

far the most expensive restaurant I've ever been in. Oh and errr, he's briefed me fully on your activities and what's expected of you, so please let's not play games."

Hamilton's mood was akin to the British weather – dreadful.

***

Patricia's problems were also compounding. As the shaded part of the umbrella moved, so did she, but her dilemma now was that she could move either the ice bucket nearer or the table on which her pina colada stood condensing in the sun. Shielding her eyes, she located Justin talking to a group of people who had just emerged from the sea with their horses. At least he hadn't mentioned cricket... yet.

Printed in Dunstable, United Kingdom